Owl IN THE OAK TREE

A NOVEL

PENNY WALKER VERAAR

GG PUBLISHING

Published by GG Publishing, Cincinnati
www.pennywalkerveraar.com

Edited and designed by Girl Friday Productions
www.girlfridayproductions.com

Cover design: Megan Katsanevakis
Project management: Sara Addicott
Editorial production: Katherine Richards and Elayne Becker

Image credits: cover © iStock/Adventure_Photo; iStock/MrsWilkins; Shutterstock/mlorenz

ISBN (hardcover): 979-8-9867343-1-6
ISBN (paperback): 979-8-9867343-0-9
ISBN (ebook): 979-8-9867343-2-3

Library of Congress Control Number: 2022919470

For Paige

REAGAN

CHAPTER ONE

2018

"Ew, they're nasty!" said one of the girls, her pouty mouth drawn downward.

"Disgusting," her partners agreed.

Reagan stopped in front of the girls and frowned. "Okay, they're gross, but stick to the discussion items, please."

She strolled around the classroom, trying to keep the commotion in her science lab to a manageable level. The gurgling of aquarium pumps blended with the murmuring of twenty-four seventh graders, six tables of four, gathered around their workstations to observe milkweed bugs in their habitat. "See if you can tell the difference between the males and females."

"Ewww, they're so creepy."

Suddenly the intercom squawked alive and bellowed, "Mr. Lock is in the building!" The students froze and turned to Reagan, their expressions a mix of fear and dread. "Not another drill . . . oh no." Whispers whizzed around the room.

Reagan groaned. "Quiet! Okay, people, you know what to do. Jamal, lock the door, lower the shade on the door's window, and everybody pack into the closet, again." Earlier that

1

morning the thermostat had read seventy-eight degrees, already uncomfortably warm. The old coat closet had no ventilation and barely enough room for twenty-five people even if they stuffed themselves in sideways. This was not going to be pleasant. Not what she'd envisioned when she had longed to be a teacher, no greater career on earth, impacting young minds. She did love it, mostly, but not today.

Why hadn't she gotten a heads-up about a drill, like the one a couple of weeks ago when they had to spend fifteen grueling minutes in the closet? Why another so soon—could there really be a shooter? She pulled out her cellphone and texted the front office.

What's going on?

Robbery at the Payless, man with a gun. We're locked down until they catch him.

Jeez. No telling how long that will be.

She pocketed her phone and looked around at her students, all eyes fixed on her. As quietly as possible while still able to be heard, she said, "There's been a robbery and, I'm sure out of an abundance of caution, the police have locked us down."

"Where? Do they know who did it?"

"The robbery was at Payless, a couple of blocks from here. I'm sure we'll hear—"

"Payless!" one of the kids said. "Who would rob Payless? That's insane. Had to be some doper."

Everyone had an opinion worth sharing, or so they thought. The noise escalated in the stuffy room until Reagan held up her hand to quiet them. Over the next few minutes, complaints periodically punctured the silence: "I'm hot. . . ." "It stinks in here. . . ." "I have a cramp in my foot. . . ." "Can we get out of here? I'll take full responsibility." The last remark brought a chorus of giggles. Finally, "Mr. Lock has left the building" came through the intercom.

"Okay, people, back to those nasty milkweed bugs. Jamal, please unlock the door."

The students charged back to their workstations to resume their study of seventh-grade genetics, and Reagan resumed her vigilance.

Nick, a gangly boy with a red cowlick and freckles, made eyes at Greta, the early bloomer in the class, who wore scooped necklines that mesmerized half the student body. His hands were conspicuously hidden under his desk.

"I'll take that," Reagan said, as she confiscated Nick's cell phone and read a half-finished text:

U wan na come to m hous after schol. parents won't be . . .

She shook her head at Nick and pocketed the phone. "You can pick it up after class." A crimson tide rolled from his neck to his face.

Already it starts, the mating rituals. "How 'bout it, guys. Can you identify any changes in their habitat?"

"Ms. Ramsey, that aquarium stinks," said one of the other girls.

Reagan walked over to the large tank and sniffed. Nothing floating on top or near the bottom, but the water was murky and the air around it foul. The loud pumps sometimes interfered with class, so were occasionally turned off. "Sorry. Jimmy's coming in after school to clean the lab. I'll ask him to look into it."

The classroom door opened quietly, and a boy scooted into an empty seat at the nearest workstation.

"Max Jarrell, where have you been?" Reagan said.

Max gave her an incredulous look and slapped his forehead. "You sent me to the office with a note for Mrs. Smith . . . before the lockdown."

"Oh. Right. Sorry." Before she moved out of earshot,

Max whispered to a nearby classmate, "Miz Ramsey's losing it."

Hmm . . . no kidding. She had to admit, she'd been a little spacey lately. The landline on her desk rang.

One of the other boys said, "Uh-oh, it's about your daughter."

Reagan's eyes widened. "What makes you say that?"

"It's always about your daughter."

She took a deep breath. *He's right. This can't be good.* Lizzie's teacher was the only one who ever called on the landline. She grabbed the phone.

"Reagan, sorry to bother you again, but Lizzie went after Kaleigh. You know her, the little girl in a wheelchair. She snatched Kaleigh's glasses off her face and threw them against the wall. The glasses are broken, and she has a nasty scratch on her forehead." The teacher's tone changed a bit, more defensive. "You know how fast Lizzie is. Our new aide was an arm's length away, but Lizzie still managed to grab those glasses." Reagan slumped into her desk chair. Of all the issues she faced with Lizzie, and there were many, that was the most difficult. Reagan had been horrified to witness Lizzie lash out at smaller children, scratch and pull hair. She was unpredictable and quick.

Reagan shook her head and frowned. "Is Kaleigh okay?"

"Well, we treated the scratch and fawned over her, but she cried for quite a while. I think she's okay, just shocked. But Lizzie could have caused lasting eye damage. We had to write an incident report for administration and call the parents."

Reagan sighed. "What can I do? I'll pay for the glasses, of course."

"I guess that's all. It's just . . . Kaleigh's father was pretty upset."

"Give me Hank's number. I'll talk to him." She focused on a framed photo of Matthew and Lizzie on her desk. Folks said her nine-year-old son was the spitting image of her with his thick, and most often unruly, red hair—although hers turned more auburn as she aged—and you could read a matchbook cover by the shine of those crystal-clear green eyes. But he had a square jaw like his father.

Her daughter—small for her age, wispy bangs below her eyebrows, pigtails past her shoulders, an upturned nose, and the most endearing grin on any child, ever—in many ways looked like a typical seven-year-old. But her eyes were telling, small and almond shaped.

More than anything, Reagan wanted to see her children happy again. Help them move through the grief of losing their father, come out the other side as well-adjusted, responsible people. She'd read somewhere, or maybe it was just in her mind, that it would take about a year to reach a new normal.

Matthew didn't cry after his father died, not at the funeral or afterward. He told her he'd promised Daddy he'd be strong. She understood that pressure because she was living it. Be strong for the children. Thank goodness Scott's hospice nurse had recommended Fernside, the nonprofit program to help grieving children. After attending group sessions, Matthew seemed to be . . . maybe not happy, but less sad at least.

Lizzie was different—nonverbal, cognitively delayed. Scott had been her protector, a hands-on parent since the day she was born. When he was at home, Lizzie was sure to be found either on his lap or at his elbow. For weeks after he died, she'd wandered around the house looking for him. Reagan had tried to explain why Daddy wasn't there anymore, but she was pretty sure Lizzie couldn't comprehend it. No wonder she lashed out. Reagan didn't excuse it, but she understood Lizzie's anger.

She hung up the phone and told the class to answer the study questions, then pulled up her bank accounts online. Less than a hundred dollars in checking. She transferred money from savings to pay Kaleigh's parents for the glasses and tide her own family over until the fifteenth, when her paycheck would be deposited.

Jennifer, one of the other teachers on Reagan's team, a tall, drop-dead-gorgeous Black woman, quietly rapped on the door and walked in. Reagan leaned toward her with a hand to her ear.

"Some of us are going to Molly's after work. Come with us."

Reagan hesitated. "I'd like that, but—"

"No *buts*. You need to get out, have some fun."

Anaya would be with the children, so there was no reason she couldn't go. It would probably do her good. Maybe if she got out more and let off a little steam, she wouldn't be so . . . spacey. "Okay, thanks for asking. I'll call Anaya, then meet you guys there."

When the god-awful bell clanged, the kids stuffed their belongings into their backpacks and stampeded toward the door. Only Nick hung back to retrieve his phone. The familiar commotion of school letting out quickly sounded from the hallway: running, lockers slamming, students calling to one another. She took one more look at the smelly aquarium, then wrote a note to Jimmy.

After locking up the lab supplies, Reagan phoned Kaleigh's home. Hank, her father, had calmed down considerably, mainly upset with the staff for letting the assault happen. He assured Reagan he didn't blame her or even Lizzie. They chatted briefly before he said, "Reagan, I just heard at Kaleigh's school you lost your husband a while back. I'm real sorry to hear that. I guess it's been hard on the kids."

The comment caught her off guard. It had been over six months, but she still ran into people who asked about her husband. She hated the awkwardness, the shocked expressions, then the condolences. One thing she couldn't abide was pity.

"Thanks, Hank, but we're all doing okay . . . really." *Who am I kidding? If I'm so okay, why do my students think I'm losing it? Why is my daughter attacking vulnerable kids?*

Before leaving the building, she made a concentrated effort to stuff down the rising tide of heartache those conversations always brought on. The bright sunshine and crisp October air invigorated her after being indoors all day in her overheated classroom. The old brick schoolhouse, built in 1914, had no central air and furnace heat that was too much for some rooms and not enough for others. While large, beautiful old homes graced a few of its streets, for the most part Norwood was a blue-collar community that had suffered economically when its largest employer, General Motors, closed their plant. Thirty years later, Norwood still had no money for a new school. Despite budget pressures, it proudly—stubbornly—maintained its own police department, fire department, and school system.

Cincinnati surrounded Norwood on all sides. The small city within a city was six miles from the downtown business district that held the headquarters of such major corporations as Procter & Gamble, Kroger, and Scripps. Norwood's students walked to and from school, some couples hand in hand.

As she pulled her car onto Sherman Avenue, angry shouting grabbed her attention. Tyler, one of the eighth-grade boys, pushed a new kid to the sidewalk. "That's my girl—stay away!" The other teen jumped up, red-faced, and grabbed Tyler's arm, but both boys hurriedly walked away in opposite directions when Reagan pulled up to the curb.

Seventh and eighth graders; thirteen- and fourteen-year-olds. Drama, drama, drama, both in and out of the classroom. Girls crying over boys. Boys fighting over girls. It's always been like that. It starts now and continues throughout a lifetime. People pair up. Animals pair up. Christ, even milkweed bugs mate and reproduce. She was alone.

Ten minutes later Reagan reached Molly Malone's. Its small parking lot was full, and cars were parked bumper-to-bumper on both sides of Montgomery Road. She circled the block twice before parking in front of a shuttered Burger King on the other side of the street. The Irish pub was in Pleasant Ridge, a community two miles north of Norwood. The room was pleasantly warm and alive with the loud chatter of men and women who had stopped in after work for their favorite bar food and a cold beer. It took a moment for her eyes to adjust to the dimmer light. Televisions lined the mustard-colored wall behind the long bar. Jennifer and several others sat at a pub table near the large storefront window. Reagan waved and walked over.

As soon as she draped her jacket over the back of the stool, a server appeared at her elbow, ready to take her order. "A Blue Moon and boneless wings. Thanks, Elizabeth."

The group gossiped about the usual stuff: students, their parents, the administration, weekend plans. It was good to be in the company of other adults, talking about trivial things.

Jennifer pointed to a man standing at the opposite end of the bar. "See that tall, nice-looking man with Joey Johnson's father? He's the guy who donated our new computer lab."

"Here you go, Reagan."

Momentarily distracted by the busy server who smacked down a frosty glass of cold beer in front of her, Reagan took a refreshing gulp before turning her attention to the man. "Really? I've never noticed him in here before," she said to Jennifer. "What do you know about him?"

"Not much. I met him when he delivered the check for the equipment. His construction company is putting that huge addition on the Humana building on Williams. You can see the crane from the expressway. I do know he's married. I asked about that right away." Jennifer made an exaggerated frown. As if the man sensed the women's stare, he turned and glanced their way. A look of recognition crossed his face. Jennifer raised both eyebrows. "I think he's coming over."

He slapped a couple of the other men on the back, said something Reagan couldn't hear, threw a luxurious leather jacket over his shoulder, and walked over. He was casually dressed in denim, shirt sleeves rolled to the elbow, collar loosened.

"Jennifer, isn't it? Good to see you again." He turned to Reagan. "I'm Jake Dekker." He shook hands with her. "You two work together?"

"We do. The scientists of tomorrow are in our hands. Hi, I'm Reagan Ramsey. How 'bout you? You work around here?"

Jake nodded. "My company's putting an addition on a building near here. I came by to take Dave, the project manager, and some of his guys out for a beer."

Loud applause erupted from the group standing in front of the bank of TVs. Jake shook his head. "That sounds like them now."

"What are they watching?"

"Hell if I know." He threw his hands up. "I lost them as soon as I signed the tab."

"Thanks again for that generous donation," Jennifer said.

"Please, don't mention it. You guys need and deserve good equipment. It made me happy that I could help. I mean that." He looked at his watch. "I was on my way out. Enjoy your evening." He walked through the crowd to the exit, got into a Jeep Wrangler parked in front of the window, and drove away.

Rush hour brought a steady stream of people into Molly Malone's, and by six it was standing room only. "That's the third time you've looked at your phone in the last few minutes," Jennifer said to Reagan over the crowd noise.

"Just checking to see if I have a text from Anaya. She's with the kids. I'm sure they're okay but—"

"Reagan, Anaya loves those kids like they were her own. You know that. Relax. The kids are fine."

"I know. Thanks for inviting me. It's been fun." It had been nice, but an uneasy feeling needled her. Maybe it was the phone call about Lizzie . . . or the comments from Hank . . . or the robbery near the school. Whatever it was, she couldn't shake it.

She caught Elizabeth's eye, signaled for her check, and counted out enough cash to cover it and a generous tip. She gestured to Jennifer and the others at the table that she was leaving, pulled on her jacket, and took out her keys. Jennifer nodded, understanding, but made no move herself.

Outside, street parking was still bumper-to-bumper, traffic heavy on Montgomery Road in both directions. Reagan waited to cross, the air thick with foul-smelling exhaust fumes as vehicles sped by, dangerously close to cars parked at the meters in front of Molly's. The sun slipped behind rooftops and cast long shadows all the way across the street. The once-bright Burger King sign, now just a shell, was partially hidden by large maple trees already a cornucopia of color: red, orange, and gold.

Daylight saving time would end in a few weeks. Reagan dreaded the long, dark nights of winter, her first as a single mom. Last winter was a blur, consumed by Scott's illness and death. A group of young people hanging out near her parked car did not concern her. Pleasant Ridge was safe, an urban neighborhood, more diverse than Norwood, with mostly modest homes, restaurants, and coffee shops. Molly Malone's sat near the busy intersection of Ridge and Montgomery, and as they were most evenings, the sidewalks were occupied by people walking to their favorite restaurant or bar.

At a break in traffic, she crossed to the middle of the street and waited for northbound cars to pass. An opening followed an approaching large black sedan with tinted windows. She couldn't see the driver. Maybe one of Cincinnati's well-known professional athletes.

Rather than keeping up with traffic, as she had anticipated, the car veered right and slowed to a crawl, hugging the curb. She'd begun crossing behind the sedan when a deafening *pop, pop, pop* sounded, and she turned toward the noise. *Someone must have thrown firecrackers from the car? From all the screaming and cussing, that group of young people didn't appreciate it much.*

An arm stretched out the passenger window. Suddenly a man poked his head out, turned in her direction, and locked eyes with her.

Her mouth dropped. Her eyes bulged. The arm swung in her direction.

A gun!

Momentarily petrified, a surge of adrenaline finally propelled her forward, but she lost her footing at the curb and stumbled.

A bullet whizzed overhead.

"Go—go—go!" Screeching tires. Screams. Cussing.

One of the young men standing by her car folded forward and went down. Others scattered. The black sedan sped north and turned right. A woman walking by the scene rushed to the victim, knelt over him, put both hands on his stomach.

What?

Reagan picked herself up, then winced when she put weight on her right foot. A stranger grabbed her elbow and walked her to the sidewalk. Within minutes sirens squealed, earsplitting as they drew near.

Three squad cars, one after the other, roared onto the scene, followed by an ambulance and a fire truck. The ambulance doors flew open, and a man and woman rushed out, each carrying a case of supplies. People poured out of Molly Malone's and joined other gawkers. A woman recorded with her cell phone. The police quickly closed Montgomery Road.

The scene replayed in Reagan's head: The gun—the arm—the face—those eyes. This couldn't be happening. Not here. Her knees suddenly turned to rubber. If she hadn't fallen, at that exact moment, she might be dead.

JAKE

CHAPTER TWO

Jake kicked at the right rear wheel until the hubcap popped off, rolled into the street, and eventually came to rest with a clatter. "Jesus!" He ran his hand through his hair.

He took one more tour around the wreckage, broken glass from the windshield crunching beneath his feet. The left front of the car and the driver's side were wrapped around a large tree. The right rear window, the only one intact, reflected the slowly rotating blue lights from the squad car.

How in the hell did anyone come out of that alive? Bile rose in his throat. The EMTs had Alex on a stretcher. He was moaning, barely conscious, and appeared to have serious injuries. Janet was visibly shaken. Always thinking, she had grabbed her medical bag before rushing out of the house into the cool, dark night when they heard the impact, only to freeze when they got close enough to recognize the rear of Alex's tricked-out Camaro, his personalized license plate: GFT4AX.

Adrenaline had surged through Jake as he tore to the car. He reached Alex first, the odor of marijuana unmistakable when he bent down over the boy. The street was dry—it hadn't rained in days—unobstructed and familiar, a block from home, yet his stepson had run off the road and hit one of the lovely trees on Shawnee Run Road with such impact that his high-priced sports car looked like a rusty piece of junk, gnarled and twisted around the large maple. Blood from a nasty cut above his right eye flooded Alex's face. His features were already distorted by swelling. He did not look like the same kid.

Janet looked pale and fragile, clutching her sweater around her chest. Jake walked over to her, put his arm around her shoulder. Silent neighbors looked on as the EMTs slid the stretcher into the back of the ambulance.

"He must have fallen asleep behind the wheel," Janet told the policeman. "He's been out studying with friends." Jake rolled his eyes as he released her, allowing the officer to help her into the ambulance with her son.

"Yes, ma'am," the policeman responded.

Jake chewed the inside of his cheek. The man had to have noticed the smell of weed, the beer cans on the back floorboard, but no comment. Prudent, maybe. Large homes in this neighborhood. Lots of lawyers.

The policeman propped his foot up on the squad car's bumper and rested his clipboard on his knee to scribble entries into his report. The ambulance left, its lights whirling lazily, its siren silent. Jake waited until the tow truck removed the car and the policeman finished with the report. He was in no hurry to join Janet at the hospital.

Things seemed better the next morning. Janet had reluctantly agreed to come home and rest after Alex was x-rayed, treated for cuts and bruises, and made comfortable. The injuries didn't appear to be life-threatening, but the films did show a fractured left ankle, so an orthopedist had been called to consult.

He would be in that afternoon. Janet wanted to be at the hospital then.

She dropped her sweater on the counter and plopped into one of the chairs at the kitchen table. Sunlight streamed through the bay window and created a halo around her light-blond hair.

She was beautiful, even this morning with no makeup, rumpled clothes. And brilliant—a doctor, no less. He still marveled that she had married him, a college dropout. He used to think he'd go back to school. But that never happened. No need, really, and no time. No time even to spend the money he made, but then the only thing he had ever wanted was to finally make his father proud, at least until he met Janet. Then it was her he wanted. Her and a family. He loved spending his money on her, not that she didn't make enough herself, and for as long as he could remember, he had wanted a son. Life had been good since their marriage in all areas but one. Alex.

Jake walked behind her now and rubbed her shoulders, then bent down and kissed her on the neck. "Want me to call your office for you?"

She patted the hand still resting on her shoulder. "Thanks, but I called from the hospital."

He took two coffee mugs from the cabinet and poured them both a cup of steaming decaf. "Here, drink this," he said, setting the cup in front of her, "then go lie down. I need to clear my schedule. I'll call you around noon."

"I couldn't do that. Alex may need me. I just want to take a shower and get back to the hospital."

"You need to rest. I'll make sure you're at the hospital in time to meet with his doctor."

"No, I couldn't. I have to get back."

"Janet, you're exhausted. He's in a hospital bed, tripping on pain meds." Oops! He shouldn't have said that.

15

She glared at him. "I knew you would blame him for this."

Jake lifted an eyebrow. "Blame him? How could I do that? The street was dry. The speed limit's twenty-five."

"You sound like you think he did this on purpose."

"No, I don't think he ran into that tree on purpose. I think he was too wasted to control the car."

Janet slammed her mug down on the table. "Not that again! If he was so wasted, why are you the only one who noticed? Why wasn't he charged with DUI?"

"Hell if I know. He may be yet. Maybe that officer was waiting for the results of his bloodwork. Janet, you had to smell the marijuana. You had to see the empty beer cans."

"No. No, I didn't." She got up from the table and faced Jake squarely. "He's just a kid, for Christ's sake. Maybe the street was dry. Maybe he was speeding. Teenage boys tend to drive too fast. Besides, what if he did have a beer or two? I'm sure you sowed a few wild oats when you were Alex's age."

Jake forced himself to calm down. He moved closer to Janet and looked directly into her eyes. "Why did you lie to that policeman? You deliberately led him to believe Alex had been studying. You know that's not true."

She speared him with a hateful glare.

Jake shook his head. "Alex could have killed himself last night. Or someone else. He's lucky he got by with a fractured ankle rather than a fractured skull . . . or worse. He comes and goes at all hours with little or no boundaries. What do you think he's doing out this late? He's only sixteen."

"You've never liked Alex. You resent the hell out of him, don't you?"

Jake grabbed her by the shoulders. "I'm worried about him. I'm worried about you." He released her and took a step back. "Alex is headed for big trouble," he said in a coarse whisper.

"He just hasn't adjusted to our marriage. He's used to having me all to himself."

OWL IN THE OAK TREE

"For Christ's sake, we've been together for almost five years. If he hasn't adjusted by now, it's time he did. The trouble Alex gets into isn't normal."

She turned to leave the room but glanced over her shoulder at Jake. "I'm going to take a shower so I can get back to the hospital. You don't need to take off work." Her voice was controlled and punishing.

Jake stared after her and shook his head, his stomach knotted. "Dammit!"

REAGAN

CHAPTER THREE

Seven thirty on Saturday, a hazy morning, too early for sunshine. Reagan struggled to push the horror of the previous night from her mind. Raw nerves and lack of sleep had left her numb. She waited in the high school parking lot for a bus that would take Lizzie, and other children with special needs, to Stepping Stones day camp. The monthly outing gave a break to the children's caregivers and a well-staffed, highly structured fun day for the children.

Grace, another parent, opened the rear door of her SUV, pulled out a large board, unfolded it like a butterfly, and hooked one end to the bumper, making a ramp to the ground. She tugged. Something appeared to be stuck. Reagan had one hand on her car door, ready to get out and help, when a heavy-looking electronic wheelchair came into view. Gravity pulled it down the ramp onto the pavement. After replacing the ramp, Grace opened the passenger door, grabbed her fifteen-year-old son around the chest, and hoisted him up from the car and into the chair. His legs were atrophied, his hands and wrists turned inward. His mother was a tall woman, and muscular. Even so, how long would Grace be able to move him around like that, several times a day, every day? She had a dark bruise on her arm, probably from moving—

A bruise . . . or something else. A birthmark? It barged into Reagan's mind, a thought that hadn't registered at the time of the incident, or when she talked to the police. A dark spot on the shooter's arm—the inside of the left one—above the wrist. Her stomach clenched. She forced her mind back to the present.

Lizzie sat in the back, content to be restrained in a large car seat, listening to music on her iPad, seeming not to have a care in the world. Her little face glowed with excitement. She gave her mother a sweet, snaggletoothed smile that made Reagan's heart squishy. She blew a kiss at the rearview mirror; Lizzie blew one back.

After Grace settled her son, she joined a group of men and women who were also waiting, talking among themselves and laughing. Despite the noticeable disabilities of these kids, this was a cheery setting, with adults in small groups chatting. The teens, many of whom had Down syndrome, had been in camp together daily in the summer and monthly since then. Now they greeted and hugged each other like long-lost friends. Young adults wearing gray sweatshirts with "STAFF" across the back milled around, talking to the kids. One blew large bubbles—translucent blue, purple, or pink—which floated across the parking lot, chased by excited children.

Like Reagan, these people had already grieved their losses, changed their expectations for their children, and appreciated the day of respite, the chance to focus on themselves and their other kids, knowing that the campers were well taken care of and having fun. This would be Reagan's first weekend without children in months, and after the trauma of last night, she needed it. Anaya, Lizzie's aide, had offered to pick her up after camp and keep her overnight. Matthew had gone to Louisville for the weekend with his friend Charley's family to visit grandparents.

After putting Lizzie on the bus, Reagan waited in a long line of cars to pull out onto Sherman Avenue. Despite all her efforts to block it, the shooting scene invaded her mind, it had happened fast, really fast: *pop, pop, pop*—screams—pandemonium. But the reruns came in slow motion: the odd-colored eyes that locked with hers, the look of surprise on the gunman's face, the arm turning toward her, the gun.

The police had gotten there within minutes. As soon as she told them she had seen the shooter, an officer took her to the police station, where she waited alone, isolated from other witnesses, for more than an hour before anyone took her statement. Her car could not be moved until CSI finished working the scene, so an officer drove her home. She sat at the kitchen table and talked to Anaya for quite a while, trying to calm down. It was after midnight by the time her car was returned to her. When she finally got to bed, she tossed and turned the rest of the night.

There was nothing like yoga to force everything from her mind, so with Lizzie safely off to camp, Reagan hurried to an eight thirty class, hoping to evade the nightmare. It didn't work. Every nag from the sore ankle quickly brought back the scene. After yoga, she took care of a few errands, dread following her like a fly buzzing just out of reach. She didn't make it to the police station until after one o'clock. There she met with a Detective Gabriel to go over her statement again and look at photos.

Dazed from lack of sleep, Reagan hunched over one book after another of mug shots. Her back above her shoulder blades ached from the tension. After two and a half hours, one of the officers brought in a Subway sandwich and chips, but she had no appetite. She took a short break and got back to it.

On the way home, she realized she'd been so focused on the mug shots she'd forgotten to mention the mark on the shooter's arm. She'd do it later. She turned on the radio and Sarah McLachlan's soulful song "Angel" enveloped her. That young man, his face ghastly white when the medics whisked him away. She hated it—knowing her neighborhood was a place where someone could get shot.

Thank god she'd be alone tonight, no one to take care of but herself. She just wanted to get home, pour herself a glass of wine, put her feet up, and fall asleep watching some mindless TV.

When she turned onto Montgomery Road, a Norwood squad car pulled in behind her. *Oh no.* She slowed slightly, hoping it would go around her, but it moved closer and its blue lights flashed once. *No, not now.* She did not need this, not tonight. She ignored it and drove on. As she turned onto Williams, the light bar stayed on, blue beam whirling slowly. Reagan shook her head and kept driving, the squad car on her tail. When she turned onto Smith, the siren squawked on and off. Undeterred, she shook her head and turned onto Kenilworth, pulled into her driveway, and parked. The music stopped abruptly.

The officer parked on the street, got out, and walked to her car, a slight paunch swelling over his equipment belt, a set of keys dangling, his gun holstered. The streetlight in front of Reagan's house cast a pale glow on the surroundings. A neighbor walking two white Yorkies glanced at the squad car, then stooped down and petted her dogs while looking toward the officer and Reagan.

He opened her car door, leaned in, and looked at her. "So . . . you didn't wanna stop?"

"Sonny, I'm tired. I've had a long day."

He propped his arm on the roof of the car and inched closer. "Rea, we need to talk. It's important."

"Can't it wait?"

"No."

"It'll have to. I'm exhausted." She got out, pushed past him, and climbed the porch steps with Sonny right behind her. She opened the door.

He threw up his arms. "Jesus Christ, Reagan, you didn't have your door locked?"

She rolled her eyes. "I told you, I don't need this tonight. Go back to work." She flicked on the lights as she entered. Scooter rushed to greet them, yapping, prancing around in circles, jumping on him joyfully.

He crouched down and casually petted the dog for a moment before turning his attention to Reagan. "My shift's been done for an hour. I've been waiting for you." He rose up, walked through the living room, and glanced into the kitchen. "Where's little man?"

"He's with Charley's family. Anaya picked up Lizzie. They're both gone for the night."

"Good. I'm going to take a look through the house."

"Who asked you?"

He turned to her, his brow furrowed. "Scott, that's who." He opened the basement door and trotted down the stairs, keys on his belt jingling.

"Whatever." She shrugged off her coat, threw it and her purse on the sofa, and stood near the basement door. When he came back up, he said, "No bad guys down there. I'll check upstairs."

"Sonny, wait. I'm tired, that's all."

"I know." He threw one arm around her shoulder into a half hug. He was a couple of inches shorter than Reagan, muscular but also thick around the middle. His sandy-colored hair was thinning on top, and his gap-toothed grin reminded her of Woody Harrelson. "It'll be okay," he said.

The stairs creaked as she followed him upstairs. Reagan's bed was unmade, a twist of sheets and blankets on the floor, clothes scattered about, a half cup of cold coffee on the dresser. Sonny grabbed the bedclothes, jerked them up with a flourish, and looked under the bed. "I see the good housekeeping fairy's been here?"

"I told you. I've had a long, hard day. I've been busy." They moved from one room to the other, looking in every closet, under the bed, behind the shower curtain. Back downstairs Sonny said, "I've seen the report from Cincinnati about the shooting."

She nodded.

"I don't want you involved."

Her head inched backward; her brow furrowed. "You don't want me involved? I didn't want to be involved either."

"Just tell them you didn't see the shooter. It was dark, it happened too fast, it's a blur—that's a common one—whatever." He paced around the living room as he threw out alternatives, the sound of his footsteps heavy on the worn hardwood floor.

"Sonny, I got a good look at the shooter. He stared right at me. It was dusk, not dark."

"Yeah, and he saw you. He may not know who you are yet, but if he's afraid you're gonna ID him, he'll find out."

She shook her head. "The police know I saw him. I've spent most of the day at District Two describing him, looking at—"

"Did you identify anyone?"

"No, but I'm going back Monday."

"Don't do that, Reagan. Eyewitness accounts are notoriously inaccurate anyway. Change your statement. People do it all the time. They think about it, get scared. Think about the kids."

She never expected this out of him. She moved closer and

studied his face. "Who are you? What happened to the man who complains incessantly about people 'looking the other way'? I *am* thinking about the kids. This is where we live. I don't want to lose one of them to a stray bullet."

"This is different. Let the police handle it."

"This is different? How?"

He grabbed her shoulders, stared into her eyes. "Because it's you, Reagan. These are very bad guys. Don't you understand? They murder people just to send a message."

"Murder?"

"What do you think? He just wanted attention? Wanted to show off his big, bad gun? Oh yeah, the vic last night—he didn't make it."

The news walloped her. She had told herself he would be okay, he'd gotten help fast. She pulled away and shook her head. "I can't do it. Norwood isn't going to turn into the South Side of Chicago if I can help it."

"Cincinnati. It happened in Cincinnati, not Norwood."

"Two miles from here. I checked it. This is our neighborhood, our home."

"Reagan, there are mean people in this world. Remember Pike County? Eight people in one family murdered in their beds. The perps didn't hesitate to kill a sixteen-year-old kid. They hunted the victims, went to three different sites. You think Matthew or Lizzie will be safe?"

Her stomach plunged. She felt dizzy, sick. *We* cannot *be having this conversation.*

"Scott was like my brother. From the first day he realized how sick he was, he made me promise, at least a million times, that I would take care of you and the kids. And that's what I'm gonna do." Sonny walked to the sofa, took off his jacket and belt, carefully placed his gun on the coffee table, sat down, and propped his feet near his gun. "I'll sleep here tonight. Starting tomorrow, a squad car will keep close surveillance, but the fact is we have a small department. We don't have the personnel to protect you twenty-four seven. That scumbag will find out who you are, one way or the other. That's why you have to change your mind." He looked up at her, his facial expression softened. "Any coffee?"

Reagan bristled. Sonny had been Scott's best friend since kindergarten and was like a brother to her too, but she could take care of herself and her children. She took a deep breath, walked into the kitchen, directly to the window, and looked out. In the ambient glow from the streetlight, the oak tree stood dark and imposing, an arm's length from the side of the house. At first glance, Bird wasn't perched in his usual spot. She scanned the tree from left to right, top to bottom. Typical for early October, the leaves were still green and dense, making her search difficult. Nothing. Where was Bird? She plugged in the coffeepot, then opened the silverware drawer, pulled out a sheaf of rolling papers from the back, and tore off a sheet. It trembled in her hand.

I need to calm down.

She was good at that. Since the early days of Scott's illness, she had been able to compartmentalize her feelings, observe herself from the outside, maintain composure. She'd had to, for the children's sake.

The bubbly sound of perking coffee filled the room. From a carousel of colorful spice jars, she took out one with *oregano* scrawled in black on a white label. Leaning back against the counter, she rolled a joint, lit it, and inhaled before she returned to the window. As she searched the tree, the sweet aroma of fresh-brewed coffee blended with the pungent smell of weed.

Where was Bird? She squinted and scanned the tree again. Her gaze lingered on a cluster of leaves, finally settling on a grayish-brown mass partially hidden by the tree trunk's shadow. Bird was there, asleep on that limb with his wings folded over his eyes. Her anxiety drifted away with the smoke she exhaled.

"Jesus, Reagan. I'm a cop!" Sonny stood in the kitchen doorway, arms akimbo, hair mussed.

She raised her eyebrows and shrugged.

He rolled his eyes, poured himself a cup of steaming coffee, and walked back to the living room, shaking his head.

Reagan took a deep breath and returned to the window. She rapped on the glass until Bird lowered his wings and his big eyes met hers. He moved to the windowsill. Then she raised the window a few inches, stooped, and said through the crack, "We've got a lot going on here. No sleeping on the job, okay?"

ALEX

CHAPTER FOUR

"Alex! Hop in." Trip slowed his silver Nissan alongside Alex, who was hobbling across the school parking lot. A horn blasted as a kid in a yellow Volkswagen darted around Trip's car, tires squealing, burning rubber.

"Yeah, right," Alex said and grinned. "Hop, with this thing?" He pointed to the cast on his left ankle just as a dark-haired girl, walking backward while she waved to a friend, bumped him. Fumbling with his crutches, he went through a sequence of frantic movements before finally steadying himself by resting against the car.

The girl stared at him, frowned, and said, "Oh, sorry," then rushed away.

Alex leaned into the car window to better hear Trip over the noise of school letting out—kids shouting across the parking lot, loud music, motors racing.

"Yeah, I see. Well, don't hop. Just get your ass in, man." Trip reached across the front seat and opened the passenger door.

A red-and-gray Beat-the-Wildcats banner decorated the side of a school bus that rumbled past them. A pimply faced boy in a band uniform hung halfway out the window, yelling something indecipherable.

"Degenerate," Alex muttered as the bus lined up with a horde of other vehicles, engines revving, each vying impatiently for its turn to cut into the busy traffic. He propped his crutches against the car and carefully maneuvered himself into the passenger seat.

"Hey, I hear you graduated from fender benders. How ya doin'?" Trip asked.

"No big deal." Alex winced as he bent down and used both hands to move the casted foot into the car and under the dashboard. He retrieved his crutches and slammed the car door. "A couple of days in the hospital and I was glad to be home, even with Jake there."

A girl wearing a short skirt casually crossed in front of the car. Trip mouthed, *"Wow,"* wide-eyed, and watched her until another car obstructed their view. "You missed a great party last weekend. Man, did I get fucked up! I couldn't even feel my arms and legs for a minute. Crazy, man!"

"Oh yeah? My mom wouldn't let me out of her sight, like she's paranoid or something. She kept looking in my room to check on me. And she's already called this afternoon demanding to know where I am, what I'm doing." Alex smiled wryly. "Lucky for me, one of her patients is in labor. She'll be off my back for a while."

"What about your car?"

"Totaled. Totally totaled," Alex said as he ran his fingers through his hair. "But no problem. Insurance will take care of it. I like those new Mustangs." He took a joint out of his pants pocket, lit it, took a hit, then held it up to Trip.

Trip shook his head and gave him one of his crooked grins. They drove past the football field where the freshman team, dressed in their practice jerseys, scrimmaged against Sycamore.

"What say we go down to the 'wood?' Jeff's having a party tonight and I need to hit Bryan up for some dope."

"Sure, no problem," Alex answered. "How 'bout I text him, let him know we're coming." He took out his phone. A text from his stepfather flashed.

Shit. Of course, Jake's got to know where I am, what I'm doing at all times. He's probably the reason Mom called earlier.

Alex shook his head. "Jake wants to know if I want to go out to dinner with him."

"Tell him you're having dinner at my house."

Short and muscular, Trip wore his sandy-colored, curly hair short, and he was polite to Alex's mother and Jake. Therefore he was acceptable. Manners and short hair, that's all it took. As a matter of fact, his mother liked Trip. He talked to her and Jake. They really liked that. It didn't matter, but it did make it easier. They didn't hassle Alex about going out with Trip.

Bryan was a different story. He wore his black hair shaved on the sides but long and angled on top, and he had a habit of flipping it out of his eyes with a toss of his head, a gesture that irritated Alex's mother. Cigarettes had yellowed his fingers and teeth, tattoos covered his arms, and he wore his jeans low. Bryan smoked and swore in front of Alex's mother. He was always himself, no matter who was around. Didn't try to please anybody. Alex liked that about him. It was cool, but he didn't tell his mother when he had plans with Bryan. Alex responded to Jake and then texted Bryan.

It was a pleasant October day, clear-blue sky. Trip turned on the radio. Rap music blared as they drove down Montgomery Road on their way to Norwood. He kept time with the music by slapping the outside of the car door through the open window. People turned and looked; the older ones scowled.

When they pulled to a stop in front of Bryan's house, Trip honked three short blasts. Bryan peeked out the window, then opened the front door. He wore jeans and a short-sleeved shirt, no socks. Trip took the joint from Alex and inhaled.

Alex's best friends: Bryan since middle school, when they had both lived in Norwood, and Trip since Alex had been forced to move to Indian Hill.

"Hey, bruhs," Bryan greeted. "What's up?"

"We've come to celebrate Alex's freedom," Trip answered as he exhaled a pungent-smelling plume of smoke. "I need weed and . . . you got any Molly?"

"Sure. Come on in? The folks won't be home until after dinner. It'll be late."

"Okay," Trip said.

By the time Alex had performed the complicated task of getting out of the car—his weight on his good leg, supported by his crutches, the joint clamped between his teeth—he was breathing hard.

"You're getting the hang of it," Bryan remarked.

"Yeah, no problem."

Trip got out of the driver's side and walked around the car. "Schmidt's having a party tonight." He raised both eyebrows at Bryan and grinned.

"Cool."

Once inside, Bryan went upstairs. Within minutes he returned with a small baggie containing weed and several white pills. Trip took a roll of money out of his pocket, peeled off a couple of bills, and handed it to Bryan. Trip always had money.

"You wanna go with us?" Alex asked.

"Nah, I have to meet up with some guys in Pleasant Ridge later. But let's have a beer, hang out for a while."

Bryan raided his parents' refrigerator and returned with three Coors. They each popped the top and Bryan flipped on the TV. Alex propped his plastered foot up on the coffee table. Each of the boys put one of the tablets in his mouth and settled back to watch a music video and talk about rap bands.

It turned dark. A car door slammed.

"What the hell's going on here?" Bryan's father roared when he walked in and saw the boys casually lounging around the living room. Empty beer cans crowded the coffee table, ashtrays overflowed with cigarette butts and ashes, and the place reeked.

Bryan scrambled up when he saw his father. "Nothin'. We was just hangin' out."

His father scowled, his face aflame. "Look at this place! How many times I gotta tell you, I don't want you punks helping yourself to my beer and smelling up the place?"

Trip jumped to his feet. "It's time for us to be getting home anyway." He passed the crutches to Alex and headed for the door. Alex, his head down, hobbled behind him.

"Wait, guys. I'm gettin' the *fuck* outa here!" Bryan followed the other two out the door.

His father yelled after them, "You kids are headed for trouble, you know that?" Bryan's mother stayed in the background.

The front door slammed. Once outside, Bryan flipped his middle finger in his father's direction. "What an asshole! There's no fucking way I'm gonna stay home with the mood he's in. He's always on my back." He crawled into the back seat of Trip's car.

The boys laughed as they peeled away from the curb. Wind blew through the open windows, music blasted, streetlights blazed. Stores and fast-food restaurants lined both sides of Montgomery Road. They whistled and waved at two girls getting into a parked Honda. The girls looked up and waved back. Everything was funny.

They headed for the wealthy suburb of Indian Hill. Once

on Sleepy Hollow Road, Trip accelerated. The road narrowed and curved, no streetlights. Trees and vines obstructed the view. Fifty, fifty-five, sixty, sixty-five.

Alex unconsciously rubbed his left leg and braced himself, but he didn't tell Trip to slow down. Bryan laughed hysterically. Sometimes those guys really got on Alex's nerves.

Eventually their headlights flashed onto a small sign that read Private Drive, and Trip turned in. The front of the house was brightly lit. Expensive cars crowded the circular driveway. Trip pulled behind a white Jaguar, and they got out. Loud music steered them to the backyard.

The three boys followed a small group of people walking on a cobblestone path around the side of the house to the multilevel patio and deck. Illumination came from charming faux streetlights, landscape lighting around a large heated pool, a flickering fire in a lower-level firepit, and the moon.

Fuck! Cobblestone. Alex carefully maneuvered down the path, lagging behind the other two. Balance was everything.

On the patio, a beer keg cooled in a barrel of ice, and a variety of liquor bottles and snacks were arranged on a small table. A large tub held soft drinks. Someone stood in the dark about ten feet away, peeing on the manicured shrubbery. Alex headed for the lower level and joined Trip. Several people sat in Adirondack chairs that circled the firepit, and others stood in small groups talking. The heavy smoke stung Alex's eyes as he surveyed the crowd, letting his crutches hold him up. His shoulders and underarms ached.

A blond girl wearing a short, tight skirt and low-cut sweater approached. "So Alex, I heard you were in an accident. I'm so glad you're okay."

He should know this person. He'd seen her before but couldn't remember where.

"Thanks."

After a couple of awkward minutes, she introduced herself to Trip. "I'm Roseanne Ackerman."

Trip said hi, then snuck a crooked grin at Alex.

He left Trip talking to Roseanne. Now he looked like some kinda weirdo. He wished he could just walk up and talk to people he didn't know, like Trip did. He had never been able to do that. He tried to casually mingle, but the crutches made him clumsy and conspicuous, so he moved into the background to watch people.

"Alex!" someone shouted from the shadows. "What are you doing here?" Jeff Schmidt stepped into the firelight. "I thought you were in the hospital. How's it going?"

Alex shrugged. "Okay, I guess."

Jeff threw an arm around Alex's shoulder. "Good to see you, man."

Alex shifted and struggled to remain balanced. His crutches dug into his armpits, causing him to wince. Jeff released him. "Did you hear why we're celebrating tonight? My brother Jimmy's been appointed to the Naval Academy."

Alex nodded. "Yeah, I heard. It don't make me feel too great to think the safety of the world is in the hands of guys like Jimmy."

Jeff laughed and nodded. "Ain't that the truth. Well, it's supposed to make a man out of him. We'll see. Hey, I'm glad you could make it. Have fun. I need to get some wood, feed the fire."

Trip danced a slow dance with Roseanne, his hands gripping her ass. An uproar exploded from a group of guys standing together with Bryan. "No way! That's fucked up!" said one of the boys, his voice high-pitched and whiny. "Holy shit! When did you hear that?" Alex trudged over to join them.

"Yesterday," replied a guy named Justin. "It's been all over Facebook today."

"Fuck, man! I told him not to do that stuff," said Bryan. "It's bad. But he said he wanted to get that ultimate high. High as he could get."

"What are you guys talking about?" Alex asked.

"Weston James. He's dead! Heroin. His mom found him yesterday morning. Life squad came but he was too far gone. They didn't even try Narcan. They told Wes's mom that rigor mortis had already set in." Justin curled his lip and frowned.

Alex's jaw dropped. He took a step back. Not Wes. He'd just seen him in class on Monday. It couldn't be him. Everybody liked Wes. . . . He was a good kid, really smart. Alex shook his head. Wes James—overdosed on heroin. That wouldn't penetrate.

"I kept telling him," Bryan said, "he should stick with my stuff. It's healthier."

One of the other guys in the group stepped forward. "Right, Bryan, that's what I always say about the stuff you deal: healthy. You should be able to sell your product at GNC." The boys laughed, but it seemed forced.

"Fuckin' right." Bryan had never gone to Indian Hill schools, didn't live in the neighborhood, and didn't really fit into this crowd. But they all knew him.

The conversation broke up when Jeff threw more wood on the fire, causing a minor explosion. Logs and kindling crackled and popped. Glowing embers with squiggly tracers shot into the dark. The night had turned chilly, and the fire captured the attention of people nearby, who leaned in to warm their hands.

On the way home, Trip drove more slowly than he had earlier, more deliberately, hugging the right side of the road, purposely avoiding the yellow center line. He was subdued. Bryan had caught a ride back to Norwood with some guys who were going downtown.

The moon seemed bigger now, brighter, casting a silvery glow on the surroundings. Alex stared out the window. Wes was dead. What was it like to get that high, so high it killed you? Kids had died before from overdosing, but nobody he knew. Being dead, going from living your life to nothingness. It just wouldn't compute.

The headlight beams danced across the surface of Sleepy Hollow and shined on ivy and gnarled grapevines growing along the side of the road. The splotchy pattern of the asphalt got bigger, rushed toward his face, then shrank again and receded. A possum, momentarily trapped by the headlights, jumped to the side of the road and scurried up a tree.

Something orange moved ahead of them—orange neon balls near the edge of the road; shimmering toads playing leapfrog, with a steady, rhythmic movement. More orange . . . a bar at chest level—

Sobering adrenaline thundered through Alex's veins. A man wearing iridescent running gear was just ahead. "Trip!"

Too late! The front fender caught the runner's hip with a thud and knocked him into the ditch.

"What the fuck was that?" Trip asked, bleary-eyed.

"You hit him, man! You hit a jogger!" Alex screamed. "We've got to stop, see if he's hurt."

Trip turned to face him, wide-eyed. "Shit, man! We can't stop. Think of the trouble we'd be in. My dad will kill me. Besides, he shouldn't be running on this road this late at night. It's too fucking late to be jogging. That's what he gets."

While Alex stared out the window, into the blackness, trying to see into the ditch, Trip, known by his family as Crawford L. Lewis III, gunned his Nissan and sped away.

REAGAN

CHAPTER FIVE

Bacon sizzled in the skillet, filling the Ramseys' kitchen with the aroma of Sunday breakfast rather than usual weekday dinner, but they had few choices. Detective Gabriel had asked her to come in to view a lineup, so she hadn't had time to buy groceries. Mac and cheese and bacon was it tonight. Lizzie sat at the kitchen table, eating Goldfish, while Reagan finished cooking. Matthew hunched over his math book and binder.

"Mom, I don't get this!"

Reagan poured macaroni into a boiling pot, then turned to her son. "What don't you get, buddy?"

"Fractions!" He grabbed his head and sighed.

Reagan wiped her hands on a kitchen towel and went to help, but commentary blaring from the living room diverted her. "It's been over a year and the city of Las Vegas is still reeling from the mass shooting that took—"

She grabbed the remote and flicked off the TV. "No, we'll not be having that with our dinner." Momentarily lost in the memory of that awful tragedy, she stood transfixed, staring at the blank screen, until Matthew screamed.

"Mom, the stove is on fire!"

"What?" She rushed back into the kitchen. The kitchen towel was in flames. "Shit!" She had thrown it too near the gas jet after wiping her hands. She grabbed the nearby fire extinguisher and sprayed the entire stovetop.

She hated to drag both children out in miserable weather, but she would have to pick up cleaning supplies, something else for dinner, and aloe vera. Her right arm had a burn that was not large, but was painful.

Typical for late October in Cincinnati, the weather had changed overnight from warm and beautiful to dark and gloomy with intermittent, bone-chilling rain. The checkout line at Kroger crept along as "Monster Mash" played over the sound system and competed with beeping scanners, one-sided cell phone conversations, and the rattle of grocery carts.

Lizzie stood in line beside Reagan, studying a huge cardboard witch behind a display of Halloween candy in a black plastic cauldron. She signed, "Eat, eat," and grabbed a package of M&M's.

Reagan shook her head, took the candy, and put it back. "No. You've already had lots of crackers. No candy."

Lizzie looked sideways at her mother, her nose wrinkled, her lips pursed.

Uh-oh. Reagan had seen that expression before, and it usually meant trouble. She clasped her daughter's hand and pulled her closer. *We've had enough drama for today.*

An older woman in front of her, slower than most, painstakingly counted coins from a change purse. The cashier made friendly conversation while carefully bagging the items. No hurry.

Reagan's chest tightened. She took a deep breath and tried to relax. Lizzie turned from observing the colorful witch to watching people coming in through the double front doors. She seemed to focus on a woman who stopped to gaze at a display of wine.

"Hi there."

Behind Reagan, a man of about thirty grinned at Matthew, whose jacket was covered with Ohio State football patches. The man held a six-pack of beer and a package of steaks.

"I see you're a football fan, but a Buckeye . . . seriously?" the man teased, his expression an exaggerated grimace.

"Oooh yeah. They rule." Matthew threw up his index finger and grinned.

"No, no, no. The Wolverines rule. The Buckeyes drool."

"Really?" Matthew took a step closer. "Then why'd they choke last week?" He grabbed his neck, eyes bulging, tongue hanging out of his mouth.

"That's 'cause your guys got a series of lucky breaks, and our guys got bad calls."

It was good to see Matthew so animated. He hadn't talked like that in months. Not since his father . . . The two of them had loved talking trash. A guy thing.

Matthew suddenly blurted out, "My dad died."

Reagan winced and moved closer.

The man drew his eyebrows together and, after a brief moment, said, "I'm so sorry." He shifted his gaze to look at her.

"Yes, well, it was a while ago," she said as she draped her arm over Matthew's shoulder, "but I think you reminded my son of him." She hated putting people on the spot. "That's a healthy-looking dinner you have there."

He looked relieved by the change of subject. "Yeah, well, I'm going to throw in some vegetables," he said with a grin. "French fries, that is. And the beer counts as a grain, don't it?"

"Well, yeah. There's that."

Lizzie yanked on her arm, so Reagan turned back around. "What, honey?"

The child signed again, "Eat, eat."

"We'll be home in a little while. We'll eat then."

The cashier, flashy in a good way, with hair as red as her

lipstick and long, dangling earrings, still chatted with the older woman, ignoring the long line. Reagan's stomach squeezed again. About five minutes of waiting was all Lizzie would normally tolerate without causing some sort of calamity.

Finally the cashier bagged the last of the woman's groceries and handed over the receipt. "Hi, Reagan, hi, kids. Sorry about the wait, but Mrs. Williams is by herself and she's lonely. Comes in here two or three times a week, I suspect just to have someone to talk to."

Reagan's cheeks burned. Okay, she wasn't the only person with problems. "Hey, Kelly." She loaded her groceries onto the conveyor belt with her left hand as she gripped Lizzie's hand with her right. Matthew bantered with Wolverine man and paid no attention.

Kelly gestured with a nod toward the stranger and muttered, "Who's Mr. Tall, Dark, and Handsome with Matthew?" She raised both eyebrows and grinned.

"No. It's not like that. I don't know him."

"Too bad," Kelly said.

Reagan shook her head. Her friends had already tried to set her up with eligible men, but she wasn't ready. Scott had only been gone six months, and like those glowing embers that pop out from a campfire, something would erupt, like with Matthew today, and she could feel the pressure of her husband's arm around her waist, smell the fragrance of his aftershave, hear him laugh.

Maybe it was only the good times you remembered. Sure, there'd been hard times too, but those weren't the memories that flared often. And Bird, the odd little owl that had shown up the day Scott was buried, still watched over them from the kitchen window. All she wanted was to be strong for her children, for them all to get to the other side of this grief. She could do that. For them, she'd be Ms. Incredible.

Kelly scanned the last of Reagan's order and totaled.

Reagan released Lizzie's hand, dug into her purse for her Visa, and handed it over to Kelly. "Can you believe this weather? I'm not looking forward to win—"

A sudden bump startled her. She sucked in a sharp breath, wide-eyed. Lizzie banged into the wine display as she bolted toward the door, her pigtails flying behind her. People coming in stepped back, their mouths agape, as bottles crashed to the floor, glass shattered, and spilled wine spread in red rivulets across the white tile.

"Shit!" She disregarded her son and grocery cart and shoved past a couple of stunned seniors to pursue her daughter. Two opposing lanes of cars moved in front of the store's entrance, apparently trying to get as close as possible so their passengers could avoid a long walk.

Lizzie cleared the threshold, but Reagan, swearing under her breath, quickly caught up and nabbed her by the back of her coat. The child casually shrugged out of it and kept running. Reagan grabbed her arm, then around her chest. Lizzie was incredibly strong for a little girl, especially one with hypotonia, which often accompanied Down syndrome. She flailed, kicked, and twisted. Reagan lost her balance and they both went down.

People slowed, gave them plenty of room, and avoided eye contact.

"Okay, okay. Cut it out, Liz." Reagan was aware of the scene they were causing but powerless to stop it. Lizzie thrashed harder. They scuffled. Reagan threw her leg over one of Lizzie's, trying to pin it down without hurting her, and held one of her arms, but the child used her other arm to push Reagan's head against the concrete, hard. Pain shot from the back of her head to her temples. Reagan lost her grip again.

Lizzie rolled outside her reach, jumped up, and rushed toward the traffic like a wild animal. A late-model Mustang rounded a corner and careened toward the front of the building. Reagan's heart slammed against her chest. A scream caught in her throat as she visualized her daughter under the wheels of that menacing Mustang.

"Hold up there, young lady. Where're you going in such a hurry?" A tall man stepped in front of Lizzie. She tried to step around him, but he sidestepped and stopped her. She looked up at his grinning face, pursed her lips, wrinkled her nose, and seemed to realize she'd been outmaneuvered.

"Thank god," Reagan said, hauling herself up from the sidewalk, her face flaming. She grabbed Lizzie's coat from the damp pavement, roughly stuffed her child's arms into the sleeves, and glanced back through the glass door. A young man in a blue Kroger shirt hurriedly placed a yellow Wet Floor sign near the spill and began sweeping glass from the pool of wine.

To make matters worse, someone said, "Hi, Miz Ramsey." One of her seventh-grade students walked by and got into a waiting car. His mother threw a half wave toward her.

Reagan shook her head, then quickly turned her attention to the man who had come to her rescue. Surprised, she recognized him as the man she had met at Molly Malone's just last week. "Thanks."

He smiled at her. "No problem." He raised both eyebrows. "That was *some* scene."

She took two deep breaths, stretched her neck, and slowly rotated her head. She'd be aching all over soon. "Yeah, I know. Would you believe we were training for the Special Olympics?" She scrunched her shoulders blades together, twisting her waist.

He laughed, revealing deep dimples. "I'm Jake Dekker and you're . . . Reagan, right?" He offered his hand for a shake like a man used to taking charge.

She got a better look at him now than she had at Molly Malone's. Tall, six three or four, dark hair peppered with silver, and soft crinkles around his eyes when he smiled. She guessed his age as fortyish. She shook his hand.

"You have a good memory. Yes, Reagan Ramsey." Lizzie looked up at her with a solemn expression. "And, of course, you've already met my daughter, Lizzie."

He directed a warm smile at the child. "Hello, Lizzie."

"Well, thanks again, Jake."

"Can I help you get her into your car?"

She let out the breath she'd been holding. "That'd be great. I just need to get my son and groceries." Her heartbeat slowed to near normal as she headed back into the store for Matthew. He was standing inside the door, looking out. Wolverine man had slipped past them while she struggled with Lizzie. He was nowhere in sight.

"Come on, buddy, let's go home." She draped her arm around her son's shoulder and grabbed her credit card, her groceries, and what was left of her pride. At home she would deal with Matthew's expression of horror.

ALEX

CHAPTER SIX

Sections of Sunday's newspaper covered the kitchen table in front of Jake, who, still dressed in pajamas, was reading the editorials and drinking coffee. Greasy plates from breakfast had been set aside, but the smoky smell of bacon lingered.

Alex eyed Jake over the comics, waiting for a chance to grab the news and see if there was any word of the jogger. There was nothing in Saturday's paper about a hit-and-run accident, and nothing on the internet, but it had happened so late that it probably wouldn't have made Saturday's deadline even if the jogger had been found.

The bacon settled in his stomach like a block of concrete and sat there. What if the jogger hadn't been found? What if he was lying in that ditch covered by vines and stuff, dying? Or maybe already dead. Or maybe he just got up and went home? He tried to hold that last thought, hoping it would ease his stomach, but it didn't. That thud played over and over in his head. He pretended to be reading *Zits*, even forced a smile, but his leg shook uncontrollably under the table. *Jake's gonna know something's wrong if that doesn't stop.*

"You're up early for a Sunday," Jake said as he laid aside the paper.

"Yeah, I know."

"Didn't you go out last night?"

"No. Stayed in. Went to bed early."

"On a Saturday night?"

"I was tired. Where's Mom?"

"She's sleeping in this morning. Late call last night."

"Yeah. I heard the phone ring."

"Well, I'm going up to shower and dress," Jake said, pushing back from the table.

When he was out of sight, Alex seized the front section of the paper and scanned every headline as he leafed through its pages. Nothing. Next he tried the Metro section. On the third page, the headline jumped out at him.

Indian Hill Jogger Victim of Hit-Skip

Michael Yeager, 34, an attorney with the law firm of Rosen, Watson and Yeager, is in fair condition today at Bethesda North Hospital after being hit by a car late Friday night on Sleepy Hollow Road. The driver left the scene. A passing motorist saw the victim and notified police. The incident is under investigation.

At least he's not dead. It's there in black and white. Fair condition. What's that mean? The room became warm, stuffy. *We're in big trouble. We'll go to jail if we're caught.* The thought struck him like a smack across the face. His heart pounded in his ears.

Sneaking around on crutches was hard, but as quietly as he could, Alex pulled himself up the stairs and hobbled toward his parents' bedroom. His mother's blond hair stuck out and her outline was visible under her blanket. The shower noise meant Jake wouldn't hear him make a phone call. He went into his bedroom and closed the door. Trip answered on the first ring.

"Did you see it in the paper this morning?" Alex asked, his voice high-pitched.

"Yeah, I saw it. So what? Nobody knows it was us."

"What about your car? What if they can match paint from your car or something?"

"You been watching too much fuckin' television, man. I told you, there's nothing wrong with my car, just a small scratch around the headlight, and I took care of that with a little touch-up paint."

"Well, how bad do you think he's hurt?"

"Look, Alex, he's okay. He's in the hospital in fair condition. That means he's okay. He shouldn't have been out jogging on that road that late anyway, man. Who does that? If it hadn't been us, it would've been somebody else. He was asking for it. Now, will you chill?"

"What if the police find out? I mean, they could ask around if there was a party near there—put two and two together, go ask who left about the time this dude was hit."

Trip hesitated, seeming to give that some thought before he came back with "Chill out. Nobody's gonna find out if you don't give it away."

The phone went dead.

Alex hopped around the bed and crouched down to the heat register near the baseboard. He lifted off the metal guard, a feat made difficult by the cast on his ankle. He fished out a baggie of pills and weed and stared at the drugs for a moment.

Maybe he should quit using. He'd gone all day yesterday without taking anything, but this pit in his stomach just wouldn't go away. He had some Xanax. He would just take one.

"I don't know why I let you talk me into this," Trip told Alex as they pulled into the Bethesda North parking lot. "We shouldn't be anywhere near here."

"I just have to see for myself that this guy's all right. I'll be able to drive myself when I get a walking cast, but right now all kinds of bad stuff keeps going through my head. Did you want me to ask my mom to drive me?"

"You *could* have just stayed home," said Trip, his voice loaded with sarcasm.

"It'll only take a few minutes." Alex maneuvered out of the passenger seat and onto his crutches.

"It takes more than a few minutes for you to get out of the fuckin' car."

When the boys reached the main entrance, Trip held open the glass door as Alex glided into a spacious, sunlit atrium. People hurried about, some in scrubs or other uniforms.

All eyes turned to a woman being wheeled toward the exit, a sleeping newborn in her lap. A second aide pushed a noisy cart loaded with yellow mums and other things. Helium balloons—a pink one (It's a Girl!) and a blue one (It's a Boy!)—floated toward the skylight. A tall, dark-haired man closely followed, cuddling another baby to his chest. An older couple trailed behind, broadly grinning.

Good. Everybody's looking at those babies, not at them. At the information desk across from the gift shop, a man told the boys that Michael Yeager was in room 431. They followed signs to the elevators and went up.

On the fourth level, spotless gray tile covered the floor, but laundry hampers and equipment that had been pushed out of the patient rooms crowded the hallway. The place smelled like the stinky stuff Jake's housekeeper used to clean the kitchen. Loud beeping sounded from room 421, like it was some kind of emergency, but no one seemed concerned. A nurse stood at a med cart, making notes into a laptop. She looked up as they approached.

Alex held his breath, put his head down, and kept moving. Maybe Trip had been right. They shouldn't be there. Security cameras could be recording them—or the cops could have the hospital staked out. They could turn around and leave, but that would be more suspicious. *No, keep walking.*

He had imagined he would be able to see into the rooms, get a good look at Michael Yeager, but most of the doors were closed. As he made his way down the hall, he tried to conjure up an excuse to walk into Yeager's room.

No, bad idea. Fuck!

Room 431 was diagonally across from the nurses' station. Tiny beads of sweat broke out on Alex's forehead. Luckily the door was open, and the nurses seemed too busy to pay any attention. He stopped and tried to glimpse in without being conspicuous.

A man in blue pajamas sat on the hospital bed with a pretty blond woman also sitting on the bed, facing him. They were laughing.

"What'd I tell you?" Trip whispered to Alex. "He doesn't look hurt to me."

"Alex! What are you doing back here? I'd think you would've had enough of this place." Carrie Newman, a young nursing student who had been on the orthopedic floor when he had his accident, smiled at him.

"Oh, uh, we thought a friend of ours was here, but I think we got the wrong room . . . or floor." His face flushed, but Carrie did not appear to notice.

"It's good to see you. You look like you can handle those things pretty well," she said, pointing at the crutches.

Alex grimaced. "I'm getting awful tired of 'em."

Carrie nodded. "How much longer before you get a boot?"

"This Thursday, the fifteenth."

"That'll be better. You'll be able to get around much easier then." She checked her watch. "Well, take care, Alex."

As soon as she was out of sight, he turned to Trip. All the color had drained from his face.

"I thought you said nobody would know us," Trip complained through gritted teeth.

"I didn't expect to run into her . . . but it won't matter. She's just a student."

Trip took a deep breath and shook his head. "Fuck!"

"Look, Trip, at least now we know this guy isn't hurt bad. We can quit worrying about it."

"I wasn't worrying. You were."

"Well, I think you're right about one thing. We need to get out of here before something else happens."

REAGAN

CHAPTER SEVEN

Reagan spread the soothing aloe on her burned arm, slipped her hands into rubber gloves, and began to scrub foam and grease from their stovetop. Her head ached but no longer pounded, and the ibuprofen she chased down with half a glass of red wine had eased most of the muscle pain. The lumbar soreness would take longer.

The room still smelled of burned bacon and grease, so she opened the window a bit and let in a refreshing breeze. Halloween, then Thanksgiving and Christmas. Just the thought made her stomach dip. The holidays were going to be tough, but they would make it through. Happier days were ahead for them; they had to be. Their last big vacation came to mind.

What a wonderful time they'd had on Hilton Head Island. Matthew had finally learned to balance a two-wheeler, and the family had spent hours biking trails that meandered through Sea Pines Plantation—Matt a little wobbly, Scott pulling Lizzie in a Burley cart. The paths took them through cool, dense woods that suddenly gave way to exquisitely manicured sun-drenched fairways. Matthew excitedly pointed out an alligator floating in a pond near one of the greens, its peering eyes barely above the water. On the beach, sand fine as sugar tickled their feet and clung between their toes. Shrimp boats, besieged by hundreds of seagulls, bobbled in the shimmering ocean. Beach clubs played loud reggae and served icy piña coladas to parents and ice cream drinks to their kids.

Nothing is ever perfect, of course, and getting to Hilton Head and back home always put Reagan on edge. As easygoing as Scott usually was, he became a maniac behind the wheel. He drove too fast on the interstate, hugging curves, crowding the cars in front. Mountains made it worse. Coming home, near Knoxville, a female driver cut sharply in front of him, forcing him to brake. Never one to mince words, he said loudly enough to be heard, "Stupid *fucking* bitch." Reagan cringed. Matthew, from the back seat, said innocently, "Daddy, we don't say stupid."

"Mom, what's so funny?" Matthew walked into the kitchen and plopped down at the table, Scooter right behind him as always.

"Oh, I was just reminiscing. Thinking about our vacation in Hilton Head."

"You said you wanted to talk to me when Lizzie wasn't around. She's asleep."

She dropped her sponge into a sink of soapy water, pulled off the gloves, and sat down opposite her son. "I just wanted to know how you felt. You looked really embarrassed to see me running after Lizzie."

"Nah, I wasn't embarrassed. It was funny until I saw that car. I was scared she was gonna get creamed."

Reagan arched an eyebrow. "Funny, huh? Your mother mixing it up on wet concrete with your little sister in front of all those people—her actually getting the better of me—and you thought it funny?"

The corner of his mouth turned into a crooked grin, and he slapped both his hands on the table. "Hilarious."

She blushed. That was her son. A kid of few words, but his expression usually said it all. That look on his face at Kroger—was the explanation really that simple? Before Scott had gotten sick, Matthew laughed freely. Belly laughs. He was a happy, sociable kid, but since Scott's death, he was quieter, and when people were around, he usually retreated into his room. Her heart ached for him. She loved watching him tease with Wolverine man. Maybe her son was becoming his old self again.

She wanted him to be a normal, carefree nine-year-old, not worried about her and Lizzie, but he seemed to think of himself as caretaker of the family. He took over duties Scott had performed: turned off the lights, locked up at night, brought in the mail. He was patient with Lizzie. If she trashed his room, he usually shrugged it off and picked up after her. He didn't complain when Reagan gave him chores, and he fed and walked Scooter without being reminded. Mostly he tried not to upset or worry Reagan. He seemed to understand she had been through a lot. He was a good kid. The kind of kid who'd pretend he wasn't embarrassed, even if he really was.

Maybe she was overthinking it. Maybe he truly had viewed the whole scene as hilarious until that Mustang drove up too fast. "Matthew"—she only called him Matthew when she wanted to make a point—"you know you can tell me anything, whatever you're feeling, right?"

He dipped his head, looked at her through lowered lashes, and gave her a lopsided grin. "I know, Mom."

"Always remember that." She shook her head, got up, and ruffled his hair as she walked by. "Okay, buddy, be gone with you." As Matthew and Scooter got up to leave, she pulled on her rubber gloves and went back to the dreadful stove.

Definitely a sucker for that kid.

• • •

The worn staircase squeaked with each step as Reagan tiptoed upstairs to peer at her daughter sleeping peacefully on top of a pink comforter, her dark hair falling over her face. Her twin bed had been shoved into a corner—the only way to fit it and a chest of drawers in the tiny bedroom. Elsa and Anna, the magical sisters from *Frozen*, sprinkled glistening snowflakes like stardust from high on the blue wall, the colorful decal straight and perfect.

What would happen to her if you weren't here?

From the time Scott had become ill, that thought was never far from her mind. Physically, Lizzie was a child, but behaviorally more like a toddler who needed constant supervision. If she did something dangerous, Scott and Reagan could never be sure Lizzie understood why she was being disciplined, or if she would remember the punishment long enough to keep her from doing it again. She didn't sleep through the night, and after she was too big to be gated in, they couldn't sleep soundly for worrying she would get up and get into trouble. Anything that could be harmful had been removed from her bedroom long ago, but it was impossible to do that in the whole house.

They had finally settled on a glass storm door to Lizzie's bedroom, locked from the outside. Since she always slept with the light on, they could easily see into her room. When she could no longer slip out of her bedroom, Lizzie began sleeping through the night. It seemed she felt more secure, as did her parents.

Satisfied that Lizzie was okay, Reagan left the room and locked the door behind her.

They had wanted more kids. She and Scott had agreed that four children, two years apart, would be ideal. For that they would need more space. Their "starter" house was small, with only one bathroom, and it was upstairs. They had saved money for a bigger one, and their plan was to move after their second child was born. But Lizzie's needs had been unexpected. Specialists, therapy for Lizzie, support groups for the family, and the adjustment to having a child with special needs—all those things took time. They put off looking for a new house *and* having another child. Reagan had wanted Matthew to have brothers like she had her sister, Jordan. But time passed.

After Scott got sick, her priorities changed. Her mind had always had a toggle switch; anytime she saw a glass half-empty, it automatically shifted to half-full. She was grateful for the two children she did have and for the good memories that dwelled in their house. Scott had bought it before they married from Mrs. Middleton, an eighty-three-year-old widow who had lived there seventy-nine years and was going into assisted living. She had raised five children there, and her granddaughter, Betty Crammer, still lived next door with her three teenagers. As was common in Norwood, the family lived close and saw no reason to move.

Downtown Cincinnati was a short taxi ride away. Major League Baseball and the NFL, bars and restaurants, theater, music festivals, parks on the riverfront—never a shortage of fun for a young couple. When Matthew was born, a large Welcome Home, Baby banner, hand-painted by the Crammer kids, hung over the door. Summer afternoons, Reagan walked with the children to UDF for ice cream. During recess at Immaculate Conception Academy, a block from their house, the street was temporarily roped off so students could play soccer. Excited squeals from kids pervaded the neighborhood. Like every community, it had its problems, but the essence of Norwood had soaked into Reagan's DNA, had permeated her soul. It was her home. She loved it and the people in it. She could not turn her back on it, like Sonny wanted her to.

A familiar screeching sounded from the kitchen, so she went back there. Outside the window, limbs from the large oak tree rubbed against the glass whenever Bird jumped from one branch to another. The streetlamp cast a shadowy light on the side yard, allowing Reagan to see him cock his head as he looked at her.

"I haven't forgotten you, don't worry." She put bits of hamburger on the windowsill. "Matt's doing his homework, fractions. Lizzie's asleep. I've been a little . . . how should I describe it . . . spacey lately. Just when I thought the three of us were moving along rather nicely to this 'new normal,' I find myself setting fire to the kitchen and, the very same afternoon, momentarily forgetting to hold on to Lizzie long enough for her to bolt. And I had seen the 'look.' You know, the one that means she's up to something."

A damp breeze fluttered the café curtains as Reagan placed several more tidbits of hamburger on the windowsill. The small kitchen still smelled like grease and onions, more than an hour after they'd eaten dinner.

Bird broke eye contact long enough to scarf up the morsels of meat, then gave her his full attention. His black pupils grew larger, almost covering the surrounding rings of yellow, his speechless expression accentuated by fine white feathers around his big eyes.

She talked to Bird as she moved about the kitchen, shoved mustard and ketchup into the refrigerator, and wiped sticky goo from the table. "I'm not so much overwhelmed with sadness, like at first. I can manage my emotions better. But I forget things, ordinary things like holding on to Lizzie. You wouldn't believe the scene at Kroger."

Bird cocked his head and looked sympathetic. Over the last six months, Reagan had come to terms with the odd little creature with the large head and catlike face. It was unlike any bird she had ever seen. Online research indicated it was possibly a saw-whet owl, small enough to perch on a windowsill. She'd decided Bird was male.

At first he had peered into the living room at people who stopped by after Scott's funeral. They noticed. It was weird the way he held eye contact with Reagan for almost a minute, like he wanted to make sure she knew he was there. And he never left.

"I won't be very far away. I'll watch over y'all. As long as you need me, I'll be there."

In his last days, Scott said that more than once. She hadn't paid much attention. Heavily medicated, he rambled, but he seemed obsessed with telling her, to make sure she understood him. *"I'll watch over you, don't worry."*

Reagan had never totally believed in spirits, but she didn't totally disbelieve either. Many things in life were unexplained. She liked knowing Bird was there. Sometimes days went by without her seeing him or even giving him much thought. But on hard days, days when she needed to vent, or cry, or just mull things over, she would find him on the windowsill, looking in, ready to lend an ear. She felt protected somehow. Less lonely. Other people talked to pets. All kinds of pets. It wasn't that odd to talk to a bird, even one that lived in the tree outside the kitchen window. Was it?

JAKE

CHAPTER EIGHT

Maisy Jefferson appeared to be sizing Jake up as she examined the books on the floor-to-ceiling shelves: architecture, construction, finance, cookbooks, and scores of novels, including the complete set of Harry Potter.

They moved around Jake's favorite room in the house, his large, comfortable study. A credenza he had built himself stood against the adjacent wall, behind a walnut desk. Several framed photos, a computer monitor, and wireless speakers sat on top. A large portrait of Janet hung above it. French doors opened into the kitchen. Frances, the family's housekeeper, hummed as she prepared dinner. The aroma of garlic and onions wafted into the room.

Maisy turned to several large trophies, one with a miniature quarterback atop a brass stand, his arm back to throw a pass. Beneath it, a plaque inscribed with Jake's name and "Ohio Northern University, 1995."

"It looks like you've played a lot of football?"

Jake peered over her shoulder. "Yeah, I did. High school and college."

Standing next to Jake, Maisy seemed tiny: the top of her head barely reached his shoulders. She looked as if she'd gotten ready for the day in a hurry. Lots of stragglers escaped the clip meant to contain the thick brown hair piled on top of her head. Thick glasses in tortoiseshell frames magnified big dark eyes. She clutched a leather portfolio to her chest, looking more like a schoolgirl than a middle-aged social worker with Big Brothers.

She turned to face Jake. "You're an ONU alumnus then."

"Yes . . . well, not exactly. My father had a heart attack my senior year. I came home to help him."

"Oh." She furrowed her brow. "That's a shame. So, you had to take care of him?"

"His business, mostly. My father was hospitalized."

Maisy's mouth dropped open. "Dekker Construction? Wow! You were so young."

Jake nodded. "The company was smaller then. I had worked for my dad since I was a kid. I grew up in the business." His father's words came to mind. *"You can work at the office. There's plenty of odd jobs that'll suit a boy like you. You have to pay for the shoes you stole and that damaged display."* Jake hadn't even wanted those goddamn shoes.

"I was an only child," Jake continued. "Everyone took for granted that I would take over when my father retired. Unfortunately he was never well enough to work after his heart attack. Good men worked for him. I brought determination and grit to the company. The crew took me under their wings and picked up the slack until I knew the ropes."

Maisy moved closer to the credenza and focused on a photograph of a man with thinning hair, smiling broadly, his arm draped around the shoulders of a teenage boy. "He looks very happy here. Very proud."

Jake smiled as he picked up the photo. "Oh, that's not my father. It's my coach." He replaced the picture carefully. "Why don't we sit down." He steered her to a leather sofa and chairs grouped around a coffee table.

"Mr. Dekker, most of our volunteers are young men and women right out of college. We do have some older, more established people, but not many. I have to ask, are you sure you want to take this on? You have a big job already, and we ask that you make the commitment of at least a year."

Jake leaned forward, his elbows on his knees. "First off, I'm Jake. Mr. Dekker's dead. Second, those good people still work for me. I can get away an afternoon each week, no problem. I'll make it a priority."

He wanted to convince Maisy, close the deal. The organization would be happy to have him. There was a shortage of volunteers, and some kids stayed on a waiting list so long they aged out before getting a match. The fact was, Maisy had no idea how important it was to him to be able to do this. As a kid, the one person other than his mother he had loved the most—the person who helped him turn his life around—was Coach Majors. He wanted to pay it forward.

"I've been incredibly fortunate. It's high time for me to give back." The clatter of dishes from the kitchen annoyed him. He got up and closed the door.

"How about your wife? Your son? How do they feel about you spending so much time with another boy?"

"My wife's fine with it. She's a busy surgeon and has late hours one day a week. That's the day I'll be with my 'little brother.' My stepson's sixteen." He raised his eyebrows and shook his head.

She threw up her hands and laughed. "You don't have to tell me. I know. The good news: the day will come when he'll want to spend time with you again. My son's twenty-nine and a new father. Needs a babysitter now. Uh-huh." She nodded slowly, grinning.

Jake's stomach sank, his smile wavered. His feelings about

Alex were complicated. Jake was an only child of only children. When he was younger, he'd longed for what other kids had: brothers to hang out with, sisters to protect, cousins, noisy family dinners at the grandparents'. Belonging.

After college, his buddies had all married and had kids while Jake had been obsessed with saving the family business, growing it, proving himself worthy to his father even after he died. Jake feared he would never have children, that part of his life had passed. The thought left a heaviness in his chest.

When he met Janet, her twelve-year-old son had been a bonus. But Jake had been terribly naive. He had no idea it would be so hard to make a happy family. At first, Alex just resisted interacting with him. One evening he brought Janet home to find Alex asleep, stretched out across her bed. Jake didn't have to be Freud to get the message. But Alex hadn't been openly hostile toward him then. That changed.

He had to admit, he didn't really know how to be a good dad. Being a good stepdad was even harder. If he was honest with himself, he didn't remember much of his own childhood. Coach said maybe he didn't want to remember because of the pain and sadness. He had helped Jake understand that his father was just as lost as Jake was after his mother died. At least rationally he could understand it. But that didn't change the feelings. The loneliness. The sense that he was invisible. That no one loved him.

Alex was making the same mistakes Jake had as a kid.

"I don't think Alex will care one way or the other. He has his own friends. His own life."

Maisy nodded, took a pen from her purse, and opened the portfolio. "Well, Mr. Dek—Jake, we have a boy I think will be a really good match. He lost his father last year when he was eight. I know your mom died when you were—"

"I'd just turned eleven."

She nodded. "You were an only child. Our match does

have one sibling, but she has severe disabilities—dually diag-nosed Down syndrome and autism, nonverbal. Aides help, but Mom has her hands full, and she's proactive where the kids are concerned. She enrolled him in counseling at Fernside after his father died, but she still worries about him. She wants him to have positive male role models, especially going into his preteen years, so she put him on our waiting list a couple of months ago. Frankly, we probably wouldn't place him so soon if your backgrounds weren't so similar."

Lost his father last year.

The enormity of Jake's commitment sank in. Maisy was describing a real kid, not some do-gooder's fantasy. A kid as lost and confused as he was after losing his mom.

The emptiness still surfaced when he thought of ways he had tried to fill the hole in his gut: A summer day, brilliant sunshine. Horns blared as angry drivers hit their brakes and skidded to a stop to avoid hitting him as he ran from a police-man. Panic when he was blocked by a squad car. Words of one cop to the other, "He's a fast little fucker. I'll give him that." Enormous relief when his father walked into the police station, then shame. Even now it made him blush. His dad must have told the cops about his mom. That always brought sympathy. People made excuses for him. He was just acting out because of his grief.

"So, Jake, what do you think? Does this boy sound like a good match for you? Oh, and another thing: he's a huge Ohio State football fan."

Jake did a double take. The OSU patches on the boy's jacket, the sister with Down syndrome. "This boy . . . is his mother a teacher? Reagan something?"

"Yes, that's right. Do you know them?"

"I wouldn't say I know them. I've met them. I didn't know she was a widow."

"Yes. It was very sad. Her husband was in his thirties.

Cancer." Maisy grabbed one of the flyaway straggles of hair and tucked it behind her ear.

"It's quite a coincidence we're talking about Reagan's son. I met her the first time two or three weeks ago, then ran into her again after that." Jake hesitated. Coach Majors stared at him from the credenza. "Yeah . . . yeah, I'd like to get started. What're the next steps?"

"So, we'll set up a short meeting to get acquainted. That'll be at Matthew's home with his mom, Matthew, you, and me. After that, if everyone agrees, you all can work out a schedule."

"Sounds great," Jake said. "I'll make myself available when it's convenient for you guys."

As he walked Maisy to the door, his thoughts returned to eleven-year-old Jake: his father dropping him off at home after the police station; the monotonous *ticktock* of his mother's grandfather clock dogging him through the lonely house; the sense of worthlessness; the desperation for something, anything. He had tried to think of a friend to call, but he hadn't talked to anyone all summer. No one had called him either. He'd finally decided any place had to be better than there. So he grabbed his backpack and headed back to the mall and got into real trouble.

REAGAN

CHAPTER NINE

Thank god for the weekend. It had been a hectic week at school, plus it had been over a month since she became the only witness to a shooting. Her home life still hadn't fully returned to normal. She left the school building, loaded down with a bulky box of posters advertising a middle school bake sale. Menacing clouds threatened a downpour. She wanted to get home before the storm. The posters she had promised to distribute around Norwood wouldn't go up today with this weather.

One of her seventh graders stood stoop shouldered outside the redbrick school's entrance, a backpack slung over her shoulder, her long, thin hair flying around her face.

"Angela, why are you still here?" Reagan had to bite her tongue to keep from asking the girl to stand up straight. She too had been uncomfortably tall at that age.

"I'm waiting for my mom. She was supposed to pick me up at three." The teen pulled her sweater tight around her.

"It's almost four. Have you called her?"

"I did, but she didn't answer."

"Well, help me get this into my trunk and I'll drive you home. It's about to storm." Reagan wasn't supposed to do that, but she couldn't let the girl get caught out in a thunderstorm.

"Thanks, Mrs. Ramsey. Where's your car?"

"It's the red Honda Accord."

Reagan opened the trunk, and the two of them struggled to push the unwieldy container in around a collapsible stroller and a couple of cases of Coke. The damp, cold wind plastered Reagan's skirt to her backside. Chill bumps peppered her arms.

"Hello, Miz Ramsey."

Surprised, Reagan pivoted to face one of her former students, a senior, standing too close, his eyes squinting at her. He was about her height and thin. His clothes reeked of cigarettes; his fingers were stained yellow.

"Bryan Butler, what are you doing here?"

With a toss of his head, he flipped his dark hair away from his eyes. "Just passin' by."

"Well, you're too late if you were going to help."

"Help? Oh, you mean with the box?"

Reagan motioned with her palms. "Bryan, personal space. Back it up, buddy."

He took one step back, his eyes squeezed into thin slits. "It's been a long time since I seen you, Miz Ramsey. Ain't it?"

A rip of lightning, closely followed by a shotgun blast of thunder, startled them both.

"Yes. It's nice to see you, Bryan, but we were just leaving. I want to get Angela home before the sky falls. Angela, get in the car and buckle up."

"I heard you seen that drive-by over on Montgomery last month."

Reagan flinched. "Who did you hear that from?" she asked, studying his face.

He shrugged. "I heard it around."

"What does that mean, 'around'?"

"I just overheard some guys. They said the dude that done it, he's a really bad dude."

"That's obvious. He murdered that young man."

"I hope y'all don't have any trouble outa 'em. They say you looked right at the guy." Bryan's stare was unrelenting.

Reagan's stomach tightened as she glanced around the parking lot. Just a few cars still there. She straightened and crossed her arms. "Why would I have trouble?"

"I just hope he don't think ya might finger 'em."

Reagan recalled the Bryan of seventh grade. A capable student, but his family didn't seem interested. She had always felt a little sad for him; he wasn't a bad kid. "Bryan, do you know who shot that young man?"

"Me? Uh, nah. Not me." He leaned toward her and shook his head, but his eyes never strayed.

"Did you have anything to do with that shooting?"

He blinked twice and answered with a flat voice. "Er . . . no, of course not. You know how word gets around. Lots of people talk."

Reagan frowned and searched his face. "Who do you hang around with now, Bryan? Don't forget, I know your mom. How 'bout I call her to ask what's going on with you?"

"If you know her so well, you know she don't give a shit about me. Go ahead. Call 'er."

Reagan's eyes narrowed. "Well, how about I talk to Ms. Ginny?" Fat raindrops began to splatter against the car roof. She opened the driver's-side door, but Bryan grabbed her arm.

"Leave my grandma alone! I told you, I ain't done nothin' wrong."

Reagan looked at his hand on her arm and arched an eyebrow as needles of cold rain pricked her skin.

He released her and leaned closer to her ear. "I just don't want anything bad to happen to you or your kids."

Reagan ducked into the driver's seat and slammed the door. A bright flash of lightning lit Bryan's face as he stood outside the window. Another loud crack of thunder followed.

Rain blew into the car when Reagan lowered her window. "You need to get out of the rain, Bryan, but you shouldn't worry about me. My brother's a Norwood cop. He's sticking to me like glue. You know what you hear around. You don't want to mess with a cop or a cop's family."

She started the car and drove away, looking at Bryan in her rearview mirror, his features distorted by the rain as he watched her leave the lot.

"That guy's creepy," Angela said. "Most of the kids stay away from him."

Water dripped from Reagan's hair down her neck, making her shiver. She cranked up the heater. "Really? Do you know him?"

"Well, I don't know him. He hangs around school a lot."

"The middle school? Why?"

"Mrs. Ramsey, geez. He deals."

Reagan froze. "Who knows about this? I haven't heard anything like that about him."

Angela shrugged. "Kids talk. It's good your brother's a policeman."

"Yeah, well . . . he's sort of like a brother." She slowed to turn onto Donner Lane.

"You can let me out here. My house is just up the street."

"Of course not. I'll take you home."

When she pulled up in front of Angela's house, the sight shocked her. Although typical of the houses built for GM workers—a well-built brick home with a covered front porch spanning its full width—a couple of the hinges were off the garage door and it hung askew. The small yard had missed the last mowing of summer, and weeds had taken over. Blinds on the front windows were broken. The place looked awful. Angela always wore nice clothes and was meticulous about her grooming.

"Thank you for the ride, Mrs. Ramsey. See you Monday." She grabbed the door handle as a crack of thunder boomed so loud it shook the car.

"Angela, wait. We can sit here until it lets up a little."

The girl shrugged. "Okay."

"Do you have any idea where your mother is?"

"It's okay if she's not home. I have a key. I'm old enough." She slipped the strap of her backpack over her shoulder.

"Of course you are. But I'm concerned about you being alone during this storm. She'll probably be home soon. I can wait a little while."

"Oh, no. You don't need to do that. I'll be fine. But thank you, though." With that she jumped out of the car and ran toward her front porch in the downpour.

Angela was a sweet kid, a good student. Her expression, when Reagan had offered to wait with her for her mother, looked strange . . . like fear, or shame. It troubled Reagan. Every school year one or two of her students needed a little more attention than the others. Help with their schoolwork maybe, or sometimes just kindness from a caring adult.

It had been like that with Bryan. She spent many afternoons after school with him, at first, when he didn't have his homework done. She made him finish it after school, no excuses. She quickly realized he didn't do his homework because he wanted that attention from her, so rather than making the after-school sessions a consequence, they became a reward. She enlisted his help in the science lab, but only if he turned in his homework with a passing grade. She made him realize he had potential. His biggest problem was his relationship with his parents. Sounded like it hadn't gotten any better.

Now here he was, a kid she hadn't seen in years, seeking her out to warn her she was in danger . . . or was it a threat?

JAKE

CHAPTER TEN

Eleven thirty Sunday morning, a beautiful November day, sunny and brisk. Jake rang the doorbell and waited on the covered porch, there to pick up Matthew for the Bengals game. He had to admit, he was a little nervous. He liked kids, had always wanted his own, but hadn't been around them much. The game would take the pressure off. He could explain the plays.

The door opened and a woman he didn't expect—sixtyish with graying hair, one thick braid that reached halfway down her back—smiled at him.

"Hi. You must be Jake. Come in." She wiped her hands on the apron tied around her waist. "I'm Anaya." She swung the door open wide for him to pass. "I came over to stay with Lizzie while Reagan gets out for a bit. She likes to run on Sunday."

He tried to place her accent—very precise English. An amazing aroma, a spice he couldn't identify, made his mouth water when he walked in. Barbra Streisand's velvety voice flowed from the kitchen: "The Way We Were."

"I'm preparing a curry for their dinner. Reagan doesn't

cook much, so the kids love it when I do." She grinned. "Reagan loves it too."

"Smells delicious," he said.

Much like the time he was there for the "get acquainted" meeting, the living room was comfortably messy—toys strewn about, a colorful patchwork afghan thrown across a black leather sofa, books stacked on the coffee table, a large teddy bear flat on the floor in front of the TV, as if it had been used as a pillow.

Lizzie sat at the dining room table, eating a sandwich and watching a video on an iPad. A children's song competed with Barbra: "Five Little Monkeys." At the appropriate place in the song, Lizzie put her hand to her mouth and ear in the universal sign for telephone and sang along with the recording. The words were soft and unintelligible, but Jake got the picture: *call the doctor.* She stopped the song, backed up the recording, and sang it again. From her studious expression, she seemed to be trying to get it just right.

"Hello, Lizzie."

A smile leaped across her face. Her two front teeth were missing. Her long, dark ponytail rested on her shoulder, and her eyes danced with some secret—possibly that she was sneaking bits of her sandwich to that small, furry dog begging under the table. She was quite possibly the cutest little girl he had ever seen.

Matthew came bounding down the stairs wearing a red-and-white Ohio State jersey over a long-sleeved sweater. "Hi, I'm ready." He held out the front of his jersey with both hands. "This is the only one I have. I've never been to an NFL game. My dad always said it cost too much."

Matthew looked anxious or excited, Jake couldn't tell which. Exactly the way he felt. They had gotten together for that first meeting, arranged by Maisy Jefferson, but hadn't talked much since.

"You nailed it, sport. That jersey's great. There'll be a ton of Ohio State fans there."

Matthew glanced down at the shirt and nodded.

The front door flew open, and Reagan blew in like a gust of wind. Tall, long legs, a solid build. She wore yoga pants and an athletic top that clung to her ribcage. Red hair in a ponytail, tinges of pink on both cheeks. He had never seen her dressed like that and without makeup, had never noticed the smattering of freckles on the bridge of her nose. He tried to avoid staring at the sweat that trickled from her collarbone to the low-cut V of her shirt. His eyebrows shot up as he blew out a puff of breath.

"Hi, Jake. I'm glad I caught you guys before you left." She grabbed a towel hanging over the back of a dining room chair, mopped her brow and the back of her neck. Her breathing was quick, her mouth wide with perfect teeth, a pretty smile. She walked to Matthew, drew him into a sideways hug, then stepped back and looked into his eyes. "Have a wonderful time, but—"

"I know, Mom, I know. Stay close to Jake, pay attention to the game, don't drive him crazy talkin' all the time." He bobbed his head from side to side as he listed all the things he wasn't going to forget. He rolled his eyes and gave her a crooked grin. "Mom, don't worry. I'll be great."

Jake winked at her. "Like he said, he'll be great."

A tiger roared from the huge scoreboard as Jake and Matthew walked up the ramp into the bright sunlight. Jake carried a tray with drinks and hotdogs, a large bag of unshelled peanuts under his arm. Matthew had a basket of nachos. They made their way through the horde of people to their seats, ten rows from the field on the forty-five-yard line. Dave Johnson, Dekker's manager on the Humana project, and his son, Joey, were already there. They were listening to a portable radio they'd brought for the game commentary. Jake had asked Dave to be there with Joey—more fun for Matthew.

The place smelled of grilled onions, fried food, and anticipation. The atmosphere was charged enough to sizzle. The Mason High School band finished a pregame presentation and marched off the field, the drumline last to disappear behind a wall painted with jungle greenery—*ba da boom, ba da boom, ba da boom, boom, boom.*

The Ben-Gals, brandishing orange-and-black pompoms, whipped folks into a frenzy. As usual, when Cincinnati played Pittsburgh, the visitors wearing black and yellow numbered about as many as those wearing orange. Just being in the jungle—the noise, the fans, the tension—made Jake's pulse quicken. He loved football, had played all through school. He wasn't sure Matthew understood the game, but that was okay. He would teach him, one of the things he most wanted to do with him.

Matthew's eyes widened as he looked around. "Wow, these are great seats. They must have cost a lot."

The comment caught him off guard. "Yeah, they were pricey, I guess. I didn't pay for them. My company buys season tickets every year. The employees take turns using them."

"Oh . . . do you think I could work there one day? What's your company's name?"

Jake hesitated. He didn't want Matthew to know he was the owner, or think of him as a rich man, someone who could buy him things. He certainly didn't want him or Reagan to be intimidated by the difference in their lifestyles. He wanted to be a friend, a mentor, like Coach Majors had been to him, but Matthew knew his name was Jake Dekker. "It's a construction com—"

Suddenly the announcer blared over the loudspeaker: "Ladies and gentlemen, would you please stand for the presentation of the colors."

Matthew hopped up as the crowd stood. Servicemen and servicewomen, with huge flags strapped to their waists, ran onto the field. Old Glory waved from the huge screen above, and Paul Brown Stadium soon resonated with the voices of sixty-five thousand people singing the national anthem.

After that, as three players from each team walked to the center of the field for the coin toss, Jake introduced Dave and Joey to Matthew. Joey was in the seventh grade, Matthew in the third. Despite the age difference, they seemed to click. Matthew immediately offered to share his nachos. The boys talked to each other, ignoring the adults. Good decision, to ask Dave and Joey along.

At the kickoff, all four of the Dekker group jumped up with the rest of the crowd and yelled at the top of their lungs. The crowd noise was deafening. Andy Dalton, the Bengals' quarterback, ran onto the field and huddled with the offense, then stepped out, looked to the bench, and squeezed his helmet to his ears with both hands.

A vendor stood in front of the first row with his back to the field, holding a case of Bud Light. People passed money down and bottles up. Jake got the boys' attention, huddled with them to be heard over the crowd. "Okay, guys, if we win, I treat us all to dinner, wherever you want to go. If we lose, we behave like men . . . and go home and cry ourselves to sleep."

The boys looked at each other, grinned, and high-fived. "Yeah!"

Dalton threw a long pass that was caught at the thirty. Matthew hollered, "Noooo!" and pointed at a lineman. "Number seventy-four held." He slapped his forehead. A yellow flag flew onto the field; a shrill whistle stopped play.

Jake furrowed his brow, glanced at Matthew sideways, and gave him a crooked grin. He hadn't noticed that hold, but Matthew had. So much for teaching the kid about the game.

Eyes still focused on the field, Matthew asked Joey, "Where do you go to school?"

"Norwood Middle School." Joey leaned forward, his elbows on his knees.

"Really? My mom's a teacher there."

"Oh yeah? What's her name?"

"Mrs. Ramsey."

"Mrs. Ramsey's your mom? No way. She's my science teacher. Best teacher ever."

Showing a full set of glistening white teeth, a huge grin stretched across Matthew's face. His mother's grin. The kind of grin that was contagious.

Joey's eyes widened. "Wait . . . so, you're *that* Matthew? Lizzie's your sister?"

"Yeah. Do you know Lizzie?"

Joey straightened and rolled his eyes. "Let's just say, I know *of* Lizzie."

Uh-oh. Jake scooted a little closer to Matthew and leaned in.

Joey continued. "Your mom tells some hilarious stories about you guys."

Matthew giggled. "Yeah, Lizzie does some really funny things, but my mom doesn't always think it's so funny at the time."

Jake continued to have one eye on the game while he listened to the boys' conversation. By the second quarter, Matthew had told Joey about his favorite NFL player, Tom Brady, even if the Patriots did cheat; his favorite class, STEM, and the STEM camp he attended during the summer; and his rock collection. Despite the chatter, Matthew kept up with the game.

"Do you like school?" Jake asked.

Matthew nodded.

"What are the other kids like?"

"Lots of pretty girls." Matthew raised his eyebrows and grinned.

"Ah . . . pretty girls, huh. Do you have a girlfriend?"

Matthew looked at Jake with an incredulous expression. "Why would anybody want just one when there are so many?"

Laughter sprang from Jake's belly.

At halftime the game was tied fourteen-all, the food was gone, and peanut shells covered the concrete. Jake stood. "Okay, who needs a pit stop?" They joined the throng of people making their way to the concession stands and restrooms. When they returned to their seats, this time with cheeseburgers, Jake told Matthew, "I didn't know you knew so much about football."

Matthew pulled his hair away from his eyes and looked up at Jake. "Well, I have been going to Ohio State games since I was little."

Jake smiled. He could see Reagan in Matthew—the green eyes, the red hair, the way his head tilted up when he smiled. He was a cute kid. "Do you want to play when you're in high school? Or maybe junior high?"

"Nah, my mom won't let me. My dad wouldn't either. He used to say he loved football, but he loved me more." Matthew blushed. "Have you heard the stuff about concussions?"

Jake nodded. In his football-playing days, concussions weren't an issue. If you got your bell rung, you sat out a couple of downs, then went back in. Nobody considered the lasting impact. A lot of players paid the price for that shortsightedness. Jake had sat out more than a few sets of downs and sometimes wondered if it would eventually catch up with him. Even if he had known the risks, he still would have played. Football and building. He was good at those, comfortable.

Matthew knitted his brows. "Have you ever had a concussion?"

The last thing Jake wanted to do was worry Matthew. "No," he lied. "Can't say I have."

"Good."

Jake sipped a Coke and made casual comments to the guys about the game. Matthew finished his cheeseburger and wadded the wrapper into a ball. Joey and Dave quietly watched the field and commented to each other.

After a while, Matthew stood up next to Jake and fished something out of his pocket, a worn three-by-five photo of a man with a toddler. He handed the picture to Jake. Creased from being folded, it looked as if it might have even gone through the wash. "This is me and my dad when I was two."

He looked at Jake's face and seemed to study him, waiting for a response. Jake nodded slowly, unsure how to proceed. He wanted this to be a fun day for Matthew, not a time to talk about sad topics, but the child was trusting him with an important piece of information, and he didn't want to mess up their connection.

"It looks like you've carried this around for a long time."

Matthew nodded and sat back down.

"I bet you miss him a lot."

"Yeah . . . he *was* my dad." Matthew left no room for the notion that a father and son would be anything other than close, loving. Jake's own father came to mind, the jumble of emotions he had tried for years to untangle. His vision blurred; the corners of his mouth pulled downward.

Matthew continued. "He liked football, too, and he was funny . . . and he took me a lot of places, like Ohio State games, and to shoot darts. We'd all go out to eat. Lizzie was always good when we were with my dad."

"That's a nice photo," Jake commented, handing it back to the boy. Then he reached into his own jacket to retrieve something from the inside pocket. Matthew watched as Jake opened a locket with two tiny pictures. "This is my father." He pointed to a man's image stuck in the left side. "And this is me when I was six. It was my mother's locket. Sometimes I wear it; other times I keep it in my pocket. Like your dad, my mom died when I was a kid."

"Oh." Matthew's face softened. The edges of his eyes turned downward as he seemed to search Jake's face for a moment. He scooted closer.

The sting in Jake's eyes surprised him. He had always sensed something was missing in his life, the bond between a man and his children, the simple act of watching a football game with his son. He was moved by this child who had suffered such a profound loss, whose family had so many challenges. Matthew, obviously nurtured with love, was so easy to be around—so polite, so happy, so sensitive. His own stepson was so difficult, so argumentative, so angry. What had he done wrong with Alex?

Matthew's attention jerked back to the game when the Bengals' pass was intercepted. He grabbed his head with both hands and yelled, "Noooo!"

The Pittsburgh fans went crazy. Chatting was impossible. The next snap, the Steelers' fullback rushed to the Bengals' twenty-five, then called a time-out. The home side grew quiet. A collective holding of breath. The Dekker group kept their eyes on the field, but apparently Matthew's thoughts were elsewhere.

"My dad still watches over us all the time. Mom says he won't let anything happen to us, but my Uncle Sonny and Mom argue over that."

"Really? Why?"

Matthew shrugged, turned his hands upward.

"Parents can be hard to understand," Jake said. "It took me a long time to understand my dad." And a lot of help.

Music blasted through the loudspeakers. The Ben-Gals, with bare midriffs and hip-hugger skirts, rushed out and danced directly in front of Dekker's section, their pompoms shaking with each beat. Jake glanced at Dave, who raised both

eyebrows and laughed. The expression on the boys' faces . . .
worth the price of the tickets and then some.

Matthew started moving with the music, alternating his
hips right and left, shoulders up and down, swinging his arms.
Joey laughed and joined the dancing.

Tension from the game drifted away as Jake watched the
kids. It had been a while since he'd had so much fun. When
play resumed, the Steelers lined up for a field goal attempt.

The music stopped and the crowd roared. Bengal fans
standing in the end zone bent over the wall as far as they could
and slapped the jungle foliage. It didn't work. The kick sailed
through the goalposts, making the score seventeen to four-
teen, Steelers.

Matthew bounced on his feet, yelling at the players. Jake's
jaw ached from clenching his teeth; his shoulders and neck
were stiff. He badly wanted Matthew's first time at Paul Brown
Stadium to be awesome, so the Bengals had to win. This was
it—the heart-pounding adrenaline rush that lured people
to the games. The thing that made normally reserved, well-
mannered folks paint their faces, scream at the players until
they lost their voices, and go insane. Impossible to explain.
Addictive.

The Bengals hurried to the line, quickly snapped the ball.
Dalton stepped back and threw a pass ten yards to the receiver,
who was brought down immediately. The Bengals sprinted to
the field in hurry-up offense. Dalton passed off to the running
back, who broke through the line. A Steeler defender promptly
tackled him, but he twirled away and kicked up speed, running dangerously close to the sideline. Jake held his breath as
he watched the screen, the camera projecting a vantage point
the fans couldn't see from their seats. The running back was
fast, sure-footed. The last Steeler defender tripped and fell at
the five-yard line as the runner crossed into the tiger-striped
end zone.

Chaos reigned; the noise was earsplitting. The Bengal Tiger roared. Adrenaline surged through Jake. Matthew and Joey jumped up and down, grabbed peanut shells off the concrete, and threw them in the air.

The players lined up for the point after and kicked the ball through the goalposts as the clock ticked down to one second. Players, coaches, staff, and fans ran onto the field as men with huge cameras got as close as possible to the players. Matthew and Joey whispered to each other, then began chanting, "We want pizza. We want pizza."

It took a few moments for Jake's heart to calm and stop pounding. Bringing the kids was supposed to be a treat for them, a sacrifice he was willing to make, but they added a whole new dimension to the excitement, the fun. He had never enjoyed a game more. Maybe he wouldn't need to teach Matthew about football, but there were other things he could teach him. Other things they could do together.

He slapped his hands on his knees, grinned, and said, "Now, pizza."

REAGAN

CHAPTER ELEVEN

Characters from *The Jungle Book*—Mowgli, Baloo, Shere Khan, King Louie, and Bagheera—decorated the colorful walls. The place smelled like bubblegum. It would take more than cartoons to put Reagan at ease. The young dental tech named Ashlee popped into the waiting room, a wide smile plastered across her face. "Okay, Lizzie, Matthew, are you guys ready?"

Was that smile genuine or concealing panic? Reagan wasn't sure. "Are *you* ready?" she asked. "That's the bigger question."

She had taken a half day off for the biannual ordeal: visiting the pediatric dentist. She and both kids followed Ashlee back to the exam room. *Hopefully it will go better this time.* Lizzie hated going to the dentist.

"Oh, we've got you covered," Ashlee said, again with a smile. When they reached the exam room, two other techs, Bree and Anneliese, according to their name tags, stood behind the exam chair. To amuse Lizzie, they held hand puppets: one a black cat, the other a yellow Tweety Bird with big eyes.

The puppets danced around, heads bobbing, each talking in a high-pitched singsong voice. "Tweety Bird, say hello to Matthew and Lizzie." They jumped up and down. "Hi, Matthew. Hi, Lizzie."

At the door, Lizzie looked at the puppets and laughed. Then a high-pitched whine coming from the next room caught her attention, and she focused on the dental chair. Much like Scooter being pushed into his crate, she stiffened her arms, splayed her fingers, and backed up. They had tried the puppets the last visit too.

Lizzie dropped Annie, the rag doll she'd brought from home, and turned to run.

Matthew said, "Oh no you don't." He and Reagan stood behind her, blocking her path. She immediately dropped to the floor. Matthew rolled his eyes and took a deep breath. "Not that again."

Reagan tried to grab Lizzie around the chest and pull her up, but her armpits seemed to disappear, and she went limp, dead weight.

"Okay, which one of you drew the short straw?" Reagan asked.

Ashlee and Anneliese both stepped forward. "We'll help."

Reagan stood over Lizzie. "Honey, we talked about this. It's not going to hurt. You'll be fine. They're just going to look into your mouth. You remember Ashlee and Dr. Litchfield. Now please, get in the chair." She grabbed her daughter's arm. Lizzie jerked it away.

"Okay, we'll go to plan B. When I pick her up, you guys each grab a leg. Hopefully we can lift her up and put her in." Reagan grabbed her around the chest and lifted.

As soon as Ashlee touched Lizzie, she screamed, "Noooo!" kicking with both feet, arms flying, torso twisting and jerking like a wild bronco. Bree tossed the puppets and rushed over to help. They yelled to each other: "Hold her there!" "Grab that leg!" "Jeez Louise!" Matthew was in the middle of them, talking to Lizzie, trying to calm her. "Baby, don't forget, if you're good, we'll get a reward when we're done. Remember last time? You got—"

Slam! Bang! They collided with the wall, knocking a framed poster down with a loud crash. The racket must have been heard in the waiting room, but Reagan couldn't help it. They let Lizzie go and she slipped to the floor again.

Ashlee said to Anneliese, "See, I told you. Lizzie is strong."

A deep voice broke through the commotion. "What's going on here?"

Everyone, including Lizzie, stopped and looked toward the door. Dr. Litchfield strolled into the room and looked down at the child splayed out on the floor. He crouched down and spoke calmly. "Well, hello, Lizzie. It's been a while. I thought I heard you in here. Why don't you get in this nice chair, and I'll take a look at your teeth?" He offered her his hand.

Lizzie seemed to consider his offer for a second, grabbed her doll with one hand, then reached out and took his hand with the other. He helped her into the chair.

Reagan felt an unexpected flash of resentment that men could manage Lizzie so easily. The exam went smoothly after that. Reagan stood on one side, holding her daughter's hand, and Matthew stood on the other, reminding Lizzie about the reward grab bag.

No longer embarrassed by these episodes, Reagan did not bother making excuses, but she worried. Even a dentist who treats only children, one who specializes in treating children with special needs, could refuse to put up with Lizzie. She was worn out by the time they were finished.

"Well, kids, you both scored in the nineties. Good job," Dr. Litchfield said. "Now help yourself to the grab bag. We'll see you again in six months. Happy Thanksgiving."

The young women looked at each other, wide-eyed, and smiled.

Happy Thanksgiving. The greeting echoed through her mind. She had known it would be a hard week and had practiced counting her blessings. Lizzie couldn't have been more cooperative when they stopped by the grocery on the way home. Considering the last time Reagan had taken her to Kroger, that was a blessing. Her head bowed, lower lip out, chin quivering, Lizzie looked at Reagan through watery eyes. With her fist closed, thumb on top, she repeatedly made a clockwise motion against her chest.

"Okay, you're sorry. I'm sorry we all had to go through that. I know it's scary to go to the dentist, but that's part of us taking care of you."

Reagan shook her head. *She doesn't understand that. When she's scared—a lot of grown men are scared of the dentist— she can't express it any other way. She's done her best to make amends.*

Reagan draped her arm around her daughter's shoulder, bent down, and gave her a butterfly kiss on the cheek.

With her thumb, index finger, and pinkie extended, Lizzie signed "I love you" to Reagan and Matthew both.

"We love you too," Matthew told her, mimicking the sign.

Lizzie hugged Annie, her doll, and jabbered to her while they waited in the checkout line.

It was two o'clock by the time Reagan pulled into her driveway. She asked Matthew to carry one of the bags of groceries, and she took the larger one, holding on to Lizzie with her other hand. As she trudged up the steps, something wet seeped through the bottom of the sack. When she grabbed it with both hands, Lizzie pulled away and jumped on the porch swing with Annie.

Reagan barely made it to the kitchen with the groceries before the bag disintegrated. She put the milk in the refrigerator, the ice cream in the freezer, and left the other things to go get Lizzie in, but her phone rang, sidetracking her.

"Hey, sis," she said.

"How'd the dentist trip go?"

"Better than last time. I only lost two teeth today, and the doc said I could get my leg out of the cast in three to four weeks."

Jordan giggled. "That well, huh? What about Matthew?"

"He'll be okay when he gets used to the eye patch." With the phone to her ear, Reagan walked to the living room window. Lizzie still swung with her doll. "How's it going in Atlanta?"

"Great!"

Reagan's terrific big sister and only sibling had flown in from her home in Atlanta six times in the eight months before Scott died. For the last two and a half months of that, she had managed her demanding real estate business, barking directives to three full-time staff, from Reagan's small dining room table. She took charge of running Reagan's household.

As much as they loved each other, they couldn't be more different. Jordan—high energy, focused, and compulsive—hated chaos and imperfection, and ran after the children to wipe down fingerprints and pick up. People who knew the two women said it was a good thing Lizzie hadn't been born to Jordan, who wouldn't have been able to cope with such a child. Reagan, on the other hand, had always been more relaxed. Different priorities.

Physically, too, they were unalike. Jordan was blond, five foot five, a size four, always smartly dressed and trendy. Reagan's friends teased that she had never owned an accessory and her weight fluctuated with the joys and stresses of her life. At five eleven, Reagan liked to think of herself as *substantial*. The only time she could have been considered slim was after taking care of Scott. She did try to keep a healthy weight, but she didn't stress over it. Besides, Scott always said he liked a woman with a little meat on her bones.

"I want you guys to come to Atlanta for some R & R. I just closed on another town house on the BeltLine. Big commission. So, I'm picking up the Ramseys' airfare for Christmas in Atlanta."

"Booyah!" Reagan threw her arms in the air and signaled to Matthew to join her.

That was just what Reagan needed. She'd been dreading Christmas. She and Matthew did a high five and a little jig, Reagan with the phone to her ear. Scooter jumped up on his hind legs, trying to take part.

"Look, Jordan, we just got home and Lizzie's outside. I need to get her. Congratulations on the sale. That's great."

"Okay, guys. Do what ya gotta do. Love ya."

"Love ya too."

"Love you, Aunt Jordan," Matthew shouted into the phone.

"Okay, little man. Let's get your sister in." Reagan went to the door and froze; her heart flew to her throat. The yellow swing was moving back and forth . . . but there was no Lizzie.

ALEX

CHAPTER TWELVE

"I don't know how this room could smell so bad when I get in here and clean it myself twice a week," Frances complained when she opened Alex's door. She walked bent over with her hand on her hip.

She was really old, but Jake loved her. Before either his mother or Jake had time to get home, Alex would air the room out good, rid it of any hint of weed or incense. But he enjoyed testing how far he could push Frances without her getting wise. For days she dusted around a bong holding an artificial daisy, and she never said anything about it. Trip had bet Alex he wouldn't leave it out for a week. Alex won.

Lying on his bed, he scowled and pointed to the phone stuck to his ear.

"Didn't you hear me call you?" Frances said. "You better get off that phone. There's a policeman here to see you, and he don't look too patient."

Alex jerked to a sitting position, cupped his hand over his mouth, and tried to whisper into the phone, but his voice was too shrill for a whisper. "Shit, a cop is downstairs. Fuck! Don't worry, I won't say anything." He ended the call. "What's he want?"

Frances shrugged. "You."

"I'll be right down."

Before going downstairs, he looked at himself in the mirror, pulled off his black T-shirt, put on a collared shirt, and popped some Tic Tacs. He looked again. Better.

A man maybe a little older than Jake stood in the foyer, examining the grandfather clock. He didn't look like a policeman. No uniform, just dark pants and a tan leather jacket. He glanced up when Alex approached.

Frances dusted just inside the living room, within easy listening distance.

"May I help you?" Alex asked.

"Alex, I'm Detective Travis." He flashed his badge. "I'm investigating a hit-skip accident that took place on Sleepy Hollow Road a few weeks ago—very early Saturday morning, October thirteenth. Do you know anything about such an accident?"

Alex's heart pounded hard enough to scare him, but he forced himself to look the detective in the eyes. "No, sir, I don't. Let me see. Uh . . . the thirteenth . . . last month. I was still on crutches." He pointed to the walking cast. "I just got this a few days ago. I had an accident myself. There's a record of that. You can check if you want. Uh . . . anyway, I wasn't going out much." He cut his eyes to the ceiling. "I can't remember what I was doing on the thirteenth, but I didn't hear anything about an accident."

"Actually, it would have been the evening of the twelfth, Friday evening."

Alex pretended to think about that for a moment, then shook his head. "Hmmm. Let me see. . . ."

"Do you know a Michael Yeager?"

"Uh, Michael Yeager? No, I don't know anybody by that name. At least I don't think I do. The name isn't familiar, but I might know him if I saw him. Does he go to my school?"

Detective Travis raised one eyebrow and studied Alex a moment before pulling a small brown notebook from his pocket. He flipped through several pages. "Do you know Jeff Schmidt?"

Be chill, man! "Yeah, I know Jeff. He's in my life sciences class."

"Were you at a party at his house on the evening of the twelfth?"

They know, they know. What can they do to me for lying? He's trying to trap you, man!

Alex tightened his jaw and hesitated. "Well, I have been to his house recently. I guess it could have been the twelfth."

"What time did you leave?" the detective asked.

Alex shrugged. "I don't remember."

"Were you driving?"

"Uh, no. I told you before, I had an accident. That happened on the fifth . . . before the twelfth. You can check." He pointed to the detective's notebook like the report of his accident could be found there. "I wasn't able to drive then."

"Who were you with that night? Who drove you home Friday night, the evening of the twelfth, or the early morning of the thirteenth?"

Trapped! He didn't want to give the police Trip's name, like some common narc, but if he didn't, he'd look guilty for sure. "Uh, I was with Trip Lewis. He drove that night."

"Trip?"

"Yeah—well—actually, his name is Crawford Lewis the third. We all call him Trip."

Surprise flashed across the detective's face. "You were with Crawford Lewis's son?"

"Yes, sir."

"Did you see a man out jogging along the road that night when you left the party?"

He swallowed hard, his mouth dry. Where was he getting his information? Was it a crime to lie to a detective? "No. We didn't see any jogger. It was pretty late when we left, if we are talking about the same night. Too late for joggers."

The detective judged him, then scribbled something in his notebook and flipped it closed. "Well, Alex, I may be back with a few more questions, if that's okay."

What if I say it's not okay? What then? Alex shrugged and closed the door behind the detective. Shit! It'd been so long— they'd thought they'd gotten away with it.

Frances stopped dusting, rested her hands on her hips, and looked at Alex. As he turned toward the stairs, she muttered, "What's that boy gotten into now? I'm thinking—trouble."

REAGAN

CHAPTER THIRTEEN

Reagan stood on her next-door neighbor's porch, shifting from one foot to the other, and rang the doorbell. She checked her watch. Two thirty-five. "Hi, Betty," she said across the screen when the door opened. "Lizzie isn't in there, is she?"

Betty Crammer dipped her chin and looked at Reagan over the top of her reading glasses. "No, hon, she isn't." Her voice was raspy from three decades of smoking. "What's wrong?"

"You know how quick she is." Reagan shook her head. "I got distracted for a moment and she took off."

"Let me grab a jacket. I'll help you." That was Betty, an I'll-drop-everything-to-help kind of neighbor. The kind you found in Norwood. While she waited, Reagan looked up and down the street. A nice day to be outside, sunny and in the low fifties, warm for late November. Sounds of children laughing and screaming drifted from Immaculate Conception Academy, a little more than a city block away. Students often played soccer in the street during recess.

Oh, that's where she is. Reagan felt a quick sense of relief.

Last month, on a rare day when public schools were closed but parochial schools weren't, she and the kids had walked past Immaculate Conception during recess. Some kids noticed Lizzie, stopped their game, and ran to her and Matthew, begging them to play. Matthew fit right in, chasing after the other kids, but Lizzie couldn't keep up, although she tried. The children were patient with her, giving her special attention. Lizzie loved that. Reagan loved those kids.

Without waiting for Betty, she ran toward the school. As usual, the short street in front of the school had been closed to automobile traffic for the soccer game. The young students were fast, agile, squealing with delight. Oh the joy of being able to run like that, being coordinated enough to control a ball with your foot, and not even realize what a gift that was. Watching them was bittersweet.

"Is she here?" Betty Crammer asked a little breathlessly when she caught up. She wore an orange Bengals' sweatshirt over her blouse.

With her hand over her brow to block the sun, Reagan scanned the area. The gray-stone church with twin towers always reminded Reagan of a miniature Notre-Dame. In the lot between the church and the redbrick school building next door, two women stood talking while they watched their students. A few cars were parked in the lot. Nothing out of the ordinary.

"I don't see her." The letdown was immediate. Reagan's energy deflated like a punctured tire.

"Well, don't worry, hon. We'll find her."

A ball chased by a girl with a blond ponytail spurted in front of the women. "Hi, Mrs. Ramsey."

"Oh, hi." She was one of the girls who had played with Lizzie. "You remember me and my daughter, don't you?" Reagan's voice was wobbly and shrill. She took a deep breath to settle herself. "Have you seen her today? Did she come by here?"

The girl moved closer to Reagan, her eyebrows scrunched together, concern in her voice. "No. She didn't. I would have noticed."

Reagan nodded. "Okay, thanks."

"I hope you find her."

Reagan nodded. Thirty-five minutes since Lizzie had been missing. She could have gone a long way in that length of time. Reagan's stomach churned.

Betty said, "Where's Matthew?"

"He went up the street toward Smith."

"Well, he probably has her already. Why don't we go back home?"

Reagan nodded. "Maybe you're right, but I want to talk to those women first."

But the teachers hadn't seen Lizzie either. On their way back, Reagan and Betty checked the backyards of all the homes on both sides of the street.

Matthew was sitting on the front porch when they returned to the house. "Mom, did you find her?"

Reagan shook her head, climbed the steps, flopped down on the swing, and tried to think. It was now after three. Lizzie could be anywhere. Scary scenarios marched through Reagan's mind. Should she call Sonny? No. If Lizzie got the idea you weren't watching her, she snuck away silently and quickly before you missed her, just for attention. That was her MO.

Street noise warned Reagan of the heavy traffic on Smith Road, one block over. Lizzie would soon be eight years old. Physically, she wasn't much different from a typical child her age; she was smaller and walked with a limp because of her loose joints and a turned-out ankle, but she could be quite quick. Cognitively and behaviorally, though, she functioned like a toddler in her terrible twos. She grabbed everything she spied—threw it, poured it, smeared it, squeezed it, or popped it into her mouth. She had no regard for her own safety. She might run out in front of a car, or grab the hand of anyone who offered, as she had this morning with Dr. Litchfield.

If she goes too far, she won't be able to find her way back home. She may already be lost, wandering around trying to find her way, crying like she does when she's scared. Reagan dropped her head in her palms. *I should never have left her on that swing.* The muscles in her neck clenched and pulled at her jaws. Her head weighed a ton. Consumed with menacing thoughts, she looked right through a tall man walking up her steps like he belonged there.

"Hi, guys. Any sign of her?"

"Jake, what are you doing here?"

"Matthew called me. He sounded upset, said Lizzie was lost." Jake stood with one foot on the top step and rested his arms on his bent knee.

"Jake!" Matthew rushed to him.

Reagan's face flushed, embarrassed that Matthew had pulled this busy man away from his work. He liked Jake, but she hadn't expected them to bond so quickly, hadn't expected Matthew to form the naive notion that Jake could solve any problem, just like his dad had. Only Scott couldn't solve cancer.

"Ah . . . buddy." She walked up behind her son, put her arms around his shoulders, and rested her chin on his head. "Don't worry. We'll find her."

Jake smiled at Matthew, then spoke to Reagan. "It's after three o'clock now. How long has she been gone and where have you looked, or not looked?"

"It's been over an hour," Reagan answered and pointed to Betty. "Jake, this is my neighbor, Betty Crammer. We've looked in all the yards from here to Immaculate Conception.

Matthew looked up this street to Smith Road. She's never gone farther than that."

"I looked in all the yards, front and back." Matthew pointed up the street. "She wasn't there," he said, pinching his lips together.

Jake glanced around the area. "If it's okay with you, I'll recruit some help."

Reagan nodded. "Yes, thank you." Embarrassed or not, she was glad he had come.

Jake took out his cell and called his office. "Dave, the crew is in for a meeting, right? Good. I'm at Matthew's house. Bring everybody over. We need help locating his younger sister. Yeah, that's the one. We're at 3525 Kenilworth in Norwood, about a block west of Immaculate Conception. Yeah, just shut it down." Jake bent down to eye level with Matthew. "They'll be here in a few minutes."

"Good. Is Joey going to be with them?"

"I don't think so, son. Dave will be coming from the office." Jake's lip curled into a crooked smile, and he nodded at Matthew, his eyes soft. "But it would be good if he was."

He shifted his attention to Reagan. "Have you posted on Facebook? Also, do you have a printer here? If so, how about downloading a map of this area and printing ten copies. Oh, and what about a recent photo of Lizzie?"

It was comforting to have someone else take charge. Reagan was so stressed she was having trouble thinking, so it was good to have something to do besides worry. Something concrete. She went inside and pulled out her laptop. The time on her computer showed 3:45 p.m. Lizzie had been gone an hour and a half.

When she returned with maps, she, Betty, and Jake worked up a plan. Within minutes, two SUVs with Dekker Construction signage pulled in front of the house and parked.

Dave, six other men, and a woman got out. Jake passed out maps to each of them with specific areas circled. Reagan had scribbled her phone number on top. The Dekker group, including Jake, moved out on foot, leaving Reagan on the porch in case her daughter returned.

It occurred to her she hadn't really searched inside the house—just a quick run-through. As much as Lizzie loved hide-and-seek, she could have slipped past her mom while she was on the phone with Jordan and hidden. "Matt, you stay on the porch. I'm going to look through the house again. Maybe she's in there somewhere."

"Okay."

She navigated over shoes and toys in the living room and headed up the creaky stairs, Scooter right behind her. Discarded clothes littered the floor in Lizzie's room. Her comforter hung off her bed, dolls of every size and shape imaginable were scattered about. Nothing amiss except no Lizzie and no Annie, her favorite toy of that week.

Lizzie's loose joints enabled her to twist and bend like a contortionist, and she liked to squeeze into tight spaces. They all thought it cute when she popped out of the clothes hamper or cedar chest. Reagan looked in all the closets, under the beds, behind the shower curtain, and anywhere Lizzie could possibly hide. Every square inch of the second floor. She didn't turn up.

A noise in the kitchen kicked Reagan's heart into overdrive. She rushed downstairs. "Lizzie?"

Bird sat on the windowsill, tapping on the glass, looking in.

Reagan raised the window. "Are you trying to tell me something? Are you looking out for her?" She wanted desperately to believe in Bird, to have faith he really was an all-seeing mystical creature that would make sure no harm came to her or the children, one that could manipulate people and world events in their favor. Believing was easy when things were going well, but now it mattered.

She had to admit that when she needed him most, he always appeared right there on the windowsill, looking at her with those big black-and-yellow eyes, that caring expression.

Bird bobbled his head, then flew back onto his perch in the tree. Was that a good sign or bad?

Reagan walked through the basement, looking behind boxes, old toys, and other discards, but there was no good place to hide down there. She returned to the porch and shook her head at Matthew.

I never should have left Lizzie on that swing. Why didn't I just let the groceries spill? Why did I answer the phone? She paced back and forth, shaking her head, until she noticed Matthew's pained expression. She flopped down on the swing with him and rocked. The wind shifted with the cooler air. Goose bumps covered her arms. She draped one around Matthew's shoulder and squeezed.

After a while, Reagan watched from the porch as Jake and, one by one, each of his people came back into view, none of them with Lizzie. They stood together on the sidewalk talking. She joined them, and Matthew followed her. Betty Crammer remained on the top porch step and lit a cigarette.

Jake said, "Reagan, they each struck out. Nobody remembers seeing her. It's after four thirty. It'll be dark in less than an hour. You need to call—"

The distant wail of a siren grew louder until it screamed onto Kenilworth. The squad car jerked to a stop at the end of Reagan's driveway. Leaving the car door standing open, Sonny Harrison shot out and approached Reagan. "What's going on? I just saw your Facebook post."

"Lizzie walked off. We haven't been able to find her," Reagan said.

"When was this? Why didn't you call us?"

"I thought we'd find her. I didn't want to bother you."

"God dammit, Rea, don't you—"

"Whoa," Jake said and stepped forward.

Sonny looked at him, then back at Reagan. "Who's that?"

"Jake Dekker, a friend of—"

Sonny glanced at the SUVs and nodded. "You called him before me—Lizzie's godfather and a cop?" His eyes squinted, the muscles in his jaw clenched.

"I didn't—"

Sonny cut her off and turned to Jake. "This woman's involved in a murder investigation. That puts her and her children at risk. We should've been notified as soon as Lizzie was out of sight."

Jake gasped; his eyes widened.

Reagan's chest tightened. She shook her head at Sonny. "I didn't think about that. Lizzie does this. You know that. Never for this long, but I think she just walked away and hasn't been able to find her way home." She crossed her arms over her chest and looked away.

"I didn't—" *Bryan Butler . . . Could he have something to do with this? No, he's just a kid himself . . . but he was creepy, threatening.* "I guess it's possible this is connected. I did have an odd run-in with an old student . . . really strange." She squinted her eyes and looked off to the left. "It was almost like he was threatening me."

"Jesus Christ, Rea!"

Her eyes stung. One traitorous tear teetered on her lower lid before spilling over. She took a deep breath and swatted it off her cheek. *Okay, enough. Pull yourself together. You've got to find your baby girl.*

"Who was it?"

"Bryan Butler. He's a senior now, but he was in my class in seventh grade."

Sonny shook his head and let out a breath. "I know him."

He took a notebook out of his shirt pocket and scribbled the information. "What'd he say?"

"It was more the way he said it. He didn't want any harm to come to me or my kids."

"So, you thought to tell"—he looked at the SUVs again— "Mr. Dekker, rather than the police." Without giving her a chance to respond, he spoke into the mic clipped to his shoulder. "This is Harrison. I'm at Reagan Ramsey's home. You know Lizzie. She's in the NICE program. She's been missing over two hours, and volunteers have been unable to locate her. Send Kurt and Murphy to 3525 Kenilworth, notify Xavier's Security and"—he turned his back to her and lowered his voice—"pull a list of all sex offenders within a twenty-five-mile radius."

Reagan sucked in a sharp breath. All the panic she'd been pushing from her mind for the last two hours pressed down on her so hard she couldn't exhale. Her heartbeat pounded in her temples as she struggled for control. It was getting dark and colder. Her baby was afraid of the dark and didn't have a coat.

"Another thing," Sonny continued. "Send Cox to talk to Bryan Butler. We have his address. We've picked him up a couple of times but never got anything solid. Ask if he knows anything about Mrs. Ramsey's daughter. I'm gonna take a walk around the house, see if I can spot anything suspicious."

Jake put his hand on Reagan's back. "Matthew, Reagan, I believe I've done everything I can here. Our presence seems to be making things worse."

"How can I thank you, Jake? I so appreciate the help from you and your team." She shook her head. "Sorry about Sonny. I can't explain his behavior."

"No need. But please, you have my number. Call me if I can help in any way. And Matthew, let me know when you find her. Let me know she's okay." He thanked the other Dekker employees and told them to go back to the office for their cars.

They piled into the two vehicles and left. Jake drove away in his Jeep.

While Reagan watched them leave, Anaya pulled up in her silver Jetta, parked, and dashed up the sidewalk.

"What's this about Lizzie?"

"We can't find her," Matthew answered.

"What can I do?"

Reagan shook her head. "I don't know." She brought Anaya up to speed, beginning with the trip to the dentist. Anaya went into the house and brought out jackets for Reagan and Matthew. "Reagan, it's bloody cold out here. Put this on." She helped both Matthew and Reagan into their coats.

Reagan loved Anaya. She had been Lizzie's aide since she had started school, but she mothered the whole family.

"Are you guys hungry?" Anaya asked.

Both Matthew and Reagan shook their heads.

"I'll wait here then." She sat beside Betty, who stepped on her cigarette and put the butt back in the pack.

Another squad car pulled up quietly. A policeman got out and opened the back door. A golden Labrador retriever jumped out.

"Murphy!" Matthew cupped his hands and held them out to the dog. The schoolchildren and teachers had all seen Norwood's drug-detecting dog, Murphy, at one time or another, sniffing around lockers and book bags. Playful, he often came bounding into Reagan's classroom after he'd finished his job to have fun with the students.

"No, Matthew, he's working now," his handler said. "You can pet him later."

"Hi, Kurt," Reagan said.

"Hey, Reagan. We'll need something of Lizzie's, some article of clothing. Maybe a shoe or something else she's worn recently." He patted her on the back. "Don't worry. Murphy will find her."

Reagan nodded and went inside. She picked up a blue Nike Lizzie had kicked off just inside the front door. "Here's something."

"That'll do." Kurt held the shoe under the dog's nose and said, "Find Lizzy, boy." His leash stretched taut as Murphy bounded forward, Kurt right behind him.

Matthew quietly opened the front door and called to Scooter. His facial expression eased into a smile when the dog jumped on him joyfully. He stooped down and put his arms around Scooter, nuzzled his neck and ran his fingers through his thick, soft fur.

Loud squawking sounded from the squad car just as Sonny returned from his inspection. He ducked back into the open car door and picked up the radio. Reagan couldn't make out much of the staticky transmission, but Sonny talked for several minutes. When he finished, he left the car and walked toward her.

"Cox hasn't been able to locate Butler. No one answered the door, and without a warrant, he couldn't go in. He's notified Cincinnati Police to bring him in if they see him, but right now we don't have anything new." He looked around, then asked, "Where's the cavalry?"

"Why be a jerk?" Reagan said, her eyebrow arched almost to her scalp. "I don't need your attitude."

She plopped down on a porch step below Anaya and Betty and wrapped her jacket tightly around her arms. One of the neighbors had a fire going. The pleasant scent of hickory hugged the air. The tip of her nose and the top of her ears had gotten cold. The streetlight in front of the house began to glow, reminding her it would soon be dark—more than three hours since she had last seen her daughter.

Kurt and Murphy came into view, walking casually, the cold wind blowing the dog's fur around his face and ears.

Sonny met them at the street; he talked to Kurt for a couple of minutes. She stiffened as he walked toward her with a grim expression, his face ashen.

"It's not good." He jammed his hands into his armpits and spoke with less anger in his voice, more concern. "Murphy caught Lizzie's scent right away and followed it to Smith Road. Then he lost it. He couldn't pick it up again anywhere around there. The only explanation, she got into a car."

Reagan threw her hands over her mouth before a scream escaped.

Sonny said, "I'm going to call Cox again. He's got to find Bryan Butler."

Anaya put her arm around Reagan and looked at Sonny. "What about an Amber Alert?"

"We'd have to know what kind of car she's in for that, and right now we have no idea. We'll put out a news bulletin with a picture of Lizzie on TV and social media. Someone will have noticed her."

"Let's go inside," Anaya said. "I'll make hot coffee and sandwiches. Betty, join us."

"Nah, hon, y'all go ahead. I'll go on home, but let me know when you find her."

Reagan, suffocating under the weight of the stress, put up no resistance as Anaya led her inside. The house was pleasantly warm, and soon the fragrant aroma of perking coffee drifted throughout the first floor. Anaya was standing at the stove, grilling cheese sandwiches, when Sonny burst in.

"Rea—"

REAGAN

CHAPTER FOURTEEN

Five thirty p.m., rush hour. "Dammit!" Sonny's squad car inched forward in the stop-and-go traffic on Sherman Avenue until he slapped on the light bar, commanding drivers to get out of his way. Flashing blue lights reflected on the darkened windows of Surrey Square storefronts.

Reagan tilted her head. "She just walked in alone and sat down at a table?"

"That's what I was told."

She sat in the front seat beside Sonny. They approached from the rear of McDonald's, which stood alone at the north end of the strip mall. She gasped when the squad car rounded the building.

An ambulance idled near the front door, and another Norwood police car sat at the curb. The parking lot was full, and cars roamed around, their drivers looking for empty spaces. Her voice climbed an octave. "I thought you said she was okay."

"Rea, she looks okay, but this is a police matter now. We

have to know if anyone abused her in any way, in case charges are brought and it ends up in court."

"I just want to take her home. Anaya and Matthew are waiting." Reagan sounded whiny even to herself, but tension had taken a toll, and she was too drained to be strong. It would do no good to argue. *It's a police matter now.*

"I know. I'll drive you guys to Children's for an assessment. That will be less traumatic than the ambulance. I'll let them know we're coming." Sonny picked up the mic. "Harrison here. Call ahead to Children's Hospital and let them know I'll be transporting Lizzie and her mother."

Before the squad car came to a complete stop, Reagan threw open the door and bolted into the restaurant, met by a rush of salty, oily smells—fries and burgers. People stood three-deep at the registers. Others stationed themselves near the counter, waiting for their orders, or moved to and from their tables, blocking Reagan's view. She scanned the room until she saw Lizzie sitting near the rear, across from a Norwood policewoman Reagan did not know. Lizzie's legs dangled from her chair. Tendrils of her thick, dark hair had come loose from her ponytail and fluttered around her face. Over her red-plaid jumper, she wore a blue Norwood police uniform jacket several sizes too big. She looked adorable, like a little girl playing dress-up.

The young policewoman was talking to Lizzie with the animated gestures you'd use with a toddler, but the child wouldn't make eye contact with her. A hamburger and fries, still in their wrapper, sat on the table between them. Lizzie's eyes roamed around the room, and when they settled on her mother, she burst into the kind of grin that was impossible not to return. She hopped up, ran to Reagan, and threw her arms around her waist.

Reagan's vision blurred; her knees weakened. She wrapped

her daughter in a tight embrace, unsure if she was laughing or crying.

Sonny walked up from behind and guided them to the table that Lizzie had occupied with the policewoman. "Reagan, I don't think you've met Officer Michelle Gardner. She's been on the force about a year."

"Hi. Thank you so much."

"Hey, no problem. One of the cashiers, Constance Riley, noticed her when she came in. Constance knew right away something wasn't right. No one came in with Lizzie and she seemed confused, like she didn't know what to do. Constance tried to talk to her. When she didn't respond, she helped her to the table and called us. Of course we were already looking for her."

Sonny dropped to one knee on Lizzie's eye level. "Hey, Lizzie Lu, you okay?"

The child threw both arms up. Sonny stood and swooped her into his arms effortlessly, in an act so familiar people watching must have thought he was her father. He whispered to her as he rubbed his face against hers. "Uncle Sonny was worried about you, really worried."

The squad car crept up Burnet Avenue, stopped at each corner by traffic lights. Reagan and Lizzie sat on the hard plastic seat in the back. Hordes of pedestrians wearing coats over scrubs, lab coats, and street clothes, a few also toting backpacks, rushed across the busy streets. The medical district of Cincinnati, commonly referred to by locals as Pill Hill, had its own rhythm. Vehicular traffic, regardless of blue lights, moved slowly.

Children's Hospital, a behemoth of towers, additions, and parking garages, stood one block north of the Shriners Hospital. Sonny bypassed the familiar main entrance and turned onto the next street, which was marked by a red Emergency Room sign. A barricade with a Road Closed to Thru Traffic sign left barely enough room for an ambulance to squeeze by. Construction vehicles and equipment, parked for the evening, were clustered around a huge fenced-in pit that would eventually hold another addition.

They drove up a steep ramp between a parking garage and multistory hospital buildings, to a circular drive in front of the emergency room door. Parked at the entrance were two white-and-blue ambulances with the colorful logo of Children's Hospital on the side. During the seven years since Lizzie's birth, Reagan had spent many hours at Children's—evaluations, therapies, a tonsillectomy that required an overnight stay. She had memorized the color-coded concourse map, learned to navigate the endless aisles and walkways, discovered the best places to park. The visits to Children's had been routine, mostly stress-free, except for the tonsillectomy. That had been a nightmare for both her and Scott, when Lizzie couldn't sleep, didn't understand why she was in pain, and fought everyone who came near her. But never had Reagan come in through the emergency room entrance, escorted by a policeman.

Sonny guided them into the spacious waiting room with walls decorated like an enchanted forest. The contrails of a shooting star swirled around gigantic trees. Green vinyl chairs and sofas were scattered around in small groups. The room smelled clean, with a hint of lemon.

Another family huddled together, talking among themselves. One of the men, face flushed, eyes red rimmed, stood talking to a woman in scrubs. Reagan didn't know him, didn't know the circumstances, but her heart went out to him.

Conversations were muted, far off. A phone rang at the nurses' station and was quickly answered. A woman walked by in high heels that clicked against the oak floor.

Sonny pointed to an empty sofa. "You guys sit here. I'll get us checked in and be back in a minute."

A second station, manned by two uniformed Cincinnati police officers, stood a few yards past the nurses' station. Their presence surprised Reagan. When she sat down with Lizzie, her baby melted into her side. Reagan draped her arm over her shoulder, and in no time Lizzie's breathing settled into the regular rhythm of sleep. Her daughter's cool skin against her arm was smooth as satin, her breath warm, her ponytail delicate as a feather when it brushed against Reagan's shoulder.

Reagan stroked her hair, kissed the top of her head, then leaned back and breathed deeply. Thoughts swirled through her mind like that shooting star. What if Lizzie hadn't been found? What if she'd been hurt? What if someone really had abducted her, like Sonny said? *She's more vulnerable than other kids. When she's scared, she fights, and she's all in when she does, like this morning. Could that have only been this morning? Unbelievable. She doesn't understand threatening situations. She can't outrun an adult, and she can't scream. She trusts indiscriminately. She trusts me. I have to protect—*

"Mrs. Ramsey, I'm Janice Lawrence with Social Services. I'll take you back now, if you're ready." The woman stood about six feet tall, slim and stately. Her dark hair fell to her shoulders, and she wore a white lab coat over her fitted red dress. A plastic sleeve hung from her belt with her Children's Hospital photo ID; there were lots of letters behind her name.

"Oh yes." Reagan gave her daughter a gentle nudge. "Lizzie, wake up, baby. We're going to talk with this lady." Lizzie opened her bleary eyes and stood unsteadily but went with her mother and the social worker down the hall without complaint.

"The officer said your daughter is nonverbal. Is that right?"

"Yes. She can say a few words, but essentially she doesn't talk."

"I understand. That's going to make things harder, but

I'll do my best. We normally use the NICHD Investigative Interview protocol: w-h questions like what, when, where, and why, and open-ended ones like 'Tell me more, what happened next.' We don't like to use yes-or-no questions."

Ms. Lawrence pointed toward two doors, side-by-side. "I hear you've both had a difficult day. I'm sorry, but I still need to ask you to watch the interview through a closed-circuit monitor in the next room. If Lizzie objects, I'll bring you in." She gestured to the door on the left. "It's all set up," she said to Reagan. "You'll be able to see and hear everything."

Then she looked down at Lizzie and smiled. "Lizzie, we're going to go in here and talk. Your mom is going to be in this room, right next door, waiting for us. Okay?"

Lizzie's brown eyes widened, but she didn't protest—no fighting, no dead-weight drops to the floor. The two of them entered a room with vanilla walls, a small table in the middle flanked by two chairs facing each other, and a small cabinet in the corner.

"Lizzie, how 'bout sitting here?" Ms. Lawrence pointed to the child-size chair. Lizzie scooted in, and Ms. Lawrence sat in the other.

"Like I said before, Lizzie, I'm Ms. Lawrence, and I know you're Lizzie Ramsey." The woman's expression changed from businesswoman to kindergarten teacher: wide eyes, broad smile, and a voice fit for nursery rhymes. She took some paper and crayons from the cabinet, sat back down, and leaned closer to Lizzie. "I understand you've had a long day and are probably tired. Is that right?" She placed the paper and crayons on the table. "Do you like to color? How about drawing a picture?"

Lizzie swatted the crayons onto the floor.

"Hmm, so you don't like to color. That's okay, but I would prefer you not throw things. I have a little girl about your age. Would you like to see a picture of her?"

Lizzie smiled and nodded.

Ms. Lawrence grabbed her purse from the cabinet, took out her phone, and pulled up photos of her daughter swinging on playground equipment. She handed Lizzie the phone. The child studied the photos, swiping through several shots.

"My daughter likes to look at photos too. Lizzie, I bet you like to swing. What else do you like to do?" She handed Lizzie a plastic poster illustrated with children engaged in several different activities, including petting a dog, swimming, dressing a doll, and climbing on a jungle gym. Lizzie looked at the pictures and pointed to the dog. "Very good. So, you have a dog, then?"

Lizzie nodded.

The social worker showed her more photos of her own family and asked simple yes-or-no questions about Matthew and Scooter. After trying to build rapport for several minutes, she took the poster and said, "You're doing great. Now, I'm going to ask you some questions, Lizzie. Would that be okay?"

Lizzie looked directly at Ms. Lawrence and nodded.

"Good. Now first, let's talk about how you can answer the questions. If I ask you a question and you don't know the answer, you can raise this hand." The social worker pointed to Lizzie's right hand. "For example, if I ask you what my doggie's name is, you wouldn't know, because you don't even know whether or not I have a doggie. Right?" She shrugged and turned up her palms. "You would raise your right hand."

Lizzie appeared to consider the instructions and held eye contact for several seconds but didn't react.

Ms. Lawrence hesitated and asked again. "Right?" Lizzie gave a slight nod and the interviewer moved on.

"Now, when I ask you if you have a dog, you will know the answer because you know you have a dog. Right?"

Lizzie nodded.

"Great. Now if I ask you a question you don't understand, shake your head." Ms. Lawrence demonstrated with an exaggerated head shake. "If you do that, I'll ask the question in a different way. So, if I asked you what is your gender? You probably wouldn't understand because a lot of kids your age don't understand the word *gender*. So you would shake your head. If I asked you if you are a boy or girl, you would understand, right?"

Again Lizzie didn't react.

"Lizzie, I'm going to talk to Mom for a moment. We'll be right outside this door. Okay?"

Ms. Lawrence left the room and went next door to talk to Reagan.

"I don't think she understands me. Either that or she's too tired to concentrate. I'm going to try another approach that we sometimes use if we're concerned about abuse. I'll try to get more information using anatomically correct dolls. But Mrs. Ramsey, I have to be honest with you, Lizzie would not be a credible witness in any court case. I recommend she not be put through it."

"I know. I agree," Reagan said.

Moving back to the monitor took all the energy she could muster. She just wanted to take Lizzie home.

In the interview room, Lizzie was resting her head on her arms on the table. Ms. Lawrence took a male and female doll from the cabinet and placed them one at a time in front of her. "Lizzie, this is a little girl, and this is a bigger boy." The child sat up and scrutinized the dolls. "Now, tell me what you think of when you look at the dolls."

"Maa." She signed "I love you" with her thumb, forefinger, and pinkie.

"Hmm." Ms. Lawrence checked her notes. "So you think this boy looks like your brother, Matthew?"

"Maa." Lizzie repeated the sign.

The social worker picked up the female doll. "What about her? What do you think of when you see her?"

107

Lizzie ignored that doll. She said, "Maa," and pointed at the male doll again.

"Okay, honey. I'm going to talk to Mom again. I think I can let you go home and get some rest. I'll be right back."

Reagan quickly joined Ms. Lawrence in the hall and waited for her comments.

"I have no reason to believe she's been abused, but I can't be sure either way. I could try to finish a thorough assessment, which would take quite some time, but I don't think she understands me, and she's also obviously tired. I'll talk to Lieutenant Harrison a moment. I can probably let you both go home and get some rest."

Reagan, Sonny, and Lizzie walked back to the squad car, Sonny holding Lizzie's hand. He said, "I'm pretty sure this wasn't about Lizzie anyway. Whoever did it, did it to send a message. You're vulnerable. We can get to you."

"Don't you think it's possible she just walked away and couldn't find her way home?" Reagan asked.

"No, I don't. We had half the town combing the area, looking for her. Murphy wouldn't have lost her scent, and there is absolutely no way she walked all the way to McDonald's without help or being noticed. You saw the traffic. That's the busiest intersection in Norwood. It's crazy that time of day. Christ, I don't feel safe crossing those streets myself.

"A few minutes before Lizzie showed up, Cox caught up with Butler about a block from his house. He swore he'd been at Buffalo Wild Wings, no idea why he was being stopped, knew nothing about a missing kid—never seen Lizzie, didn't know her. Cox said he looked convincing. Anyway, while he had the kid stopped, the call came out that she'd been found, so he let Butler go." Sonny shrugged. "That kid's a con. We're going to find out for sure what happened. I'm having Cox pull all surveillance tapes in the area. Although I have to say, those guys have been pretty good at avoiding cameras."

Reagan grew silent. She tried to disconnect from her frightening thoughts and focus on each step—the way one foot struck the pavement, then the other; the way her sock rubbed against the heel of her shoe—but she still felt her heartbeat in her temples, her blood rush through her veins. She struggled to exhale but couldn't quite clear her lungs.

For the first time, she got it. They were in danger. There were those who would do her and her children harm. For a brief moment she felt she might splinter, fly off in a million different directions. No. She couldn't do that. She had children who needed her more now than ever.

An ambulance pulled up to the emergency room door. She watched the driver get out and mosey into the hospital. How could he be so unconcerned when the world was such a mess?

"Are you okay?" Sonny asked when they reached the car.

"Yes . . . I'm okay. I'll figure something out."

JAKE

CHAPTER FIFTEEN

Crawford Lewis—actually Crawford Lewis Jr., but no one called him *junior* anymore—fit the image of the high-priced lawyer he was. His dark tailored suit no doubt cost a thousand bucks or more, and his leather briefcase was embossed with gold initials. Thanksgiving afternoon, and Jake was still frustrated from events earlier in the day, but he'd agreed to meet when Lewis said it was urgent. Now Lewis sat in Jake's living room, discussing the investigation of a hit-and-run with Jake, Janet, and Alex.

"Sorry to intrude on your Thanksgiving, but this couldn't wait. Actually, they have nothing on the boys at all. They're just fishing." He looked at Alex. "The police have a hit-and-run and, after almost a month, no suspects. You weren't involved. You've clearly stated that—to them, to me. Don't let it concern you. It's in my hands."

Jake observed Alex and frowned. "Alex, do you know anything about this accident?"

"Well, of course he doesn't, Jake," Janet said.

Jake said, "I asked Alex. Do you know anything about this incident?"

Alex appeared calm now, not rattled like before. Why not? He had his mother on one side of him and his lawyer on the other. Jake suspected he had taken something; he was too relaxed for the circumstance. But then, why shouldn't he be relaxed? He'd never had consequences for his behavior. Just today, before Thanksgiving dinner, he was presented with a new Mustang. Jake had been adamantly against it, but it didn't matter. Janet argued that it wasn't a gift; the insurance company had merely reimbursed him for the loss of his Camaro. He got the cast off his ankle and a new car within a week. No consequences . . . just like when Jake was a kid.

Eli came to mind, the sixteen-year-old who had hung out at the mall some thirty years ago and recruited younger kids to do his stealing for him. He was Fagin to twelve-year-old Jake's Oliver Twist. Jake had been so starved for attention, confused, and angry—not unlike Alex—that it felt good to be noticed by a cool older guy, or anyone. And the drugs Eli gave him, they had worked fast and sure.

Alex said, "No, sir, I swear. I don't know anything about it."

The corner of Janet's mouth turned into a half smile—more like a smirk. Jake hated that. He turned to Alex.

"Then why all the questions? Why do they suspect you?"

"Jake! Jake, this happens all the time. It's routine," the lawyer bellowed. "They've got an accident they must investigate, and if they can pin it on some young guys who'll be intimidated by their badges, and unable to afford adequate counsel, they're gonna give it their best shot. Anything to keep their clear rate decent. Problem is, they're gonna get more than they bargained for if they harass *my* son."

Wonder where Eli is now—still locked up? If not for Coach Majors, I'd be right there with him.

Jake stared at the lawyer. "So, you don't think Trip could have been involved in this?"

For the first time that evening, the lines around Crawford's mouth turned downward, and he looked older. "Don't worry, Jake. Just leave it to me. You won't hear anything else about it."

REAGAN

CHAPTER SIXTEEN

Reagan pulled to the curb on Erie Avenue and parked. The sidewalk in front of the District Two building was crumbling. With its low roof and small windows, it looked like a library built in the fifties, not a police station.

A light rain—*Could that be sleet?*—peppered her windshield. Gusts of wind picked up crumpled leaves and tossed them aside like broken promises. Late November in Cincinnati: cold, damp, and gloomy. She ignored the passing traffic while she considered what to do.

She could go home, call later—maybe after work. Leave a message on his voice mail. But she wouldn't. That wasn't her style.

Oh well, let's get this over with.

She got out of the car, turned her coat collar up, and crossed the street.

Two police officers, a blond woman and a man with graying hair, sat at a desk behind a glass barrier in the small lobby. The woman put down a bagel and leaned forward. "May I help you?"

"Hi, I'm Reagan Ramsey. I have an appointment with Detective Gabriel." She glanced over the officer's shoulder at a wall clock.

The woman nodded and picked up her phone. "Ron, Ms. Ramsey's here for you. Says she has an appointment." Opposite the front entrance, a door with a keypad led into another part of the building. Within minutes, the plainclothes detective, middle-aged with a sandy-colored crew cut, stood in the doorway.

"Reagan, good to see you." They shook hands. "Come on back."

His shoes squeaked on the concrete floor as he led her into the secure area of the station. An empty wooden chair sat in the tight landing between steps going half a flight up and half a flight down. The name Sonny Kim was carved in the back of the chair. A rope lay across the seat, and below that was the inscription "Saving a place for a fallen hero."

Kim had lost his life when he was ambushed by a mentally disturbed man who wanted to commit suicide by cop. The day of his funeral, along with hundreds of other heartsick mourners, Reagan waited on Montgomery Road most of the afternoon for the solemn hearse carrying his body to Gate of Heaven Cemetery. She got home in time to watch the Last Call ceremony televised live from the gravesite; in spirit, she stood in the rain among hundreds of men and women in uniform as the haunting "cleared for home" pronouncement rang out over the somber grounds.

For days, the faces of Kim's wife and children, the memory of the last call, the distraught expression of fellow officers, had preoccupied Reagan's mind. These officers were never sure what they would encounter when answering a call, yet they went anyway.

"Want some coffee?" The detective led her into his cramped office. The room smelled like greasy food. Her queasy stomach turned. "No thanks, but please, have some yourself."

"Nah, I've already had more than enough."

An open Styrofoam to-go box on his desk contained a half-eaten burger. Besides his leftover lunch, there were stacks of manila folders, a yellow legal pad, and scattered newspaper clippings. A man in the middle of something. The room was barely big enough for the metal desk, with one chair behind it and two chairs in front. A four-drawer file cabinet sat against the wall. Detective Gabriel pointed to the chairs in front of the desk. Reagan lowered herself into one. He sat in the other, opposite her.

"I was glad to get your call yesterday. Maybe you've remembered something else about our guy?" He had a twinkle in his eye, a look of anticipation.

"Actually, no. It's just the opposite. I'm not going to be able to help you." She twisted her purse strap and watched his eyes narrow. "It's just . . . really, I'm not sure anymore. I don't even clearly remember what he looked like." She lowered her gaze to the floor and shook her head.

What a lie. That face stares at me several times a day.

With the back of her hand, she swiped tiny beads of sweat from around her hairline. "I don't want any . . ." She let out a sigh. "I'm sorry. I just can't help you."

The detective moved closer to Reagan. "What happened? You've been so sure of yourself until now, so committed."

"I'm sorry."

He opened his mouth to speak, then paused, as if to collect his thoughts. "Reagan, you're the only person who got a good look at this guy, and you got a very good look. You make a valuable, credible witness. We think it's probable the bullet was intended for someone other than our victim. Some sort of territory dispute between two drug dealers. We pulled security tapes from businesses near the scene. We couldn't get a good look at the driver of that car, but the tapes did show a guy with priors for selling drugs in the group of kids with our victim, who most likely was just a poor kid hooked on heroin—in the wrong place, at the wrong time to make a buy."

The detective locked eyes with hers. "We need your help." He put his elbows on his knees and clasped his hands.

Reagan shifted upright and drew her purse tightly to her chest. She couldn't risk it. It was too much. "I want to help you, I do. I just can't now."

He cocked his head. "Did someone get to you?" He anchored his gaze on her. "Don't you have a brother, or cousin, or something with the police department in Norwood? What will he say if you withdraw your statement?"

His scrutiny made it hard for her to catch her breath. She unbuttoned her coat and averted her eyes, her gaze settling on a framed photo on top of the metal file cabinet. A young girl about Matthew's age.

Detective Gabriel noticed. "Hey, I'm sorry. I shouldn't be coming on so strong, but this is personal for me. The kid in that photo, that's Chelsea." He jerked his head in the direction of the picture. "Her mother was a friend of mine in high school. Four of us were going home one night after a ballgame when our car was broadsided by a drunk driver. We were all scraped up pretty bad, but Kathy, her mother, got the worst of it. Her leg was broken in several places." He picked up the photo and looked at the girl.

"It took a long time, but her leg healed well enough for her to walk. After high school, we drifted apart. You know, some of us went away to college. Some stayed around here. The last time I saw Kathy was at our high school reunion. She looked great, bragged about her toddler, took out her cell and showed us . . . oh, maybe a hundred photos of Chelsea. Kathy was always a terrific writer, and she had just published a children's book. She sounded so happy. Ten days later she was dead of a heroin overdose."

Reagan gasped.

"That was eight years ago; Chelsea was two. Way before the god-awful scourge of heroin laced with fentanyl we have now. We, Kathy's friends, learned she'd been struggling with addiction off and on since the accident. It started with pain meds. None of us had any idea. I'm a cop and even I didn't understand it. How could someone so beautiful, so smart, with so much to live for, OD on heroin?" He shook his head. "It just didn't make sense."

His eyes drilled into hers. "And even scarier, that could have been any of us. Me even. I can't honestly say that if it'd been me that broke my leg, in constant pain, I wouldn't have had the same problem."

He put the photo back on his desk. "Chelsea takes after her mother. I see her pretty often. She sends me a new school picture every year, and I keep it there to remind me. These are not just stats. They're people who have loved ones." His phone rang. He glanced at the screen and sent the call to voice mail.

Reagan caught a shift in his voice, less energy.

"The young man you saw get shot? His sister calls me every day to ask if we have anything new. That's the only thing she can do for him now. Make sure the guy who did it pays. We've had too many cases like this. Too many." The detective shook his head; his jaw muscles pulsated.

Reagan steeled herself. It made sense that the shooting was related to their out-of-control drug problem. Two of the kids at school had lost family members to it: one lost a parent, the other a sibling. The kids were devastated by grief and shame. Every time it happened, the staff gathered in the teacher's lounge and exploded. How can this keep happening? Somebody should be able to do *something*. But she couldn't be that somebody. There was too much at stake.

She couldn't tolerate sitting there another minute, so she got up to leave. *This was a mistake. I should have called.*

"If I think of anything, I'll call you, but now I have to go. I want to be there when my son gets home."

He threw up his hands. "Okay, I guess we're done." They both knew she wouldn't be back.

Lizzie was lying on the floor in front of the TV when Reagan entered the house. Curious George raced across the screen, the Man with the Yellow Hat right behind him. Cartoon music blared throughout the first floor.

"That's too loud!" Reagan grabbed the remote and turned off the TV.

Lizzie got up, frowned at her mother, and went to her room.

The heavenly smell of yeast rolls drifted from the kitchen. Anaya was checking something in the oven when Reagan walked in. "What are you cooking? Smells wonderful."

"Lamb roast. It'll be ready in a little while. So, how did it go with the detective?"

"Okay, I guess." At least she'd talked to Detective Gabriel. Hopefully she would now be able to get that off her mind. "I feel guilty."

"Rubbish. Reagan, give yourself a bloody break. You did not shoot that kid. There were other people there. Someone had to see something."

What a cop-out. Someone else can do it. Someone who has nothing to lose. "I don't want to talk about it." Reagan threw her purse on the kitchen counter and slipped out of her shoes. "I guess Matt went out with Jake?"

"Yes. Jake was here right after we got home. He said they'd be home by six. I'm not sure where they went, but they took Scooter."

"Really?"

• • •

"Mom! Where are you? Come 'ere," Matthew yelled as he bounded through the front door an hour later, Scooter on his heels.

Reagan darted into the living room, carrying a large wooden spoon. "What's going on?"

Jake walked in behind Matthew. Their cheeks were ruddy, like they'd been out running in the cold. Jake's powerful physique seemed to fill up the door frame; he carried himself like a well-conditioned athlete. He shot Reagan a crooked smile.

"Hello."

Something stirred in Reagan that she quickly shoved down. "Hi, guys. Where'd you go?"

"Washington Park," Jake answered. "It's dog friendly, so we could play with Scooter there." He and Matthew took off their jackets. Matthew tossed his on the sofa and Jake hung his over one of the dining room chairs.

"Mom, where's Lizzie?" He bounced on his feet, his eyes dancing. "I want to show you guys a new trick we taught Scooter."

Reagan raised her eyebrows and grinned. Matthew was more excited than he'd been in months. "Why don't you guys come into the kitchen. Anaya and Lizzie are both in there."

When Jake and Matthew joined the others, Reagan said, "Okay, let's see it."

Matthew palmed something from his jacket pocket and called Scooter. The dog trotted into the kitchen, nails clicking on the vinyl floor, shaggy fur flouncing around his eyes. Matthew said, "Okay, people. Watch."

"Matt, you have our undivided attention," Reagan said. "Show us."

"Okay." He raised his arm and the dog sat upright in front of him, ears perked, eyes fixated on Matthew. "Scooter, would you rather be a Wolverine, or would you rather be dead?"

Matthew raised his thumb and pointed his index finger at his pet. On cue, Scooter rolled over on his back, drew his front paws to his chest, and cocked his head, mouth open, tongue hanging out.

Laughter erupted from the group. Matthew grabbed his knees, howling. Lizzie giggled, clapped her hands, then walked over to Scooter and rubbed the dog's belly. When Matthew calmed down, he slipped Scooter a reward.

Reagan's eyes stung. How long had it been since she'd seen her son belly laugh like that? Too long. Not since his father got sick. She glanced at Jake, who laughed like it was the first time he'd seen the trick. She walked over to him.

"Thank you, Jake. Matthew loves the time you guys spend together. There's been a big change in him since you came into his life."

Jake smiled. "The feeling is mutual. Matthew's a great kid."

"Anaya's cooked a lovely dinner for us. Would you like to join us? She's a very good cook."

"Dinner smells great. I'm sure Anaya is a good cook, but Frances is expecting me. If I stand her up, she'll seek revenge. And it won't be pretty."

"Frances? I thought your wife's name was Jan or Janet."

"It's Janet. She has office hours late on Thursdays. That's when Frances gets to torture me. Tonight it's liver and onions." He made a face. "I don't particularly like it—neither does my stepson, so he always manages to be somewhere else on Thursdays—but Frances has been like a mom to me since I was a kid, and she knows how to scare me, so I eat it anyway." His cheeks caved into dimples.

Despite the meeting with Detective Gabriel, and for only the second time that day, Reagan found herself laughing.

After the children were in bed and Anaya left, Bird stared from his usual perch in the tree as Reagan poured "oregano" into a joint, lit it, and exhaled through the open window. "No judging and don't look so righteous!"

Bird jumped from the tree to the sill, inches from Reagan's face.

"So, I know you're disappointed in me. I get that. I always thought of myself as doing what's right, a good citizen. But I'm not brave. I'm not. I just want us to get through this, this grief and worry that something's going to happen to one of the children . . . or me. I can't lose either of them—and they can't lose me. I'm all they've got."

The light from the kitchen window reflected in Bird's eyes. Okay, maybe that was an expression of concern with just a tad of judgment. She took another hit of weed.

"One question: That was quite a coincidence, Jake being mysteriously matched with Matthew after helping me with Lizzie at Kroger. Did you have anything to do with that?"

JAKE

CHAPTER SEVENTEEN

"ABC National's conference is in Hawaii this year," Jake said as he moved around the kitchen island. "The Four Seasons on Oahu again." He pulled an onion, a bell pepper, and eggs out of the refrigerator and closed the door with his hip. "That's where I learned my incredible ukulele skills, remember?"

"Oh yeah. I remember," Janet answered from her seat at the kitchen table, where she was reading emails on her iPad. She didn't keep office hours on Wednesday, and unless one of her patients went into labor, she had one morning a week to unwind. "My guess is everybody in the hotel bar remembers your incredible ukulele skills."

"You think?" He directed his most charming grin at her. "We could make a real vacation out of it. Think about that phenomenal beach." He peeled and chopped the onion, then poured olive oil into a cast-iron skillet.

"Aren't you supposed to be working when you attend those conferences? Isn't that what you tell your CPA?"

"Absolutely. I'll pick up new trade info. Network with guys

from all over the country. I'm taking Dave and Peggy too. You'd be surprised how much I'll learn." He threw the onion into the hot skillet like Guy Fieri, creating an explosion of mouthwatering fragrance.

Wednesday mornings were Jake's favorite of the week. Alex was in school, and so he went to work late to be with Janet—one of the perks of being the boss. He enjoyed making a big breakfast for the two of them.

"Yeah, like playing the ukulele."

"And other stuff too. You and Peggy can lie by the pool and order drinks with those cute little pink umbrellas or visit that killer spa. You never got to Pearl Harbor last time. You could check it out."

"Jake, you know I hate to fly. The thought of spending all that time on an airplane gives me heartburn."

"I'll spring for first class. You'll be in a comfortable cocoon."

"Besides, I hate to leave Alex alone for so long."

Jake hesitated. *I could offer to take him. That's not what I had in mind, but maybe it'd be good for the whole family. The three of us vacationing in the tropics. Why not? I know why not. He doesn't want to have anything to do with me.*

Jake said, "We could take him."

"Jake, he'll be in school, and he *cannot* afford to miss a day, much less a week."

"Well, Frances could be here, or maybe he could stay with Trip's family."

"I'll think about it."

"Good." Jake finished up the omelet, served half to Janet and half for himself. He poured them both another cup of coffee and sat down at the table.

Janet frowned at her iPad.

"Of course, if you really don't want to go," Jake said before taking a bite of his breakfast.

"Oh, it's not that. I was trying to remember what woke me

last night," she said, stirring her coffee. "Did you hear anything unusual? Did it storm?"

"If it stormed, I slept through it. Why?"

"The house made some funny noises."

"What kind of noises?"

"Like a slam, I think near our room. I can't describe the other noises."

"Was Alex home?"

"Yes. You were in your study when he came in last night."

Jake shrugged, palms up. "Let's eat first. We'll look around afterward. Possums got into the Johannsens' attic. Maybe some critter crashed our place. Or you could've been dreaming."

When they finished eating, Janet took their empty plates to the island. "You've made quite a mess over here."

"It's okay. I've got an arrangement with Frances. She'll take care of it."

Janet shook her head.

"Don't worry. She loves me," he said.

"Oh, don't I know it."

On the second floor, the first room they came to was Alex's. The bed was unmade, and clothes were strewn all over the room, with one big heap in the corner. Dirty dishes lay on the floor by the bed. Wet towels were on his bathroom floor.

Janet sighed. "Well, nothing's amiss here."

Just the sight of the room spoiled Jake's mood. It was a mess. He'd made a mistake coming up there if he wanted to enjoy the morning. The clothes that Janet gave Alex carte blanche to buy, he simply stepped out of and left on the floor. Jake headed toward the gigantic heap in the corner, kicking designer jeans and expensive shoes out of his path. With each step his temper climbed. One of Alex's shoes stuck partially out of the pile. Jake gave it a swift kick.

"Holy *shit*!" came a masculine cry from under the clothes.

Janet and Jake both took a step back, their mouths agape as

shirts and sweaters flew off what they thought was just a pile of clothes.

"What the fuck's going on?" A disheveled, scraggly, dark-haired boy stood unsteadily.

"That's what I'd like to know," Jake said.

Janet's face turned bright red. "Bryan, what are you doing here?"

"Sleeping, till I got the shit kicked out of me."

"How did you get in here? When?" Janet asked.

"Alex let me in through the window," he replied, rubbing his eyes.

Jake walked to the window, which faced the front of the house above the portico. He guessed it was possible for someone to climb onto the roof and step in—with help. "Get your things and get out of here!" His voice quivered with rage.

"Okay, *okay*! I'm going." He looked around the room before spying his jacket on the floor near the window. He glared at Jake, who snatched it up and threw it at him.

Janet and Jake followed Bryan down the stairs to the front door. He casually donned his jacket and turned his coat collar up. Before strutting down their drive, he hesitated long enough to light a cigarette and flip hair out of his eyes with a toss of his head. Then he turned a corner and was out of sight.

Again Jake hesitated. When he was this angry at Alex, he usually said the wrong thing and only made matters worse between him and Janet. Dammit! So much for his pleasant morning at home.

Janet, still red-faced, turned toward him. "What does Alex see in that kid? Why does he hang around him when I expressly forbid it?"

Jake thought about his words and purposely controlled his voice. He didn't say, "I told you so," or, "You shouldn't have given him that car in the first place," or, "He's headed for trouble."

He looked at Janet steadily. "Jan, Bryan's one of his best friends. You can tell a lot about a kid by the company he keeps."

"Well, I'm not having it! You're right, Jake. I'm going to have to be more forceful with him. He is not going to turn out like that young hoodlum."

JAKE

CHAPTER EIGHTEEN

"Because he got in a fight with his mom," Alex yelled, apparently trying to justify slipping Bryan in through the window the night before. "What's the big deal, anyway? We got plenty of room."

Jake stood in the living room with his elbow resting on the mantel, saying nothing. His intention was to be there to support Janet—and, if he was honest with himself, to make sure she carried through on her promise. Alex and Janet sat on the edge of the leather sofa.

"What about his parents? They must have been worried sick about him."

"Nah. They don't worry about Bryan anymore."

"Well, that makes no difference," Janet said as she became more agitated. "I've told you repeatedly not to hang around with Bryan. He's a bad influence. And, the idea of you sneaking him into our home." She stood, looking down at her son, pointing with her index finger. "No way, Alex. I have no idea what Bryan's into, but I bet it's no good. I don't want him here, and I don't want you running around with him."

Alex stood, too, facing her. "He's my friend. You can't tell me who to hang with. What happened to this being my home too, when you made me move here against my will? If this is my home, I should be able to have *my friends* spend the night."

"I'm your mother. I can tell you who you can and can't bring into our house."

"My mother? Big deal. When did you ever care what I did as long as I didn't keep you from running off to . . . wherever? You've always cared more about your patients. You wouldn't even bring this up if it weren't for him." Alex pointed an accusing finger at Jake. "And he has *no* right telling me what to do. He is *not* my father."

Janet's face turned crimson. Alex had obviously pushed a button, struck a nerve. At Alex's age, Jake would have given anything to have his mother back. The way Alex talked to Janet enraged him. The kid had weaponized her drive to get through medical school so she could make something of herself and take care of him. He made it sound like she ignored him, but if anything she had been too caring, too soft.

"Don't talk to me like that," Janet demanded. "You sound just like Bryan. That's what you pick up from hanging out with him. There's going to be some changes around here from now on, Alex. For a start, you're grounded. I want your car keys. You can have them back when you've earned them."

"No way! It's my fucking car and you're not getting my keys!" He turned to walk away from his mother, but she grabbed his arm. "Let me go!" He shrugged it away from her.

Jake stepped in front of Janet, put his hand on Alex's shoulder. The look Alex gave Jake could have ignited a blaze. They stood, squared off, each challenging the other, for what seemed like a long time. Jake could picture the boy trying to take him down, but Jake was bigger, stronger. They both knew that if it got physical, Alex would lose.

"Okay, okay. I'll get the fucking keys. Just let go of me." Alex pulled away from Jake and stormed out of the room.

Jake sighed and slipped his arm around Janet's waist. At least she stood firm this time. That was huge. For several minutes they stood in the living room, waiting. Janet squinted, the way she did when she had one of her migraines.

"What could be taking him so long?" Jake said.

Janet shook her head. "I have no idea. I'll see." With Jake right behind her, she entered Alex's room just in time to see him sitting on the ledge of the open window, ready to climb out.

"Oh no you don't," Janet shouted as she rushed across the room and grabbed his arm, roughly pulling him back inside so that he lost his balance.

With both his arms and all his might, he pushed Janet into Jake. She hit the back of her head hard on Jake's chin.

"I'm getting the *fuck* outa here," Alex shouted as he turned and climbed out on the roof, then dropped the short distance to the driveway.

Janet looked dazed. She stared after him.

Jake rubbed his chin. "Are you okay?"

Janet pivoted on her heels. "You just made things worse."

Jake took a step backward. "What?"

"Alex wouldn't have acted like that if you hadn't pushed him into it!"

"You're the one who asked for his keys. You're the one he shoved. Alex is in trouble. The only difference between him and Bryan is a couple of years. You saw the real Alex this evening. Up until now, he had you conned."

"There you go again, accusing him of things you can't prove. You've never liked him. You're jealous of him . . . of our relationship." Janet stood with her hands clenched, tears running down her cheeks.

"Janet, that isn't true."

"You've never had kids. You don't really know what it's like."

"Janet, I—"

"I don't want to discuss it anymore. I have a splitting head-ache." She walked around Jake and out of the room.

REAGAN

CHAPTER NINETEEN

Reagan glanced at Matthew, who was quietly gazing out the window as they rolled north on Montgomery Road.

Taking my son to do his Christmas shopping is supposed to be fun, remember?

Scott had always loved it—two guys out shopping for their women—until last year, when he told Matt he couldn't take him shopping after all. The look on Matt's face—like he finally got it, something was terribly wrong. She never wanted to see that expression on her son's face again.

It's got to be better this year.

With the weather cold and overcast, and the ground wet from melting snow, some Norwood snowbirds had already migrated to Florida for the winter—bare hardwoods and brown landscape left behind for palm trees, tropical flowers, and sunny days in the seventies and eighties. Those who had family in the area usually waited until after New Year's.

"So tell me again," Reagan asked, "how much money do you have and who are you shopping for?"

"Eighty-eight dollars. Jake, Anaya, Lizzie, Aunt Jordan,

Uncle Sonny, Mrs. Morris, and Mr. Seacrest. Jake said he would take me Thursday to buy your present."

"If that's the case, how much can you spend on each gift?"

Matthew rolled his eyes and answered with the exasperated tone that reminded her so much of Scott. "Mom, I know math. That would be ten dollars 'cause there's tax."

At the intersection of Pleasant Ridge and Montgomery, the traffic slowed, allowing Reagan to take a good look around. She had avoided the area since the shooting, but a pileup on the expressway made Montgomery the quickest way to get to the mall. A big Keep Out sign now hung on a high fence surrounding the shuttered Burger King. *Might as well say,* "No drug dealing—no murders allowed." *Why couldn't they have put up that fence earlier, before—*

"Mom, that place burned."

On the other side of the street, the shop next to Molly Malone's was dark—the large storefront window gone, the insides charred. Happy hour at Molly's. Lights were on, but the place looked empty. No cars parked bumper-to-bumper on the street, no overflow needed at Burger King. A lone man walked out, got into one of the four cars in the bar's parking lot, and pulled out onto the busy street. Before the shooting, the area had been alive with people walking dogs, jogging, or rushing into the local bar and grill for a quick bite and a cold beer.

That cool neighborhood. Look at it now. That's what happens when the locals allow gangs to take over.

Detective Gabriel came to mind—his heavy sigh, the bitter smile when Reagan reneged on her promise to help him. Her stomach dipped. She shook her head and tried to chase away that image. Both she and Matthew remained quiet the rest of the way to Kenwood.

A huge banner with a colorful Santa and "Welcome" written in glitter hung from the second-floor railing inside the mall. Red poinsettias in green pots stacked into the shape of a gigantic Christmas tree stood in the food court. Kiosks that only came out for the holidays crowded the center aisles, offering ribbon candy and chocolates, costume jewelry, electronic gadgets, and other gift items. "God Rest Ye Merry Gentlemen" drifted out of Williams-Sonoma.

If this can't put us in the Christmas spirit, nothing can.

Matthew, his hands shoved into his pockets, stopped at a kiosk displaying costume jewelry. His eyes widened when he spotted a gaudy ring, a large blue stone surrounded by rhinestones, on sale for $9.99, half price.

"This is pretty."

Reagan tilted her head slightly and pursed her lips. "For whom?"

"Mrs. Morris?"

"Why don't we look around a little more? There are a lot of nice things. We can always come back to this if you like."

He nodded.

The yeasty aroma from Auntie Anne's made a pretzel irresistible, so they bought one apiece and grabbed the last two empty nearby seats. The pretzels, warm and delicious, coated their fingers with sticky butter that they licked off, one fingertip at a time.

"Where do you want to go next?"

"Macy's," Matthew said.

Ah, right, Macy's, where a few years ago Scott took Matthew to Christmas shop and let him buy Rosie for my present, the red stuffed panda he's slept with every night since.

Reagan smiled at her son and put her arm over his shoulder as they moved on.

Inside the store, Matthew found a display of gift items tailored for teachers—paperweights and coffee mugs with funny sayings. They spent several minutes browsing through the stuff, picking up an item, reading, laughing or not, and carefully replacing it on the table.

"Mom, this is my favorite." He handed her a mug that said, *"Teaching is easy. It's like riding a bike—but the bike is on fire, the seat is broken, and the tire is flat."*

Reagan laughed. "Oh, that's perfect."

She grabbed a strand of her unruly hair and secured it behind her right ear. "I like this one too." She picked up one with *"Keep Calm and Pretend It's on the Lesson Plan."*

"That's another good one for a teacher." She raised both eyebrows.

After reading all the mugs, they bought *"Lesson Plan"* for Mrs. Morris and *"Bike on Fire"* for Mr. Seacrest, and scratched both names off Matthew's list.

They'd been at the mall more than an hour when they got to Macy's men's department. In there, another mother was helping her child with Down syndrome buy a gift. The young girl looked about Lizzie's age but higher functioning. She handed the clerk money, waited patiently for the transaction, listened to instructions from her mother, and said thank you when the clerk handed her the package. Her face glowed with excitement.

Most people wouldn't notice such an ordinary thing, but that child pricked a tiny hole in Reagan's heart. She longed to see that glow on Lizzie's face, the expression of amazement at all the glitz and glitter, that over-the-moon excitement when she got a gift. She would love to include her daughter in the holiday events she'd loved as a kid: Christmas shopping, breakfast with Santa, mailing her wish list to the North Pole, and sitting inches from the TV on Christmas Eve to get the latest sightings of the sleigh.

But just because those activities delighted other children didn't mean Lizzie would enjoy them. She had no concept of the future, and anyway, she couldn't write a letter to Santa.

Like many autistic children, she was supersensitive to lights and noise, unpredictable, sometimes uncontrollable. Waiting in line for Santa was out of the question; she couldn't be trusted around other children not to pull their hair or grab their glasses. The last time Reagan had taken her shopping in a crowded mall with loud music, Lizzie clamped her hands over her ears like she was in excruciating pain, bolted away from her, and narrowly missed crashing into a man using a walker. Reagan wasn't sure she could manage her daughter alone.

Thank god for Anaya. She fussed over the children, and her too. Reagan would have asked Anaya to move in with them, but the house wasn't big enough for another family member.

Strolling around the men's department while Matthew studied a selection of toiletries, Reagan found herself looking through a stack of Calvin Klein sweaters. Scott had favored that brand. She pulled out a navy blue turtleneck, medium, and imagined him in it. The color was great with his complexion, those big brown eyes that pulled you in, suggesting X-rated behavior. Abruptly she replaced the sweater.

I'm supposed to be having a good time with my son. This isn't helping.

She meandered through the department until she noticed Matthew, still at the toiletries, staring down at something on the table. When he saw her walk toward him, he ducked his head and looked in the opposite direction. That was odd. She walked over to him and put her hand on his back.

"Buddy, did you find something you like?"

He shook his head.

"Matt, look at me."

When he turned to her, water pooled in his clear-green eyes, his face red and tense. Reagan understood when she saw the gift box on the table: Star Wars Empire Toilette Water for men. Matthew had bought that for his father last Christmas.

The bottle still sat half-full on his parents' chest of drawers. She draped her arm around his shoulder.

"Buddy, we can finish this another time. You ready to go home?"

He nodded and leaned against his mother as they walked back to the car.

She took the interstate on the way home. Pleasant Ridge was too depressing, and she had a vague notion she was responsible for that.

"Ahhh." Reagan breathed in a mouthwatering bouquet as she stepped into the house. Reagan loved being greeted with heavenly aromas when she opened her front door. A splendid cook, Anaya was more like an international chef than someone hired to take care of a child with special needs. Even on school days, she often made gourmet meals for the four of them and did amazing things with coconut milk, chilies, and lemongrass.

Matthew immediately ran upstairs to his room with his package and slammed the door. Scooter trailed after him and sat outside his bedroom, yapping, until Matthew let him in. Lizzie sprawled out on the living room floor watching *Frozen*. "Let It Go" blared from the TV.

"What's with Matthew?" Anaya appeared from the kitchen. She looked tired—no, stressed. The creases around her eyes and mouth were deeper than usual, her familiar smile replaced by a thin mouth and firm jaw.

Reagan took a deep breath and shook her head. "Froot Loop moment." Months ago, while casually shopping in Kroger, Reagan fixated on a big box of Froot Loops. Scott had loved the cereal and snacked on fistfuls straight from the box. She went from neutral to meltdown in a split second—left her grocery cart in the aisle and rushed out of the store before causing a scene. Ever since then, they all referred that way to those overwhelming waves of grief.

"Ah . . . well . . ." Anaya shook her head, pivoted, and walked back into the kitchen.

Reagan followed. "Something smells wonderful."

"I thought I'd have a go at a new recipe I found. It'll be ready about six. I hope Matthew didn't eat a bunch of junk at the mall and ruin his dinner."

"He'll always eat your cooking, you know that. Lizzie too." Reagan bent down and opened the oven door to take a whiff. "Yum."

Anaya flashed a weak smile and nodded.

Apparently the aroma captured Lizzie's attention too, or she'd tired of *Frozen*, because she left the TV blaring and sauntered into the kitchen.

"Oh, I didn't notice her pajamas." Reagan spun the child around by the shoulder. "Where'd those come from?" The one-piece footie pajamas looked like a unicorn costume and were on backward, as usual, so she couldn't reach the zipper and strip during the night, a behavior that apparently brought her no end of enjoyment.

"I picked them up at Nordstrom last week," Anaya said. "They were so cute I couldn't resist." She seemed to be preoccupied with putting a salad together.

Reagan shrugged out of her jacket and hung it on the back of a kitchen chair. "I drove through Pleasant Ridge for the first time since the shooting. Anaya, you wouldn't believe how it has changed in such a short time. It felt creepy."

"What do you mean?"

"It was just dead. Almost no one out."

"It's cold. People want to be home. It'll probably pick up, Rea. Don't read too much into it. Even the most popular places have occasional slow nights."

"You think? I hope so. It's just . . . I'm concerned it's going downhill." She took a stack of plates out of a cabinet and placed them around the table. "Are you okay? I've never seen your jaw clench like that."

Anaya sighed and looked at the ceiling, then at Reagan. "I'm okay, but I do have something I need to talk to you about."

Instantly Reagan was back in Dr. Walker's office, clutching Scott's hand, waiting for the results of a PET scan, each trying to be strong for the other. She took a deep breath, held it in, and braced herself. "What is it?"

"I have to go to India. I'm sorry to do this now, Rea. I don't relish leaving you and the children when I know how much you need me, but my sister is very sick, and I must go to care for her. It's different there in our village. They don't have the resources we have here in the US. You'll be able to get another aide for Lizzie, but my sister has no one else."

Reagan blinked and swallowed hard, struggling to take it in. Anaya was leaving. A tingling spread from her chest to her fingertips. She had to grit her teeth to keep them from chattering. Anaya was going to India. How would she manage Lizzie without Anaya? Would she come back? How would she tell the kids?

She glanced out the window. Bird sat on the sill, looking in with a sympathetic expression. She shifted to the defense she'd practiced so often, had become so good at, focusing on one detail at a time.

At least it's not cancer.

She took the salad bowl from Anaya, set it aside, and folded her into an embrace. "Of course you must go. We'll manage until you get back. You *will* come back. Right?"

ALEX

CHAPTER TWENTY

The porch light next door shone through the black night, making the raindrops on the window sparkle like sequins. Alex sat on the floor with his back propped against Bryan's bed, looking out, mesmerized by the glitter. The raindrops seemed to be dancing against the windowpane. Awesome! He started to tell Bryan . . . but didn't.

Across the room, Bryan leaned against the wall, watching a music video on TV. Both guys had been smoking weed since early afternoon. They'd gotten together to play Grand Theft Auto V but eventually tired of that and turned to YouTube.

When Alex tried to push himself up off the floor, his hand brushed against something partially concealed by the bedspread. "Hey, man, aren't you a little old to be playin' with dolls?" He laughed as he held up a small rag doll he'd scooped out from underneath Bryan's bed.

Bryan stumbled over, his brow creased, his eyes glassy. "That ain't mine." He stared at the doll for a moment before his bleary eyes focused, then his face turned red. "Oh yeah, I remember, my niece left it here. Give it here. I'll take it to her."

"Likely story. Sure you weren't doing something nasty with her?" Alex lifted the doll's skirt and waved it in Bryan's face.

"Fuck you." Bryan grabbed for the doll, which flew out of Alex's hand to the floor. Alex laughed harder, swaying as he bent over and grabbed his knees. "Okay, okay, chill. I was messing with you like you mess with me. Like we used to do all the time. I wish I still lived in Norwood. I was happy here. Just me and my mom. She didn't care what I did. Always too busy."

His mom didn't get why he was so upset at having to move. Nobody even asked him if he wanted to—like anybody would have been happy to live in some big house in Indian Hill; like he hadn't lived in Norwood all his life; like his best friend didn't live a block away.

His fists automatically clenched. "I wish she'd never met Jake. Ever since then, everything changed."

Bryan rolled his eyes. "Not that again. What if Jake was like my ol' man? But you're right. We could do anything we wanted back then—my ol' man locked up, my mom happy he was out of the house." He curled his lip, slowly shook his head. "Even if I stay in Norwood, as soon as I'm eighteen I'm getting the fuck outa here."

"What about college? My mom's constantly grilling me about college." Alex scaled his voice higher, imitating his mother. "You've got to get your grades up. You'll never get into a good school. You don't know how lucky you have it to be able to go right into college after high school. I had to save money and work my way through."

Bryan shrugged. "I ain't going to college, dude. Can you see me living on some college campus like some fuckin' schoolboy, joining some fraternity and shit? I'll have a helluva lot more fun. I'll have my girl, and I'll make way more money than my ol' man."

Alex jerked his head back. "Your girl? What girl?" Bryan

made all kinds of comments about girls, like all the guys did, but he had never shown an interest in having a girlfriend.

"She's new in school. A real looker."

"Have you, like . . . talked to her?"

"Of course. What'd you think, I'm some fuckin' retard or something? She likes to talk to me, and we hang out when she can get away from her ol' man."

A jolt of jealously surprised Alex. Bryan was *his* friend. His best friend since fifth grade. The day they met, when they snuck into the Reds game, was the best day of his life. Bryan and Trip were his only real friends, and he hadn't met Trip until he moved to Indian Hill.

"Well, from what I hear, college kids buy a lotta dope," Alex said. "Going to college might be good for business. You could branch out. Become a kingpin. I could even sell for you."

"I ain't gotta go to college to sell to college kids. I'm growing my business now and those guys will—"

Without warning, Bryan rushed to the window, almost tripping over Alex. He looked up and down the street. "Shit, I heard a car door slam and thought it was my parents. Not, though." Despite the rain, he cracked the window to let in some fresh air. "I don't want to give my ol' man something else to rag on me about. He's got no time for me."

"That's not so bad," Alex said. "Jake's got too much—always watching me, telling me what to do, what not to do, getting between me and my mom. How long have we been here, anyway? I can't remember when I was supposed to be home."

Bryan shrugged.

"Well, I'll just tell 'em I was with Trip." He figured he was coming down, since he was concerned about his parents. "What else you got, man?"

Bryan went to his bookshelf and took down a green book, actually a secret stash box he had gotten at a head shop in

Clifton. He removed a bag of weed and three rolled joints and offered Alex the box containing an assortment of pills.

Alex ran his tongue over his lips as he moved the tablets around with his finger.

He had been only twelve four years ago, the first time Bryan gave him drugs. Alex had asked then, "Where'd you get them?"

"From my mom's medicine cabinet."

"What if she finds out?"

"Don't worry. She ain't gonna find out. There's three different bottles with the same stuff in 'em. One day you take a couple outa the blue bottle, next day the yellow label, then the big bottle without a label. She's got so many she ain't never gonna miss 'em."

"What'll they do?"

"Take one. You'll find out."

He knew he shouldn't. The DARE officer at school and his teacher constantly hammered on the kids in his class not to do drugs. But he'd been bummed about his mom getting married. He'd plucked one of the white tablets from the box and popped it into his mouth. Nothing really big happened at first, but within a few minutes he felt . . . mellow . . . cheerful. But mainly it was no big deal.

Bryan pushed a button and became subdued, engrossed in YouTube.

Alex swallowed one of the tablets and quickly lost interest in the dancing raindrops, the doll, and Bryan's hypothetical girlfriend. He soon began to feel tingly and weird. He tried to ignore it, but weird turned into queasy, which turned into panic. What had Bryan given him?

Wes . . . is this what he felt like before he died?

He shouldn't have taken that last hit. His heartbeat cranked up. He couldn't catch his breath. Wes. He couldn't stop thinking about Wes.

"Bryan, man," he could hardly cough out the name. "I think I'm going to be sick."

Bryan stared at YouTube and didn't respond.

"Bryan," Alex screamed. "I don't feel so good. I think I'm going to puke."

"You think what?"

"Something's wrong, man. I don't feel good."

Bryan's blank stare morphed into a look of recognition. He jumped up and grabbed Alex's arm to pull him up. "Not in my house. You gotta get the fuck outa here."

"Wait, man. I'm not feeling good. Don't," he said as Bryan pulled him to his feet. "What if I can't make it home?"

"That ain't my problem. You've gotta go. My folks are already on my ass, and I don't wanna have to deal with their shit tonight." Despite Alex's protests, Bryan dragged him out of the bedroom and practically pushed him down the stairs to the front door.

"But . . . but . . . I can't drive, Bryan, I—"

Bryan opened the door and shoved Alex out into the cold rain. Alex turned around, but before he could speak, the door slammed in his face and the lock clicked.

He turned up the collar of his jacket, shrugged, and walked to his car in the rain, shivering uncontrollably, pushing down tears.

Twenty minutes later he was standing in his bedroom. He couldn't remember how he had gotten from Norwood to Indian Hill, but he was thankful neither his mom nor Jake was home. He did not want to deal with parents. He stripped to his skin and crawled into bed, his thoughts fragmented, out of control. He was done with Bryan. He would quit using. Maybe he wouldn't even wake up. Would anybody care?

REAGAN

CHAPTER TWENTY-ONE

Large, lacy flakes of falling snow turned Kenilworth into a living Christmas card. Reagan sipped hot coffee and watched through the living room window as the children across the street put the final touches on a snowman: button eyes, carrot nose, and, to add panache, a red-striped scarf around the neck. The streetlight decorated with a red bow and holly completed the picture. "Do You Hear What I Hear?" flowed from the TV. The faint scent of evergreen drifted from the Christmas tree in the corner of the room.

Enough. I'd better get a move on.

Their flight to Atlanta was scheduled for 3:15 p.m., and Reagan wanted to get to the airport by at least one o'clock. Security lines would be longer than normal. Boarding usually started more than half an hour before departure, and she needed to be there in time for preboarding help with Lizzie. Leave nothing to chance. They could eat lunch at the airport. She took her empty cup to the dishwasher near the kitchen window. Snow covered the roof of the large birdhouse Reagan and the children had painstakingly painted for Bird, now in outline, a child's drawing. Bird stood just inside the door, his head poked out, with an expression of surprise.

"You're not going to leave too, are you—fly south for the warm weather? You'll be here when I get back from Jordan's, right?"

"Mom, it's snowing harder." Matthew strolled into the kitchen, pulling his Batman suitcase, his backpack already on his back. His excitement was obvious by his shining eyes and wide grin.

"Yes, I know. It's beautiful, isn't it?"

"We'll have a white Christmas."

"Buddy, it's not snowing in Atlanta."

"Oh yeah, right. But maybe it will."

Reagan glanced at Bird. "Well, stranger things have happened. You could be right. Are you all packed?"

Matthew nodded.

"Let me see what you've got in there." Reagan put the suitcase up on the table and opened it. Rosie, his red panda, threadbare in areas and patched in others, lay on top. Underneath was a stack of pants, shirts, and underwear; and two pair of pajamas: one Spider-Man themed, the other red covered with Ohio State logos. In the pocket were a toothbrush and a comb.

"Looks good. What's your sister doing?"

"She's in her room."

"Will you keep an eye on her while I finish getting ready?"

Reagan had been looking forward to the trip for weeks. She needed it. Anaya's leaving was a blow that had left her stressed and depressed. The children hadn't had a good home-cooked meal since she left, and Lizzie, whose behavior in the best of circumstances was unpredictable, had been whiny and uncooperative for days. The only positive: Reagan had been too busy trying to fill the void to worry about what happened in Pleasant Ridge.

The doorbell rang. *Oh, Sonny's early.* Scooter raced to the door, the most energetic he'd been since he first spied the suitcases, his frantic bark competing with the music channel on TV. Reagan opened it.

Jake, ruggedly handsome in woolen clothing crusty with snow, stood on the front porch leaning on a snow shovel, his face red from the cold.

"Jake! Hi. I'm surprised to see you here."

"Hi, Reagan. I hope I'm not intruding, but I was out and thought I'd take the opportunity to teach Matthew to shovel. He tells me he's the man of the house." He raised both eyebrows and grinned. "It's a great time to show it."

She laughed at the reindeer antlers stuck on top of his Jeep, which was parked in front of her house. A big red nose clung to the grille. "That'd be great but—"

"Oh, I know. I should have called first. I'll just—"

"Oh, no. No, that's all right. Honestly. That's exactly what I want you to do with Matthew: the man stuff. I'll get him."

Eleven o'clock. We've got time. She went upstairs to get her son.

Over the next hour, Reagan took care of last-minute items. She dressed Lizzie and stuffed her backpack with toys to keep her busy on the plane, downloaded boarding passes to her phone, adjusted the thermostat, crammed Christmas presents into an empty suitcase, and positioned the luggage by the front door.

Between each task she peeked out the window at Jake and Matthew. Jake had a habit of putting his hand on Matthew's back when he talked to him. Matthew, wide-eyed, seemed to hang on every word. The snow swallowed the normal sounds of the city—traffic noise from Smith Road, barking dogs, chimes from Immaculate Conception. Reagan heard only the scrape of shovels against concrete, the murmured speech of Jake and Matthew, and, every so often, Jake's distinctive deep, boisterous laughter.

Lizzie limped into the living room, her backpack over

her shoulders, tugged on Reagan's arm, and signed with her fingers to her mouth: "Eat, eat." Under her arm she carried a doll, this one rubber. Annie, her favorite, was still among the missing.

Matthew burst into the living room. His face was reddened, his eyes were watery, and his nose dripped, but he hadn't complained about being cold. "Mom, come look! We shoveled the whole driveway and walk." He pulled off his hat and turned to say something to Jake, who was walking back to his car. "Jake, come in."

"Buddy, we need to leave soon. It's after twelve and Sonny will—"

"Look, he's bringing in presents!" Matthew jumped up and down and met Jake at the door. "Are those for me?"

Jake carried in three boxes, beautifully wrapped, one with Tinker Bell paper, one with Captain Hook, and another in red foil with a gold Godiva sticker. "This one is," he answered and handed Matthew the largest of the three gifts.

"What is it?"

Jake laughed. "Why don't you open it?"

"Can I, Mom?"

Reagan smiled. "Sure. Go ahead." She glanced at her watch, trying not to be conspicuous. Jake handed her the other gifts.

"Reagan, this is for Lizzie, and I hope you like chocolates."

She chuckled. "Oh, no. None of us like chocolates. We prefer spinach and calf's liver. Don't we, Matt?" She made an exaggerated smiley face at Matthew.

"Right, spinach . . . and liver," he yelled as he tore into the gift, throwing scraps of paper into the air. He pulled out a black-and-orange Bengals jersey. "Oh man, I love it!" He took off his coat and pulled the jersey over his head.

"You left something in the box."

Matthew pulled out the tissue paper and found a small envelope underneath. "What is it?"

Jake grinned. "Tickets to the Ravens-Bengals game on the thirtieth."

"Awesome!" Matthew said as he held up the tickets. "There's four."

"I thought we'd ask Dave and Joey. How about it?"

"Yeah!" Matthew squealed. He ran to retrieve a gift from under their tree. "This is for you." He handed Jake a present wrapped in red paper and string. "You have to wait until Christmas to open it."

Jake stuck out his lower lip. "Well, that's not fair."

Matthew laughed and bounced on his toes. "Just kidding. You can open it now."

Reagan cranked up the TV volume. "Jingle Bells" blared into the room. Matthew looked on as Jake opened the package and uncovered a gift set of cologne. He opened one of the bottles, sniffed the scent, and grinned. "Star Wars. I knew it'd be good. Thanks, sport."

Matthew flashed a satisfied grin and nodded.

Jake stood, tucked the package under his arm. "When are you leaving for your aunt's?"

"Today," Matthew answered.

"Well, I'll go and get out of your way. Merry Christmas."

"You too, Jake, and thanks so much for today, and—" *Uh-oh. Where's Lizzie? She said she was hungry.* "Excuse me, Jake." Reagan rushed to the kitchen in time to see Lizzie unscrew the cap from a half-full gallon of milk. "No, wait—"

Too late. Lizzie poured milk all over herself and the counter, down the front of the cabinet, and into a large puddle on the floor. The only dry spot: the inside of Lizzie's cup.

Well, she said she wanted to eat.

"Sorry, honey, I got distracted." Reagan, grateful when she heard the door close behind Jake, grabbed a roll of paper towels, tore off a handful, and threw them on the counter and floor. "Honey, I know you want to do things for yourself, but we've talked about this. Some things are too heavy for you."

Matthew came through the door, Scooter right behind him. The dog immediately trotted to the puddle and began to lick up milk.

"Scooter, get out of here." She tore off more paper towels and dabbed at the front of Lizzie's shirt. "Honey, we have to change your clothes."

"Noooo," she signed. "Eat, eat."

Scooter walked through the puddle, leaving milky paw tracks on the floor.

"Arghhh." Reagan shook her head and glanced at the clock on the stove. Twelve thirty.

Well, Sonny's not here yet anyway. We won't get there by one, but we can grab something and eat on the plane.

She finished cleaning up the milk, took Lizzie by the hand, and walked out of the kitchen.

The front door burst open, allowing in a blast of frigid air. "Hey, y'all about ready?" Sonny stomped snow off his boots and entered. He was dressed in street clothes, a heavy coat, and gloves. "Who was in the Jeep with antlers?" Scooter pranced up to Sonny, shaking his behind.

"Jake. Uncle Sonny, did you see I shoveled the drive?"

Sonny cocked his head, furrowed his brow, and studied Matthew. "You did that?"

"Yeah . . . me and Jake."

Sonny's gaze drifted from Matthew to Scooter and he crouched down to pet the dog. "Well, Scooter, it looks like it's gonna be just you and me for Christmas." He noticed Lizzie's shirt. "What did you do now?" He grinned at the child and shook his head.

Lizzie rotated her fist against her chest with a clockwise motion.

"Sorry?" Sonny bent down to her eye level. "You should say sorry to your mother, not me."

Reagan said, "She was trying to pour milk herself and accidently spilled it all over herself and the kitchen. I need to change her."

He stood. "I know I'm a little late, Rea, but the streets are a mess out there. I just checked on your flight. Wouldn't you know, it's on time. Go ahead, change her, but we need to get going. Matt, are you going to your Aunt Jordan's or a Bengals game?"

Matthew looked down at his jersey. "Jake gave me this for Christmas. Isn't it cool?"

"Yeah, sure. If you're ready, let's put these things in the car." Sonny pointed to the suitcases. "Your presents are in my car. Sorry it doesn't have horns, like Mr. Dekker's."

Reagan ignored Sonny's snarky remark and headed up the stairs with Lizzie.

They finally got on the road at twelve forty-five. Several inches of snow still covered the side streets, but Smith Road had been treated and was better. They had two hours to get to the airport, get through security, and preboard. Typical travel time to CVG was about twenty minutes. Lizzie had been super cooperative and contrite since spilling the milk. They had time.

Sonny took the Norwood Lateral to I-71 South. Traffic was slow but moving steadily, and everyone in the car was in good spirits. Scooter sat in Matthew's lap and watched the world go by as they traveled south. Matthew and Reagan sang along to "A Holly Jolly Christmas" on the radio.

As they approached downtown, the snow kicked into high gear, coming down fast and hard—whiteout conditions. The traffic slowed to a standstill. Scooter became unsettled and barked incessantly. Lizzie started crying, loud wailing without tears. One o'clock. No movement for fifteen minutes. Scooter calmed down and so did Lizzie, but Sonny fidgeted, blew out puffs of hot breath, and finally pulled out his phone. He checked the Delta site again. "The flight's still on time. Siri, call the Norwood, Ohio, police department." He drummed his fingers on the steering wheel until a voice came on the line. "Hey, Jerry, I'm on my way to CVG. Reagan has a three-fifteen Delta flight to Atlanta and we're stuck in traffic near downtown. What gives?" After a moment he said, "Oh gawd!" and pounded the steering wheel.

Reagan's stomach sank. She braced herself for bad news.

"Semi jackknifed coming out of the tunnel." He shook his head. "Worst-case scenario. It takes hours to straighten out, and that's when the weather's decent and you don't have everyone and his brother leaving town for the holidays. Shit!"

They'd had their tickets for weeks and it was Christmas; flights were sold out.

"We're stuck. What should we do?" Reagan kept her voice calm and confident even though her insides had turned liquid, a skill she'd perfected over the last several months.

"Aren't we going to Aunt Jordan's?" Matthew, wide-eyed, sounded alarmed.

Sonny glanced in the rearview mirror. "Don't worry. Y'all are gonna get to your Aunt Jordan's for Christmas if I have to drive you all the way there. Let me think. . . . You still there, Jerry? What's going on with you guys? Yeah, maybe . . . I can see a little daylight. . . . I can probably squeeze over there. Jerry, you're a lifesaver. I owe you one. . . . Sure thing. We'll be here. We ain't going anywhere, that's for damn sure. Oh, one more thing, Jerry. Will you call ahead and have a wheelchair waiting for us? Thanks, Bud." He put his phone in the cup holder.

Sonny turned on his right blinker. "Okay, Jerry said it's pretty quiet in Norwood. We're gonna get in the right lane, and he's coming on the shoulder to lead us out of here, lights and siren if needed."

Reagan slumped against the car seat, let out a huge breath,

and mouthed "thank you" to Sonny. Until then she hadn't noticed the slight tremble in her hands. While they waited, she sat sideways in her seat and made small talk with the other three. Every few minutes, she glanced out the back window. The snow continued to fall, but more gently now. Twenty minutes after the phone call, Reagan spied rotating blue lights approaching from the rear on the right shoulder. "Look, Matt. Here he comes."

Matthew drummed his feet against the floorboard, excitement written across his face. "He's here. We're gonna make it!"

Lizzie clapped. As usual, Matthew's excitement rubbed off on her.

When Jerry reached Sonny's car, he flashed his headlights and Sonny pulled onto the shoulder behind him. They took the Reading exit, circumventing the tunnel, and picked up I-71/75 from Sixth Street. Christmas lights twinkled from Cincinnati skyscrapers as they sped through downtown. At the river, Jerry waved off and headed back north.

Sonny crossed into Kentucky and made good time the rest of the way. At 2:10, he pulled up to a Delta curbside check-in, off-loaded the luggage, and stuffed his presents for the family in one of the suitcases. Scooter yapped incessantly and jumped repeatedly from the back seat to the front.

Reagan helped Lizzie out of the car. Snow swirled around them, "Little Drummer Boy" blared over a loudspeaker, horns honked, car doors slammed, parents shouted to their kids, and scores of people dressed in heavy coats and boots rushed in and out of the building as Lizzie watched them with narrowed eyes. Matthew hugged Scooter around the neck and got out of the car.

"Okay, folks, three suitcases checked to Atlanta." The Delta agent looped tags around the handle of each suitcase. "Your plane's on time, leaving from gate B3. They'll be boarding in just a few minutes. Have a nice flight."

Sonny peeled off a five-dollar bill and tipped the agent. "Okay, guys, I would come in, but I can't leave my car here. Anyway, someone should be waiting with a wheelchair." He bent down and made eye contact with Lizzie. "You be good, okay?" He gave her a hug, then Matthew. "Tell your Aunt Jordan I said hello and have a wonderful Christmas. Scooter and I will pick you up when you get home."

"Thank you so much, Sonny. If it hadn't been for you, I'm sure we would've missed our flight."

"No problem." He gave Reagan a hug. "Have a good time. You deserve it."

Reagan grabbed Lizzie's hand and headed through the terminal as fast as she could with her daughter in tow. There was no attendant waiting, and she didn't want to take the time to look for one. Matthew followed.

Oh no! The lines to get through security snaked all through and around the gigantic room: people with laptops, children, luggage. Just taking off heavy coats and shoes to go through the scanner made the process slower than usual, and B3 stood at the end of the concourse, the farthest away from the elevators.

They showed their boarding passes and Reagan's ID to an agent. Another directed them to a line to go through the scanners. That line crept forward. They were soon sandwiched between businesspeople trying to get home and families headed to parts unknown.

Reagan's phone said 2:25. *They're probably already preboarding.*

A woman in a red jacket unhooked the rope barrier by Reagan and motioned for her and the children. Her name tag read Louise Duncan.

"Sorry I didn't meet y'all at the front door, honey. I got sidetracked. Some man wouldn't take no for an answer. I figured it was faster to take care of him than argue. Anyway, you can go through this scanner, and I've got your wheelchair. Don't worry, I won't let you miss your plane." She pointed to a scanner on the far side of the room, with only a couple of people waiting.

Reagan could have kissed her on the mouth. She helped Lizzie out of her backpack and into the wheelchair. Even with the help, by the time they traveled through the underground transportation tunnel and back up to terminal B, it was 2:45. When they reached gate B3, "Boarding Zone Two" sounded over the loudspeaker. "Anyone holding tickets with zone two may board at this time." Lizzie looked at her mother and signed, "Eat, eat."

"Ms. Duncan, thank you for your help." Reagan fished her wallet out of her purse.

Louise Duncan put her hand over Reagan's.

"No, honey, no need. You just get your little ones on that airplane and go where it is that you wanna go. And y'all have a merry Christmas, you hear."

No preboarding, but at least we made it. Reagan thanked Ms. Duncan again and herded her children to the end of the line.

Travelers around her were happy, excited, rushed. Lots of commotion: a cart with a flashing yellow light and recurrent beeping, loud boarding announcements, shouting, running. Stimulation. Lizzie covered her ears with her hands.

"Boarding Zone Three, everyone holding tickets with zone three may board at this time."

In the Jetway, passengers in zone three crowded in behind Reagan and the children. On the plane, they moved single file to seats 22A, B, and C. People regularly stopped forward movement to cram carry-ons, coats, backpacks, and other belongings into overhead bins and under their seats. Reagan stopped again for a man in front of them to take off a heavy coat and stuff it under the seat before sitting down. Their seats were two rows back. Apparently that was the last straw for Lizzie, because she abruptly dropped to the floor.

Oh no! "Honey, get up." Her daughter was a sizable heap under a unicorn backpack. Only one side of her face was visible; that one eye stared blankly at her mother. Behind her, Matthew slapped his head with his palm. A groundswell arose from the startled passengers who wouldn't be able to get around her in the narrow aisle.

"What's the holdup?"

"Now what?"

"I think a child had a seizure."

"Oh no."

Reagan's face burned. She gritted her teeth and leaned in close to Lizzie's ear. "Get up, now."

Lizzie was unmoved, literally. Reagan silently pleaded with someone unseen. *Please, please, please, don't throw us off this plane.* She positioned herself behind her daughter, slipped her backpack off her shoulders, handed it to Matthew, and grabbed her around the chest. She heaved upward, but the child slipped out of her mother's grasp. Disappearing armpits.

One of the flight attendants said, "I need to get by—excuse me—let me squeeze by," as she made her way past the passengers stuck in the aisle behind Reagan and the children.

"What's the problem here? Should I call the paramedics?"

"No, please don't. If you could just help me get her into her seat. We're only two rows back . . . 22A through C."

The flight attendant—Ellen Page on the name tag—seemed skeptical as she looked down at the child, but couldn't see Lizzie well because she was on her stomach, her face partially pressed against the floor.

"Are you sure she's all right?"

"She'll be fine, I promise. If you could help me lift her up."

"I'll try." She glanced at the people lined up, looking on. "Please move back."

Reagan directed her to wedge between the seat and Lizzie's hips; she situated herself on the other side. "On my count of three—" Both women heaved upward, like they'd seen a million times on hospital sitcoms, but Lizzie did not move. The crowded space, the awkward positioning, and Lizzie's dead weight all made it impossible to lift her from the floor.

"I'm going to have to get the captain." Ms. Page turned and addressed the passengers standing behind her. "Please move back into the Jetway."

Reagan took a deep breath and exhaled slowly, trying to quell the anxiety and embarrassment. *This is my fault, I know. She said she wanted to eat, more than once, and I didn't listen. I was going to get something on the plane, but how did she know that? And I know she gets overwhelmed, overstimulated. What was I thinking? This is the only power she has. If they usher us off this plane, I'm to blame.*

"Well, hello, Mrs. Ramsey," said a smiling man in uniform. He looked too young to be a pilot. His name tag read Charles Bone. "It seems we have a situation here."

"Yes, so it seems." Reagan stood erect; her chin pointed upward in her most self-assured pose. It was fake, of course, all an act. But her pride wouldn't let her beg him not to throw them off the plane. She felt powerless—the way Lizzie must feel all the time, unable to express herself or grasp simple concepts. She wasn't exactly powerless now, was she?

By that smirk on his face, Charlie Bone seemed to see right through her. Infuriating! What did he know about parenting a child with special needs?

"Have you asked her to get up?"

Double infuriating! "Yes, of course."

"Do you mind if I talk to her?"

"Of course not. Go ahead."

"What's her name?"

"Lizzie."

He asked the passenger in the seat next to Lizzie to move for a moment, which he did. The copilot then sat down, propped his elbows on his knees, and leaned in as close to Lizzie as he could get in the cramped space.

"Hello, Lizzie, would you like for me to help you to your seat? I think we can find some ice cream, but you have to be in your seat to eat it." He offered Lizzie his hand.

Some of the nearby passengers stood to watch, and a few took out their phones.

Just when Reagan felt sure they would all three be escorted off the plane, Lizzie nodded, took his hand, and got up.

"Yes!" cried one man. "Hallelujah!" said another. Applause broke out around them.

After Lizzie was belted into 22B, safely in the middle of the row, Reagan tilted her chin again and turned to the copilot, who now looked amused and quite proud of himself.

"I'm from Delta Quality Control," she said. "My children and I are mystery passengers, and this was an assignment to make sure the staff dealt appropriately with a challenging situation. You were being graded."

He threw back his head and laughed. "Well, Miss DQC, Delta picked the wrong scenario to trip up this first officer. I have a niece, you see, very much like Miss Ramsey here, who drives my sister up the wall with this very same behavior, but she will do anything for her Uncle Charlie. Especially when I offer ice cream."

Reagan scooped a loose strand of hair behind her ear. "Well, Mr. Bone, you did receive a passing grade. Good job."

None of the other passengers complained when the flight attendant brought Lizzie lunch, a pasta casserole, apple slices, milk, and ice cream. Matthew had a ham sandwich and cookies. Reagan had white wine, just white wine.

After a smooth ride for about an hour, the intercom squawked. "Ladies and Gentlemen, we are approaching Hartsfield-Jackson International Airport in Atlanta and will be on the ground in fifteen minutes. Local time is four forty-five p.m. Temperature is fifty-five degrees. We very much appreciate being able to serve you and hope you will again choose Delta. One more thing: You all have a merry Christmas, especially Mrs. Reagan Ramsey, Mr. Matthew Ramsey, and you, Miss Elizabeth Ramsey. You made this trip memorable."

The bell dinged, indicating it was safe to move around the cabin. Most of the passengers seated on the aisle hopped up like they had been waiting forever to stretch their legs. Lots of loud commotion as people pulled suitcases from overhead bins, gathered their belongings, and talked on their phones, but Lizzie seemed okay with it. Matthew crammed his stuff back into his backpack, and Reagan loaded Lizzie's.

Passengers in front of Reagan moved into the aisle one row at a time to make their way off the plane. The wine, the gentle vibration of the aircraft, and most of all the relief in finally having reached Atlanta and her wonderful big sister left Reagan comfortable and happy. She and the children stood and waited patiently for their turn, her mind wandering to thoughts of last Christmas.

They'd made a pact, she and Scott, to enjoy the holidays, to appreciate the joy of living no matter what. Was this to be his last Christmas? They hadn't known for sure. Neither had expressed the notion, but it had hovered in the back of her mind. That trip to Atlanta was what they needed, a reprieve from doctor's appointments, work, and worry.

And they had enjoyed it—at least she believed he had. A new friend for Matt, the boy who lived next door to Jordan. Gourmet food, good wine, and classic Christmas movies, only those with happy endings. Scott didn't have much of an appetite and alcohol wasn't appealing, but he loved the movies and watching his family have fun. That's what she needed now. Time to be loved and nurtured by the little family she had.

Suddenly she stiffened; the noise of movement and voices faded. A man three rows closer to the exit reached for his luggage and a coldness raced through her midsection. *That's him . . . wait . . . maybe not . . . I don't know.* As she leaned forward and stared at his profile, her heartbeat quickened. It looked like him. A lot like him. The dark man-bun, the prominent chin, the muscled arms. If she could only see his eyes.

She looked at the children and then toward the man, her stomach churning, her thoughts racing. *What should I do? Hide? I definitely can't let him see me or the children. On the other hand, if I could just identify him—if I knew he was locked up—it would be such a relief.* Then he turned toward the exit.

She stared at his back until he moved onto the Jetway. His long-sleeved, red knit shirt had the outline of a large whale on the back. As long as he didn't put on the coat he had fastened to his suitcase, he would be easy to follow.

ALEX

CHAPTER TWENTY-TWO

The basement was cool and dusty, lit by a single bulb. The furnace rumbled, then cut off, startling Alex. *Christ, will you relax!*

He blew on the top of a large cardboard carton. A cloud of dust formed and fell. How had this dirt escaped his mother's watchful eye? She was always looking for something to straighten, clean, disinfect. Not that she did it herself. She just demanded it be done.

He heaved the box to one side and glanced behind it. Not there. Other things—empty boxes that normally held the Christmas tree and decorations, several tangled strings of unused lights, a shopping bag of leftover wrapping paper ready for next year—lay scattered in the wake of his search. Not what he was looking for. He scanned the room again. His skateboard and two bikes propped against the wall. An old chest of drawers stuffed with discarded clothes. There, in the dim corner, he spotted them; he moved closer. They looked good at first glance. He grabbed a T-shirt from the chest and dusted off the top of the bag: four woods, a hybrid, one through nine irons,

PF wedge, sand wedge, putter. A complete set, an expensive set, and it would be three or four months before anyone looked for it. By then he would have bought them back. No sweat. He lifted the bag over his shoulder.

Heavy. Jake must be strong as an ox to carry this, but then, he rides a cart mostly. He's not that strong.

Alex climbed the stairs, careful not to let the bag bang against the wall, leave marks as evidence, and turned off the light. Before opening the door, he listened, although no one was home.

Paranoid! Jake's company Christmas party. They'll be the last ones to leave.

He walked straight to the garage, where he had parked his Mustang to avoid being seen loading the clubs. With a sigh of relief, he allowed the hefty load to slide from his shoulder, opened the trunk, heaved the clubs up and in, then quickly slammed it shut.

"Bruh, these are great. We should be able to get at least a couple hundred for them." Bryan took off the head covers and examined the driver, then the three-wood.

"What if this guy, Leo, thinks they're stolen?" Alex asked.

"Leo couldn't give a shit, man. And besides, they ain't stolen. They're your ol' man's."

"Right. It's his fault I don't have money in the first place. Mom would give me plenty if it wasn't for him, and he's loaded."

Bryan nodded in agreement.

Alex couldn't stay mad at Bryan long, so they were friends again. He'd thought about quitting and didn't use for a few days after his panic attack, but that didn't work out; getting high was all he could think about. He needed more stash, so he went to Bryan. It was as though nothing had ever happened, and neither one of them said anything. After all, it was only a panic attack. Besides, if not Bryan—and Trip—who would

Alex hang with? The scene at Bryan's house was no big deal anyway.

"I heard Lytle Tunnel is closed today 'cause of a wreck. Which way do I go?"

"Leo's place is on Meteor, near downtown Newport." Huge clumps of dirty snow lined the interstate. They passed a silver Nissan that had slammed against the rear of a Honda; a wrecker was stationed nearby. "That's the second crash we seen since Norwood. Let a little snow fall, and Cincinnati is fuckin' paralyzed."

Alex slowed, the condition of the roads making him nervous, his anxiety bleeding over to his driving. Bryan directed him through Newport, a city with a seedy past. A huge Going Out of Business Sale sign covered an entire storefront, next to a women's shoe store with a solitary string of Christmas lights over the window, then the pawn shop. They drove around the block, looking for a parking place, then pulled into one directly across the street from Leo's and stopped the car.

It was four thirty, almost dark, and cold—even for December. Most of the businesses had closed early for Christmas Eve, and the icy sidewalks were almost empty.

They could see through the window that Leo had a customer, a Black man in a Marine uniform.

"You look nervous, man," Bryan said. "Ain't nothin' to it. I've hocked lots of things. Leo has the best deals."

"I'm not nervous. I just want to wait till that dude leaves. No use asking for trouble." Alex blew into his hands to warm them. "You don't think he'll close early, do you? After all, it's Christmas Eve."

"He don't look like he's in no hurry."

"Okay, we'll wait." Alex started the car again, for heat and the radio, and watched the pawn shop window. The Marine talked to Leo, shooting the breeze.

Tap, tap, tap from the window on the passenger side. Alex

jumped, turned down the radio, lowered the window from his side, and saw a gaunt man stoop over and gaze inside. Bryan's eyes bulged. The man's hair was matted and his pupils were dilated into big round disks, the whites red. He looked wired, obviously high on something. He leaned in the window, haphazardly waved a gun, its shiny metal glistening in the light from a streetlamp.

Alex froze.

"You been following me?" the wild man asked in a husky voice.

"No, man." Bryan, apparently recovered from his initial shock, answered like it was an everyday occurrence, having a gun waved under his nose. "We ain't been following you."

The man leaned in farther, took a good look around the inside of the car, the back seat. The putrid smell of booze and BO smacked the boys.

"Somebody's been following me. It ain't been you?"

"No, but we seen some dudes around the corner back there. Could've been them," Bryan pointed behind him.

"White dudes?"

"Yep, white dudes."

The expression on the man's face changed—like he was thinking, or confused. He looked down the street where Bryan pointed and nodded his head. "Yeah, could be them." He rose up and staggered off in that direction.

"Holy shit!" Alex threw his body back against the seat. "That guy was fried." He shook his head as he mumbled under his breath. "Probably used to be some high-powered executive."

Bryan slapped him on the back of the head. "Bruh, would you mind raising the fuckin' window just in case he comes back . . . and next time don't be so fuckin' quick to lower it."

Alex raised the window and coughed out a laugh. "You're something, man. 'No, we ain't been following you, but we seen some dudes around the corner back there. Could've been them.'"

Bryan cackled. "Spooky, man. He was *fuckin'* spooky!"

Funny then, the electric thrill of fear shared. They were friends again, he and Bryan, and Alex was glad. Bryan was the coolest.

When the Marine turned to leave, they got out of the car, locked it, then checked the doors to be sure. Alex grabbed the clubs from the trunk. They waited for a car to pass, then crossed. A bell above the door rang. Inside, the walls were a grimy off-white. All sorts of things—musical instruments, guns, tools, jewelry—cluttered the front room.

"Hi, Leo."

A weaselly looking man with pocked skin, an unlit cigar stub hanging from his mouth, looked at them over his glasses. He took the cigar from his mouth and held it between yellowed fingers.

"So you're back, kiddo. What have you brought today?"

"My friend here has these golf clubs." Bryan helped Alex lift them onto the counter. "They're PING. Best you can buy."

Leo took the clubs from the bag, removed the covers, and examined each one carefully, running his hand along the metal shafts, the wood heads. Then he looked up. "How much?"

"Two hundred," Bryan said. "They're worth way more than that."

"So, kiddo, this look like a country club setting to you? These clubs gonna be in great demand?" He threw up his hands.

"Ah, come on, Leo."

"One hundred."

"Don't shit us, man. I know people come to your shop from all over. These clubs are worth over a thousand bucks, easy. Give us at least one fifty."

Leo hesitated, looked at the clubs again while chewing on his cigar. Finally he bobbed his head. The deal was made. "So, whose name goes on the receipt? Yours or your silent partner's here?"

"Mine. Uh. I'm the one who'll be picking them up," Alex sputtered.

"I'll need a picture ID."

Alex pulled out his driver's license, the fake one that had cost him $150 and had to be redone three times before he could pass as twenty-one. He laid it on the counter.

"This the current address?"

"Yeah."

Leo nodded. "Well, I guess a guy who lives on Shawnee Run could have a set of PINGs."

"Yeah, sure."

Leo scribbled Alex's name and address on a receipt and shoved it in front of him, along with his license. "Sign here, by the *X*."

Alex signed.

Leo pulled two bills off a wad from his pocket and gave them to Alex, along with his license and a yellow copy of the receipt. "Keep the receipt. You'll have ninety days to pick them up."

From Newport they crossed the river again and drove to Clifton, a melting pot of old mansions, narrow row houses, apartments over storefronts, and student housing. Inner city. Street and pedestrian traffic were light. Most of the students had gone home for the holidays. Alex parked in front of a one-story clapboard house with peeling paint.

"Do you want to come?" Bryan asked.

"Sure, if it's okay."

"Better that you come than sit in the car. He can be real paranoid. If he sees you sitting in the car, he'll take it wrong."

Alex and Bryan walked up to the door and knocked. It opened a fraction. Through the narrow crack, a young woman said, "Yeah?"

Bryan mumbled, "We're here to see Mose. I called already."

"It's okay," a deep voice shouted from the background. The woman opened the door wider. She was thin, with ears that stuck through wispy, shoulder-length blond hair, big vacant eyes, darkly circled. The house was uncomfortably warm.

"Hey, man. Been expecting you. All ready." He patted a stack of plastic bags on a nearby chair. He was huge like The Rock but had hair longer than his girlfriend's, tied behind his neck. A muscle shirt showed off mammoth arms. He glared at Alex as he walked in behind Bryan.

"This is Alex, Mose. He's cool."

He locked eyes with Bryan. "You didn't tell me you was bringing company. Not good."

"He's just a friend. He's cool. He takes a lot of the stuff I buy from you. We just came from Leo's. He needed money for his stash." Bryan talked too fast, his voice high-pitched.

The hair on Alex's arms stood up. The dude didn't look too friendly. Definitely not someone he wanted to piss off.

Mose eyed Alex from head to toe, then turned to Bryan. "You say he's cool? He better be."

"Hi, son. It's late. Where've you been?" It was a friendly question. No accusation in the tone.

"Just hanging out. How was the Christmas party?" *Change the subject. Jake loves talking about his fuckin' company.*

"Fun as always." Janet put her arm around her husband's waist and gave him a gushy smile. "Jake spares no expense when it comes to the Christmas party."

"Great." Alex avoided eye contact with either parent as he headed upstairs.

"Don't be long," Jake called after him. "Candlelight services begin at eight."

REAGAN

CHAPTER TWENTY-THREE

Reagan jerked a dark scarf from her neck and tied it around her head, covering her most distinctive feature, her long, auburn hair. She pulled sunglasses from her backpack, slipped them on, and felt sure that, at a glance, she would be unrecognizable. A tall, slim woman in a red uniform jacket, Tinker Davis, waited in the Jetway with a wheelchair. After situating Lizzie in the chair, the group joined the chaotic rush of travelers in Atlanta's airport, by some accounts the busiest in the world.

Reagan, desperate to keep Red Shirt in sight, held Lizzie's hand as she hurried past gate after crowded gate, shops, and newsstands.

"The plane got in a little early," Ms. Davis said. "No need to rush. Your little guy's having a hard time keeping up."

"What . . . oh." Reagan blushed. Matthew leaned forward under the weight of his overstuffed backpack and trailed about ten feet behind. While they stopped to let him catch up, Red Shirt turned into a souvenir shop.

She called to Matthew. "Sorry, buddy. I thought I saw somebody I knew."

Matthew's shining eyes danced. His grin stretched all the way across his face. He still believed in the magic of Christmas, or maybe it was the rush of people or flying that exhilarated him. Whatever, she loved his look of wonder, but Lizzie seemed disturbed by the commotion—people running in all directions, children wailing. CVG on steroids.

As they approached the shop Red Shirt had entered, Reagan slowed again; turned up her collar, hoping for a little more cover; and glanced in. He was standing at the counter, his coat still strapped to his suitcase. She stopped in front of the wheelchair and pretended to check on Lizzie. If she could only get a glimpse of the inside of his wrist, but his sleeves covered his arms. No use.

Lizzie's eyes darted from one side of the wide corridor to the other as they rolled past the bright McDonald's sign and through the pleasant scent of hazelnut at a coffee shop. Loud laughter from folks waiting to get into Buffalo Wild Wings caused her to slap her hands over her ears and frown. Reagan stroked Lizzie as she glanced back, searching for Red Shirt.

"We'll take the elevator to the transportation tunnel." Tinker Davis pushed the down button and waited. On the train platform, she pointed to an electronic sign above the doors. "Trains to the terminal run every two minutes. That sign there tells us one is coming in eleven seconds."

Reagan scanned the people rushing to get on the train but didn't see him. When the doors opened, Ms. Davis squeezed them all into the crowded car, motioning people aside like Lizzie was royalty.

Jordan was leaning against the wall in baggage claim. She glanced past Reagan but noticed the children, rushed to them, and said to Ms. Davis, "I can take Lizzie." She gave Matthew a quick hug and helped her niece out of the chair. Matthew bounced on his toes, eyes sparkling, mouth going faster than a jet at takeoff. As soon as Lizzie was free of her restraints, she clapped and bounced around, then hugged Jordan too. Reagan wanted to enjoy the moment—her children were obviously overjoyed—but Red Shirt—

"Rea, you don't look like yourself. I wouldn't have recognized you if it weren't for the children."

"Your luggage is on carousel six," Ms. Davis said. "You want me to help with that?"

Reagan shook her head. "Thanks, Ms. Davis, but we can manage."

"Y'all take care and merry Christmas." She walked away, pushing the empty wheelchair.

Reagan left Jordan and the children and walked to carousel six. He had to come through baggage claim, didn't he? What could she do? Follow him to his car? Take down his license number?

A loud ringing sounded, even more god-awful than the school bell. The luggage conveyor rumbled awake and luggage from their flight emerged. The Batman suitcase appeared first. Dammit! If she'd been in a hurry, that would have been last. She couldn't just hang around waiting for Red Shirt. She jerked their three suitcases, one at a time, off the conveyor.

"Mom, I'll take mine," Matthew said. She had been so engrossed in searching for Red Shirt that she hadn't noticed Matthew walk up. He took the Batman suitcase and she pulled the other two. Maybe she should have had Ms. Davis help with the luggage. She could have left—

Wait a minute! Was that him, Red Shirt? It didn't register at first, but a flash of red passed her going in the opposite direction. She turned. The back of his shirt—that whale outline—went out the glass doors and disappeared into the crowd.

Absurd ideas raced through her mind. Leave Matthew

with the luggage and chase after him, but Jordan and Lizzie—what about them? She could call the police . . . and say . . . what? The longer it took to decide, the slimmer her chances of catching up with him. She stood motionless, staring at the exit, and her whole body sagged.

Jordan, holding on to Lizzie, walked up to join Reagan. "We'll drop the luggage off at the house, grab something to eat. I've got tickets to the Botanical Garden."

"On Christmas Eve?"

"Oh, yeah. Garden Lights, Holiday Nights—the busiest time of the year at the garden. It's fabulous. I couldn't let you miss it."

During the short drive from the airport to Jordan's home, Reagan berated herself for letting Red Shirt slip away. What were the chances it was him, anyway? That he would end up on the same plane as her? That would be a monumental coincidence, wouldn't it? But then what were the chances her daughter would have both Down syndrome and autism? What were the chances that at age thirty-five, Scott's itching would end up being fatal? What were the chances an odd-looking bird would show up the very day her husband was buried and make its home in her backyard? She had learned not to discount long shots.

One thing was sure, she would never be free of this anxiety until the authorities captured and convicted the gunman. Chances of that happening without her help were minuscule, less than the chance that she and the gunman would fly to Atlanta on the same plane.

Jordan's chic town house covered three floors, lots of stairs, but the location made up for any inconvenience. A few steps outside her door, the Eastside leg of the Atlanta BeltLine—a wide, paved pedestrian path—connected the Old Fourth Ward to Piedmont and Inman parks. Urban Atlanta. Restaurants, bars, stores, and parks lined the trail or were within easy walking distance.

The weather had been glorious all afternoon: sunny, fifty-five degrees, light jacket weather. Jordan called days like this chamber-of-commerce days, great for promoting Atlanta to outsiders.

They walked the half mile to Park Tavern in Piedmont Park to eat on the patio. After being cooped up in an airplane, it was wonderful to stretch out, get a little exercise, feel the soft breeze on her face. Lizzie, at last untethered to anyone or anything, ran ahead of the adults, laughing. Matthew, always the big brother, ran with her, stopping her every once in a while to allow the others to catch up.

Even on Christmas Eve, folks were out on the BeltLine walking, skating, biking, taking advantage of the weather. The family stopped for a while to watch a young man paint a colorful mural under a bridge, then moved on past high-rise apartment buildings and condos.

When they reached Park Tavern, they grabbed an outdoor table overlooking the park, with a breathtaking view of the Atlanta skyline. The sun, low on the horizon, streaked the sky with layers of gold, pink, blue, and magenta, like the sand sculpture Matthew had given her for Mother's Day.

A boys' choir stood under a canopy singing "O Holy Night." For the first time since leaving the flight, Reagan forgot about the gunman and let the music envelop her. "I'm glad to be here, Jordan. You can't imagine how much I've been looking forward to this trip."

Her sister's smile, though wide and beautiful, didn't quite reach her eyes. They ordered and chatted while waiting on their food.

"You should have seen Lizzie on the plane, Aunt Jordan. The flight attendant had to make people get off because she wouldn't let them by." Matthew raised his eyebrows.

Jordan winced. "You're kidding."

"Nope." His slow, restrained smirk spread into a wide mischievous grin, and Reagan felt a pinprick to her heart. That was his father's grin. The flash of memory took her breath, and she hesitated before shaking her head and throwing up her palms.

"No, he's not kidding."

Soon they were laughing at stories, one after another—many about the situations they'd found themselves in with Lizzie, a few they told every time they got together. Lizzie was happy being the center of attention.

"We shouldn't talk about her like this." Reagan retrieved a pack of wipes from her purse. "She's enjoying it entirely too much and understands more than you think. I don't want to reinforce that behavior."

"We need to get going anyway," Jordan said. "By the time we walk back and get the car, it'll be time to go to the gardens. Our tickets are for seven. It's a short drive."

Several blocks before they reached the gardens, bright red and white pointed stars sparkled high in the inky-black sky. White lights and a large green wreath completely covered the building at the entrance. The surrounding trees and shrubs gleamed green, red, blue, and purple. Matthew's face glowed, his eyes wide and shining.

"This looks awesome," Reagan said, "but I don't know how Lizzie will tolerate the stimulation."

Jordan slapped her palm against her forehead. "Rea, I'm so sorry. I can't believe I didn't think about that. We don't have to go in. That's fine. We can always go home."

"Mom, let's give it a try," Matthew pleaded.

Reagan hesitated. "Okay, let's try it."

They rented a stroller with a tray. Reagan scattered Goldfish crackers across it to, hopefully, distract Lizzie. She scrutinized her daughter's face as they joined a crowd on the main path that meandered through the gardens. Millions of colorful lights glimmered and twinkled. "Jingle Bells" played from small speakers strategically placed in shrubbery, hidden from view.

"It'll be okay, Mom. She likes it." Matthew's expression conveyed hope and excitement.

Other children, too, ran around, laughing and clapping. *Oohs* and *aahs* competed with the music. Lizzie closed her eyes and put her head on the tray.

Good. Maybe it would be okay. They stood on an elevated walkway, mesmerized by the Radiant Rainforest, a forty-foot cascading curtain of blue, green, and pink lights.

Farther down the path, the huge Earth Goddess sat by a pool and dipped her hand in the water. Thousands of tiny blue lights made up her flowing hair. A large Chihuly glass sculpture stood on top of a fountain that flowed into the pool. Reagan watched for signs that Lizzie would erupt.

They smelled wood burning and saw a group of excited children roasting marshmallows over an open fire, their parents looking on. They called to Matthew and offered him a marshmallow. His face glowed in the light of the fire as he joined the other kids and then thrust the gooey treat into his mouth. Next they walked through a tunnel with a shimmering canopy. All the while, Lizzie kept her head down.

When they reached the point as far from the entrance as possible, a blaring instrumental choreographed with lights flashing on and off jolted her out of her complacency. She jerked up straight, put her hands over her ears, and howled.

"You're okay, you're okay." Matthew put one hand on each side of her face and tried to settle her. No use. Lizzie continued to scream. After several minutes, Reagan, Jordan, and even Matthew came to the inevitable conclusion that their Holiday Night at the Botanical Garden was over. They turned around and retraced their steps. The incoming crowd parted enough to allow Jordan to squeeze through with the stroller. Behind them, Reagan and Matthew hurried to keep up as they headed to the exit. Reagan glanced at the onlookers' faces as she pushed through the crowd. Lots of scowls, looking the other way, or expressions of *Glad I'm not you.*

When they returned the stroller at the front entrance and Jordan picked up Lizzie, her screams faded to a whimper. Jordan repeatedly whispered, "You're okay," and rubbed the child's back as she carried her to the SUV. Lizzie calmed completely as soon as they got into the car; she fell asleep on the short ride home.

When they got back to Jordan's, the wonderful scent of evergreen met them at the door. A nine-foot Christmas tree stood in the corner by the fireplace, the angel on top almost touching the high ceiling. The spacious first floor, a combined living room, dining room, and kitchen, was something out of the December issue of *Better Homes and Gardens.* And to think, when Reagan needed her, Jordan had left this to sleep for weeks on a secondhand pullout sofa in their living room.

"I'll get Lizzie ready," Jordan said. "She's sleeping with me."

"Really? Do you know what you're in for?"

Jordan's eyes widened. "Oh yeah."

"Well, thanks. She's worn out. She should go right down."

When Jordan returned, Reagan said, "Your tree smells fantastic. Everything looks beautiful." She drew closer, eyeing specific ornaments. "Oh, I remember this one. It's the one Matt painted for you in kindergarten."

"I love it," Jordan said. "He was so cute when I opened it; his chest puffed out a mile." She picked the globe off the tree and handed it to Reagan for a closer look.

Reagan rubbed the smooth glass, smiled, and glanced around the room. "Where's Matt?"

"He went next door," Jordan said. "Tony's been over twice asking when Matthew would be here. My guess, they're going to play Fortnite."

"Is that okay with Tony's mom? This is Christmas Eve."

"His mom was more excited than Tony when I told her Matt was coming. There aren't many boys in this development."

After Matthew got home and both kids fell asleep, the women strategically displayed items from Santa and placed presents from each other and Sonny under the tree. Then Jordan handed Reagan a glass of pinot noir and they sat at the kitchen island, drinking wine and reminiscing.

"I thought I saw the gunman today."

Jordan put down her wine and stared at Reagan. "What? Where?"

"On the plane. Three rows in front of me. I didn't notice him until we landed."

"Are you sure it was him?"

"No, but it sure looked like him, and I felt the same menacing aura when I noticed him." Reagan propped her elbows on the counter and laced her fingers together. "I wanted to block him from my mind for the few days we're here, but I think I brought him with me. I'd know for sure if I could have gotten close enough to see his eyes or his left wrist. I tried to follow him, but it was impossible with the kids and the crowd."

Jordan moved closer and shook her head. "Rea, did you really try to get close enough to see his eyes?"

"Yes, but there were too many people. I never did."

Jordan threw up her hands. "Did it occur to you that if you saw him, he saw you? What were you thinking? You had the kids with you." Her voice became loud, shrill. "What if he noticed you following him, doubled back around you, and followed us here? We could all be in danger."

Reagan shook her head. "You said yourself I looked different. He never even glanced my way. I just wanted to . . . I don't know. . . . I don't know what I wanted."

Jordan's voice mellowed and she put her arm around Reagan. "Okay, let's be rational. I have a well-placed friend at

Delta who owes me a favor. He may be able to tell us who occupied that seat. We can find out a lot about a person just by
googling. Are you sure you know his seat number?"

"The aisle seat three rows in front of us, 19C."

"Okay. I'm a little hesitant to call Bill on Christmas morning, but he's a good friend. I'll see if I can get through to him."

REAGAN

CHAPTER TWENTY-FOUR

Christmas morning, Matthew played Santa—handing out the presents, waiting until each person opened their gift before retrieving another one from under the tree. When all the presents had been opened, Jordan served quiche, a fruit salad, and sweet rolls. Midmorning, Tony rang the doorbell and asked Matthew to come to his house.

One would have thought Jordan had cooked for a crowd rather than two adults and two children who would have been more than happy with mac and cheese, but Jordan did not do anything halfway. The whole house smelled like Christmas. The fragrance of roasting turkey and yeast rolls blended with the piney smell of evergreens. Jordan prepared a salad, fruit, and sweet potatoes. Desserts included chocolate chip cookies, red velvet cake, pecan pie, and ice cream. They all stuffed themselves, even the children.

"That was almost as good as Anaya's cooking," Matthew said, rubbing his stomach. The women looked at each other and shook their heads.

Sunshine flowed through the large kitchen windows. Lizzie sat on a barstool at the island and looked on while the women cleaned up sticky remnants of Christmas dinner and stuffed leftovers into glass containers.

A vague feeling nagged Reagan. Several times since arriving, she'd noticed Jordan's jaw clench, and she hadn't been as jovial as normal, even yesterday at Park Tavern. Reagan chalked that up to the stress of entertaining them. Her sister always wanted everything to be perfect.

Jordan surprised her by putting a laptop on the island.

"Rea, I made that call this morning, and Bill got back to me within the hour with a name: Dr. John English." She booted up her computer. "I googled him. He's a marine biologist who contracts as a consultant with the Georgia Aquarium, in Atlanta, as well as the one in Newport, Kentucky. Is this the man you saw?" She turned the screen toward Reagan.

Several photos of a well-built man with muscular arms. He wore his long dark hair down in a couple of shots, tied at the nape of his neck in others, or up in a man-bun. He looked straight into the camera in one photo. Big dark-brown eyes, not the unusual light brown of the gunman she'd seen the day of the murder.

"This doesn't sound like a gangster who would kill someone for the hell of it," Jordan said.

As Reagan stared at the photos, heat traveled from her face down her neck and across her chest with the slow, agonizing pace of a three-toed sloth. How could she have made such a mistake? That man wasn't the gunman. Maybe his profile sort of fit, but—

"Rea, there's something I wanted to discuss with you even before yesterday."

Reagan stiffened, her mind on overload. "Okay, what is it?"

"Have you thought about placing Lizzie in a residential facility?"

Whoa. She hadn't expected that. "No, never have."

"Rea, I discussed it with Cheryl and—"

"You did what?"

"Remember, you added me to Lizzie's Circle of Care on her Medicaid contract, so Cheryl was free to discuss her service plan with me. I don't see how you can possibly keep her at—"

Reagan's face flushed. "That's for me to decide."

"Well, of course, it's up to you, but hear me out. You don't have Anaya anymore to jump in at the last minute, take her for a sleepover—"

"She didn't do that often, just occasionally when I was super stressed, like after I was almost murdered."

"You are under so much pressure. No wonder you jumped to conclusions about that passenger. And what if that *had* been him? Suppose you run into him, face to face, in Cincinnati or somewhere else? What do you think would happen? He'd try to silence you the best way he could. That's what. All this stress has impaired your judgment." Jordan reached for Reagan's hand. "How can any of you be safe? But at least you and Matt can protect yourselves. Lizzie can't."

Reagan pulled away. "Why would he hurt Lizzie? She can't identify him. She's safe."

"No, she's not. I agree with Sonny. I don't think she took off on her own, stayed away for hours, and just casually walked into McDonald's when she got hungry. Think about it! You can't possibly watch her every minute. Dammit, Rea, you're a young, single woman who deserves happiness."

"I'm not a single woman. I'm a widow."

"You *are* a single woman. You need to meet someone. That's what Scott wanted so badly that, on his deathbed, he put it in writing. Remember?"

Remember? How could I possibly forget the letter I read so often the edges are tattered—the letter Jordan handed me the day after his funeral, the letter I could repeat by heart?

"How can you date when you always have to be with Lizzie? Cheryl said it was getting really hard to find aides. And Medicaid will fund residential care."

Reagan tilted her chin and shook her head.

"If you're not concerned for yourself, think about Matthew. It broke my heart last night to see how much he wanted to stay at the garden but understood he had to leave. It's always like that. Matthew comes in second. Everything revolves around Lizzie."

Reagan's chin quivered; her eyes teared.

"I'm only thinking of you. I love you, all three of you. You looked exhausted even before Anaya left. Cheryl says there's room for Lizzie, and you could take her out for visits whenever you wanted. She would be well taken care of in the meantime."

Jordan had crossed a line. How dare she go behind Reagan's back and discuss such a thing with Lizzie's social worker. Jordan had chosen career over marriage and children—at least that's what she said. How could she understand the bond between a parent and child? She might understand from the outside in, but not from the inside out.

With Matthew and again with Lizzie, seeing her newborns had been like falling in love for the first time; every time she closed her eyes, she saw the babies, smelled the talcum powder, ran her hands over their smooth skin, and felt the fuzzy hair at the nape of their necks. Thoughts of them dominated her waking hours and her dreams.

But with Lizzie, the need to protect and defend increased exponentially. As she developed, her issues became more complex: her inability to talk, her dual diagnosis of autism at age five. With every setback, she and Scott grieved a little, then changed their expectations and declared, "We've got this."

She was tiny and precious, and she needed them. They never considered placement.

Both women were quiet the rest of the day. So many

thoughts crowded Reagan's mind that they jumbled her thinking. She tried to identify the reason for the hazy guilt that disturbed her. Guilt for being angry at Jordan, the person she counted on more than anyone? Possibly. Guilt because of Matt's disappointments? Maybe. But something else nagged her, something more complicated: guilt for even considering the possibility of freedom.

REAGAN

CHAPTER TWENTY-FIVE

Reagan leaned against her desk and faced her students, laughing. "I'll admit, I wouldn't want one to bite me either."

Charmayne, a new student from Lexington, sitting near the front of the room, spoke with the genteel southern accent Reagan adored. "It wouldn't even have to bite me. If it got close enough, it would scare me to death." She drew her hands to her chest.

"Right," Greta yelled from her workstation, turning the heads of every seventh-grade boy in the class. "They're so icky."

"Don't worry. I'll protect you girls," Nick said, brandishing an imaginary sword.

Impertinent comments came from several directions. "Don't be such snowflakes," Max hollered from the back.

It was nice to be in the classroom after winter break, distracted from obsessing over the gunman, and Jordan, and Lizzie—sending one child away to benefit the other—all the unbearable notions that had preoccupied her every moment during the holidays. She couldn't deal with them head-on, but they were always on the edge of her consciousness, threatening to pull her under like quicksand.

But here she was in her element: confident, safe. She knew how to do this, and her students could be such fun. Reagan strolled over to the wall thermostat. Seventy-six degrees. Argh. Let the room get the least bit warm and the place smelled like dirty socks. "Guys, don't forget, you need to shower every day and wear deodorant."

Like Quick Draw McGraw, two of the boys pointed at each other.

Reagan sat behind her desk. "Okay, enough about last night's *The Walking Dead*. We need to get back to milkweed bugs. But first I want to talk to you about a new contest." She picked up a bulletin and read. "Samsung's Solve for Tomorrow contest challenges students in grades six through twelve to show how STEM can be applied to improve their community. Selected schools receive equipment and technology." She looked up. "People, could we use more equipment? Do we need more technology?" She expected a resounding yes, but she got blank faces from her students. Nobody showed *any* enthusiasm.

"This says the state finalists get twenty thousand dollars' worth of equipment!"

No go. They weren't interested.

"Okay, people, what gives? You know Samsung. Most of you have Samsung phones."

Jamal Washington stood up. "It's just that we do all this work, and we never win. The bigger schools do."

Reagan arched an eyebrow. *He's right. The richer schools usually do, the ones that already have equipment and can make more elaborate projects. I can't let them get away with such a defeatist attitude.*

"Well, one thing's for sure; you won't win if you don't try.

What about those kids in Phoenix who competed against MIT students for the best underwater robot—and won? Remember, we talked about that. They weren't even in college and went up against some of the smartest people in the country, maybe the world. They were poor kids, from poor families, from a poor high school. Did they tell themselves they weren't going to enter that competition because they never win anything?"

Jamal rolled his eyes. A collective moan rose from the future scientists of Norwood. Max stood up. "I heard Mr. Anderson told his class he would shave his head and paint tiger stripes on his car if his class won."

Huh? Dave Anderson shaves his head every summer, and he's a maniac when it comes to the Bengals. He already planned to paint his car when football season starts. Probably already bought the paint.

"I'm not shaving my head or painting my car. You'll have to come up with something else."

Kids threw out ideas like they were pitching for the Reds: pizza party, no homework for a week, a month, a trip to Ollie's, dye your hair—

Suddenly, all twenty-three kids were fully engaged. Angela, the only one absent. They chanted, "Dye your hair! Dye your hair!"

Reagan had never been a fashionista. She didn't much care for jewelry or accessories and wasn't above perusing the clothing racks at Snooty Fox or the Goodwill Store, but she took pains with her hair. She frequently got unsolicited compliments from total strangers about it. She didn't want to mess with it. She hesitated. Oh, they were probably right. They wouldn't win anyway.

"Okay. What color?"

"Not pink or blue or purple. They're too common," Greta said with a decisive nod.

"Green," someone shouted from the back.

"Green?" Reagan squinted.

"Yeah, green." That lone suggestion morphed into the matter settled.

"Okay, but only if you guys are state finalists. Now you have to decide on a project by the end of next week."

When all the students had gone and Reagan was packed up to leave, she noticed someone peeking through the window of the science lab door. At first glance it looked like Mrs. Hamilton, Angela's grandmother, but Reagan wasn't sure. When she moved closer to the window, the sight alarmed her. Mrs. Hamilton was petite, but she walked tall—a proud lady, always immaculate and well dressed, like Angela. This woman was stooped, her chest caved in, her red-rimmed eyes glassy as porcelain, her demeanor so unlike Mrs. Hamilton's Reagan wasn't sure it was the same person.

"Mrs. Hamilton?"

"Yes."

"Are you okay? Is Angela okay?"

The older woman twisted a tissue. "I'm okay . . . Angela's okay . . . but I've come to withdraw her from school." She took a deep, ragged breath. "My daughter, Beverly, Angela's mother, died Friday evening." She looked at the floor. "Heroin overdose."

Everything stopped: voices from the hallway, the slamming of locker doors, the traffic noise from Williams Avenue. *No, no, no. Not another one. Not Angela's mother.* Speechless, Reagan could only stare at the older woman.

The grandmother shook her head slowly before continuing. "When your husband was sick, Bev asked me to make a chicken pot pie so that she could take it to your family. She always loved my chicken pot pies." She lifted her head, eye level with Reagan. "I thought that was a good sign, her caring about someone else. She would do that—clean herself up, go through good periods—and I would have hope. During those times I would do anything she asked, just to keep her from slipping back. But there were vultures always hanging around, tempting her. They didn't want her to clean herself up. They wouldn't leave her be."

She stared down the empty hallway. "I tried to tell her she was killing herself. When she was using, I thought I could deal with her death easier than her life—doing anything to get her heroin, begging, stealing from me and other people close to her . . . forgetting she had a daughter who loved her." Her voice cracked. "I only wish I never allowed that thought in my head. I tried to get Angela to move in with me, but she was desperate to take care of her mother."

Reagan stood transfixed by Mrs. Hamilton's musings, bombarded by ugly thoughts she couldn't bring into focus.

"I'm sorry about your husband, Reagan. You know what it's like to watch someone you love die right before your eyes. That's what I was doing too, watching my beautiful daughter waste away . . . degrade herself . . . and there was nothing I could do to save her."

She shook her head. "Nobody brought us casseroles. We didn't want anybody to know, anyway, and those who knew didn't understand. They got angry and told us to practice tough love. They were disgusted with her. Angie and I were ashamed. I knew Bev was sick. . . . She didn't want to live like that, but she couldn't help herself. I didn't want to be tough . . . but I tried." Mrs. Hamilton grabbed Reagan's hand, looked her in the eyes, and said, "It's the most powerless you'll ever be, having a child on drugs."

Reagan wanted to jerk her hand away, run. This wasn't about her, but she was blindsided anyway. She'd been holding herself together, barely, and now this. Guilt on top of every-thing else. The community she loved, the place she and her children called home, was in the middle of an epidemic. People were dying and their loved ones were suffering heartbreak, and she had turned her back. For some reason she couldn't explain, she felt sure that the man who had pointed a gun at her was the same man who had sold Beverly her heroin.

ALEX

CHAPTER TWENTY-SIX

Students spilled out of Norwood High School in hordes—laughing, talking, yelling across the parking lot to friends. They seemed happy to be back at school after winter break. Indian Hill was still off, so Alex was meeting Bryan in Norwood to pick up weed and hang out. Frances's day off, no one would be the wiser.

A boy named George walked up behind them and slapped Bryan on the back. "Got weed?"

Bryan glanced over his shoulder. "In my car, bruh."

The three boys joined a group of kids leaving the schoolyard, then stopped at Bryan's rust-spotted, ten-year-old Pontiac parked on the street a block away. Alex stood beside the car as Bryan made the deal. George got out of the car and stuffed the baggie into his jeans. Alex got in.

"There she is now," Bryan remarked to Alex. Stephanie Benedict, wearing a heavy coat and knee-high boots, her hair stuffed under a knit beanie, casually glanced their way. Bryan gawked at her wide-eyed, grinning from ear to ear.

"She looks like she wants to come over," Alex said. Bryan

actually blushed as he pulled up his jeans and turned up his coat collar. Strange. Bryan never tried to impress girls. But his eyes sparkled as Stephanie approached.

"Hi, Bryan." The sun made her squint.

She was even better looking up close. Her cheeks were pink from the cold air, and a dark mole at the corner of her mouth, like a beauty mark, made her look more mature than the other girls.

"Hey, Stephanie. This is Alex Petersen, a friend of mine."

She shaded her oval eyes and turned them toward Alex. "Hi, I don't think I've seen you around before. You aren't in any of my classes, are you?"

"No. I go to Indian Hill. We don't go back until tomorrow, so I came down to see Bryan."

"Nice to meet you." She turned her attention back to Bryan. "Are you good at math? I got a D on my math quiz, and my dad will have a fit if I fail. I need a tutor."

Bryan hesitated, as though he had a dozen scenarios running through his mind, before he finally answered. "No, I suck at math."

She rolled her eyes. "I feel so stupid in that class. It's always been my worst subject."

"Yeah, mine too," Bryan said. "How you doin' otherwise?"

She sighed. "Okay, I guess. It's hard going to a new school your senior year." She rounded her shoulders. "The other girls don't like me. I don't know many people at all."

Bryan smiled at her. "You know us."

She looked at Bryan and returned his smile. "I suppose you're right. What are you guys up to?"

"Just hanging," Alex said. "Killing time."

"Yeah," Bryan added. "We got nothing special to do. How 'bout you? You want to join us?"

She pursed her lips and slowly shook her head. "I have to get home and babysit my sister. It's such a pain. Will you guys be around later?"

"Yeah, sure."

Bryan watched her walk away, and Alex watched Bryan, his eyes narrowing. Just as another boy climbed into the car with Bryan, Stephanie glanced back over her shoulder and threw them a quick wave before getting into a late-model Toyota.

Later Bryan and Alex sat in Bryan's car, talking.

"I tell you, my ol' lady and I just don't connect. I don't do nothin' right in her eyes. Shit, I'm making more money than her and my ol' man put together, and I don't have to sit in some fucking office all day, pushing a pencil, playing kiss ass." Bryan's lip curled.

"Then why don't you get yourself a better set of wheels? This one's a piece of junk." The inside of Bryan's car looked like the outside, dilapidated, and it always smelled like cigarette smoke mixed with grime.

"Hey, don't say nothin' bad 'bout ol' Spike here." Bryan patted the dusty dashboard, feigning annoyance. "We've been through a lot together. My parents ain't like yours. Nobody's buying me nothing. A new car would raise too many questions." He gazed out the window, ran a hand through his hair. "But I'll tell you one thing, when I'm eighteen, I'm out of there. Then I'll get new wheels."

"Me too. If Jake's still around when I'm eighteen, I'm gone. But I don't think he will be."

"Oh yeah?"

"He and my mom are barely speaking. I even let him catch me with stuff, 'cause it always causes a fight between them. I hate him, always fucking things up between me and my mom, like he can tell me what to do. But I don't think he's getting any these days. She hardly speaks to him. You'll see. He won't be around much longer."

"Put it there, man," Bryan said, grinning, giving Alex a fist bump.

◆ ◆ ◆

The next weekend, Alex made another trip to Norwood, but Bryan seemed more interested in connecting with his wannabe girlfriend than hanging out with him.

"Stephanie said she was going to the library. I'm hoping to meet her there, but you can come along if you want."

Alex's throat tightened. Since he was twelve, Bryan had been his best friend. He only had two real friends, Trip and Bryan, and Trip had always been more interested in chasing some girl. Now Bryan at the library? That was serious.

"I don't know." His options: go back home or . . . what? "Okay, I'll tag along." Alex's shoulders drooped as he followed Bryan to his car.

When they got to the library, Bryan didn't go in, but waited outside for Stephanie. After a while, she came out clutching two huge books to her chest.

"Hi," Bryan said as they fell in step beside her. Bryan was always cool, nonchalant, but around Stephanie it looked forced.

"Hi, guys. What's happening?" She slowed her pace.

"Nothing much," Bryan said. "Thought you might want to hang out or something."

"I don't have enough time for that. I wish I did, but I have to do the babysitting thing. My folks are going to some political meeting."

Bryan grinned. "You want me to go with you, keep you company?" He glanced at Alex with an expression like *You understand, right?*

"I'd like that, but my dad is a paranoid maniac. No guys when he's not there. He's so hard to please I just don't bring anybody around. It's embarrassing, having him check guys over the way he does." She cut her eyes toward Bryan. "You'd never pass."

The remark seemed to roll over him.

"Every time I get a phone call, he gives me the third degree.

It's like he doesn't want me to make new friends, and he's the one who moved us here." The traffic on Montgomery Road sped by, spewing foul-smelling exhaust. "You're the only person I've even given my number to."

Bryan got a shit-eating grin on his face.

"Maybe I could meet you somewhere tomorrow. I don't have to babysit then." Stephanie stopped and looked at him; a strand of black hair was pulled out of her cap and curved around her chin. "Get high, maybe."

Bryan's eyes widened. "Yeah, we could do that."

"I haven't had my own plug since we moved here," Stephanie said.

Bryan nodded. "I can get you anything you want."

"Cool." Her eyes flashed and locked with his.

Alex's face burned.

REAGAN

CHAPTER TWENTY-SEVEN

The casket, white with gold highlights, stood at the front of the room, a blanket of pink and white flowers on top of the closed lower lid. The sweet fragrance from funeral sprays and the sound of people talking in whispers coalesced into a memory that pushed Reagan off balance. Only ten months ago, it was all for Scott. Her stomach roiled; she sank into a nearby chair and tried to steady herself.

She didn't remember much about the day of his funeral—mostly the numbness, the pressure to hold it together, the disconnect between being in her own home after the service but being lost. The shock of Scott's diagnosis had been numbing. He'd been tired and his appetite was off, but everyone gets rundown occasionally. No big deal. It was the itching that finally sent him to the doctor. He complained that even his tongue itched. How could itching be that bad?

So many flowers, their fragrance sickeningly sweet. Afterward, people crowding in at home, a warm day . . . stuffy. Jordan hovering, tending to everything. Food, a spiral-cut ham, a colorful fruit salad, so much food crammed onto the dining table. As if she could eat. As if food would make it better. And Bird showing up out of nowhere—the odd-looking creature staring into the living room, locking eyes with her.

Angela stood at the head of the casket, talking to a group of kids about her age, none of whom Reagan recognized. She looked exhausted, her eyes glassy, her shoulders stooped. The teens took turns hugging her, stroking her hair.

Reagan hoped to talk to Mrs. Hamilton—offer her condolences and ask about Angela. She'd been so shocked at the news, she couldn't remember what she'd said, or even if she'd said she was sorry. But Mrs. Hamilton wasn't in the room. Visitation would last until nine o'clock, but Reagan had left Lizzie with Betty Crammer and didn't want to impose on her. She couldn't wait long for Mrs. Hamilton.

As Reagan approached the casket and Angela, she focused on her breathing, on the purse strap on her shoulder, on the thought that she must stay strong and comfort Angela, not run away and hide. The people there didn't know, anyway, how she had let them down.

Beverly, dressed in a lovely blue print dress, looked to be not much older than her daughter. Her long straight hair, blond like Angela's, swept across her forehead and pooled on the satin pillow.

Sleeping peacefully. Maybe that was consolation for those who loved her, mired with her in the struggle to overcome her addiction.

Angela noticed Reagan and excused herself from her friends. "Thank you so much for coming, Mrs. Ramsey."

Reagan bit her lip and reached out to hug Angela. She could count the child's ribs when she pulled her close. She smelled a hint of lavender. "I'm so sorry, Angela. I'm just so sorry."

Angela's eyes watered. She twisted a tissue like her grandmother had done. "She'd been sick for a while."

"Yes, I know. Your grandmother told me." Reagan stepped back from the embrace. "Your mother died from an illness. She would have gotten well if she'd been able. You know that, right?"

The girl nodded, tears spilling.

"We'll miss you in class."

"I'll miss you too. Max and Charmayne were here earlier with their parents. I'll come back to visit, for sure." Angela glanced over Reagan's shoulder and smiled at someone approaching, so Reagan gave her hand a squeeze and moved on.

As she walked out of the funeral home, Detective Gabriel approached. *Why would he be here?* She could duck into the ladies' room, or out the side door, but they had made eye contact and there was no way to avoid him without being obvious.

"Hello, Reagan. Nice to see you." He cocked his head. "How do you know Beverly?"

"Her daughter, Angela, is in my class."

"I see." His eyes narrowed.

"And you?" Reagan asked.

"We're cousins. Angie's grandmother and my grandmother are sisters." He flashed a weak smile. "You know how it is around here. Everybody's related."

"I thought you might be here to look for the dealer who sold her the heroin."

"Nah. That's TV stuff. Dealers don't go to wakes; they couldn't care less."

During the days that followed, Mrs. Hamilton's words looped through Reagan's mind like a broken record. *Desperate to take care of her mother; forgetting she had a daughter who loved her; nobody brought us casseroles.* She lost weight, felt hollowed out and heavy at the same time. It had all been too much: losing Scott, the love of her life; losing Anaya, her surrogate mom;

almost losing Lizzie; losing her connection with Jordan; losing her belief that people were good, that *she* was good.

The dark days, bare trees, and frigid, wet weather didn't help. Last winter was supposed to be the worst, watching Scott's life fade away. It had been almost a year; things were supposed to be better. Could she possibly make it till spring?

JAKE

CHAPTER TWENTY-EIGHT

Jake slouched at the children's library table, knees around his elbows. Matthew meandered around the crowded room, taking his time, picking up one book after another, paging through it like he was looking for something specific before shaking his head and putting it down. Jake couldn't recall ever seeing him with such a serious expression. He was patient with Matthew, normally. But struggling to force his six-three frame into one of the tiny chairs strained his composure.

A beautiful day, sunny and warm for the last day of January, Jake had planned to take Matthew and Scooter to Washington Park, let them both run off pent-up energy from being indoors. Inside all day himself, he had looked forward to getting some fresh air, but much to his surprise, Matthew had other ideas. He asked to go to the library.

Jake looked forward to afternoons with his "little brother," sharing the things he loved with him. Despite his surprise at Matthew's choice, it pleased him. It reinforced his notion that he and Matthew had a lot in common. Jake loved reading even more than football.

He had tried to share his love of books with Janet, but she had no interest in the ones he wanted to discuss, and she didn't get his appreciation of fantasy, like *Lord of the Rings* or the Harry Potter series. She accused him of being in his second childhood, but it wasn't his second. He hadn't had a first. He was ten when his mother got sick, about the time kids graduated to chapter books at school. From then on, paperbacks were his escape and constant companions.

He had never been in the Norwood branch of the Cincinnati and Hamilton County Public Library, but the building, which was impressive from the outside, was smaller on the inside than he'd imagined, crammed full of books and crowded with people. Sunlight shone through the large library windows, overheating the room. Sitting on the pint-size furniture, he felt conspicuously like a clown.

Matthew came back to the table, his eyebrows squeezed together, and sat down next to Jake.

"What are you looking for, Matt? Maybe I can help you find it."

He pursed his lips. "I'm not sure, but I think I'll know it if I see it."

"What's it about?"

Matthew leaned in, close to Jake's ear, even though no one else was paying the slightest attention to them, and whispered, "Humping."

Jake jerked upright. "Oh . . . humping."

"Yeah. Some boys at school laugh and tease about humping a lot. I laugh about it, too, but I don't get what it means."

Boys at school, laughing. Several thoughts rushed into Jake's head. How his tormentors laughed, calling him stupid, *sooo* stupid. That slick magazine, the one Donny brought to school . . . His face burned at the memory.

Dangerous territory. Jake was unsure how to proceed with Matthew. This was important. He loved the way Matthew looked up to him, and his response could determine how much Matthew—and his mother—trusted him with sensitive stuff.

Confusion, that's what he remembered. He'd had no one to talk to about sex, no one to ask—certainly not his sick mother. And his father was seldom home, working ten, twelve hours a day, hiding out from the inevitable.

"Did you ask your mother?"

Matthew flashed a *No way* expression.

Jake understood. Even if you didn't get it, you knew you didn't want to ask a girl about it.

"Matt, sometimes boys make fun of things they don't understand, and it's easy to go along because you want to fit in. I'm happy to have this conversation with you, but I also think your mom would want to be involved." The lines around Jake's eyes softened as he looked at Matthew. "I had lots of questions about 'humping' when I was your age. Everybody does at some point because it's about growing up, becoming a man or a woman rather than a kid. It's important to get good information." Unfolding his lanky body, Jake stood. "Why don't we call your mom? If she says okay, we can pick up a couple of pizzas on our way to your house and we can all talk."

Matthew dipped his chin and looked up at Jake through hooded eyes. "Okay . . . I guess."

Jake sat at the Ramseys' dining room table behind two large half-eaten pizzas, a bottle of Heineken at his fingertips, casually paging through a large picture book while he waited for Matthew and Reagan to return. The room smelled of tomato sauce and cheese. The ceiling creaked overhead from Reagan's footsteps as she checked on Lizzie, who had eaten and gone to bed before he and Matthew got there. Matthew chattered away in the kitchen as he fed Scooter.

The librarian had suggested a book written and illustrated for children with anatomical drawings of a pregnant woman, a cutout view of her uterus with a baby, and correct terms for body parts.

"Just as I thought, she's down for the night." Reagan's chair scraped against the hardwood floor when she pulled it from the table and sat. Matthew sat down, picked a piece of pepperoni off the pizza, and dropped it into his mouth.

Reagan glanced at each of them, raised both eyebrows, and gave Jake a weak smile.

She didn't seem like herself. Maybe she would prefer to talk to Matthew about this subject alone. But she had insisted he come over. It could just be the time of year. Most people need time to recoup from all the holiday stress.

Jake took a deep breath and got down to business. "Well, Matthew said some of the boys at school were laughing and teasing about humping. He pretended he understood what they were talking about, but he didn't, really, and he wanted to."

Reagan stroked Matthew's hair. "Buddy, I know that's something you would have wanted to talk to your dad about. Isn't it great to have a friend like Jake who you can talk to?" She propped her elbows on the table, folded her hands, and turned to Jake.

Guess that means she, the science teacher, wants me to take the lead. "Well, Matt, like I told you in the library, everybody at one time or another has questions like yours because it's about growing up. Sometimes people make jokes and talk like it's dirty, but it—"

"It is inappropriate to talk like that." Reagan stared at her son.

"Your mother's right. We'll answer your questions, but this is something kids should discuss with their parents. I don't want you telling the guys at school—or anywhere else—what we talk about here. If they ask you questions, tell them to ask their parents."

Jake waited for agreement from Matthew before

continuing and, after further thought, closed the book and set it aside. He didn't want to talk down to Matthew, and part of the book was geared for younger kids. But he had to start somewhere.

"Every species has a way of making offspring—if they didn't, their species would die out, wouldn't they?"

"Yeah, like dinosaurs."

"Right. Humans and animals are either male or female, and each have special body parts for making babies."

Matthew tilted his head—big eyes, all ears.

"Besides peeing, a man's penis and his scrotum function for that purpose." Jake tried to gauge Matthew's understanding, but the boy was unreadable. Reagan leaned on her elbows, her mouth hidden behind her fist—like Matthew, unreadable. "Females don't have a penis," Jake continued.

"I know. Mom says Lizzie's developmentally disabled. When I was little, I thought that was why she didn't have anything between her legs."

Matthew giggled but Reagan looked shocked. "Matthew, that has nothing to do with it!"

He rolled his eyes. "I know that now, Mom."

Reagan shook her head.

"Like I said," Jake continued. "Females don't have penises, but they do have something between their legs, it's just harder to see than your penis. On the outside, they have the opening to their vagina that leads to the uterus. The uterus is where babies grow."

Beads of sweat penetrated Jake's hairline. He was afraid he was going too fast, skipping something important. He paused and glanced again at Reagan, who was still hiding her expression behind her hand, before turning back to his "little brother."

"Any questions?"

Wide-eyed, Matthew shook his head.

Jake squirmed in his chair. "Besides a uterus, females have ovaries inside their bodies. They're attached to the uterus by tubes. These ovaries have very tiny eggs in them. When girls grow up, every month an egg floats down one of the tubes and lands in the uterus. If the egg is fertilized, a baby is made and attaches itself to the uterus, where it will grow."

"I don't get it. What's that got to do with humping?"

Jake ran his hand through his hair and crossed his ankle over the other knee. "Well, sperm is what fertilizes the egg. It is made in the male's testicles and comes out the penis. That happens during sex. That's what the boys referred to as humping."

Matthew threw up his hands. "I still don't get it. How does it get in the female?"

Jake cleared his throat. "Remember, I said the female has an opening to the vagina between her legs. The male's penis fits into that like a puzzle."

"I do not understand."

"When a man and woman get married and want to become a family . . . with children, well . . . think of a puzzle. When their pieces come together, sperm comes out of the man into the woman."

Matthew furrowed his brow and stared at Jake until his mouth dropped open. His eyes became saucers. He slammed both palms on the table and yelled, "Yuck!" He gawked at his mother. "You did that? You must have really wanted a baby."

For the first time that afternoon, Reagan flashed a genuine smile. "I did, buddy. I really wanted a little boy just like you."

Jake leaned forward, mirroring Reagan's pose—elbows on table, hand over mouth—and clenched his jaw to stifle the snicker trying to make its way out. More than anything, he did not want Matthew to feel stupid or embarrassed. "Matt, it's not as unpleasant as you think now." He avoided Reagan's gaze.

Matthew looked like he couldn't decide whether to be

pleased that his mother had wanted him so much or disgusted by what his parents had done. Either way, Jake had more to say about the topic.

"Matt, these parts of each body, the male and the female, are our private parts. The parts we keep covered by our clothes. If anyone ever tries to touch your private parts and you don't want them to, or if they make you feel uncomfortable about it, you should tell your mother or your teacher, even if—or especially if—they told you not to tell. You shouldn't be embarrassed. Your private parts are yours. You should tell. And that also means that you should never touch someone else's private parts if they don't want to be touched or said no. Even if you think she or he would like it. No means no, and you never want to go along with others who don't appreciate that, right?"

Matthew and Reagan both nodded. Jake pushed back from the table. "I'm going to leave this book. It has some drawings you may want to look at. Anyway, you can read it if you want. We'll return it to the library next Thursday."

Matthew grabbed the book and opened it to the pictures. Jake put on his jacket, took out his keys, and walked with Reagan to the front door.

"Well, that was fun," Reagan said.

"Oh yeah? Watching me squirm? You enjoyed that, did you?"

"Yep, that's about right."

That was more like her. She was cute. *An understatement. Tall, built, long legs, that stunning smile. An amazing mother. What's not to like?*

"Jake, really, thanks so much. Obviously Matthew wanted a man to talk with, and you handled that just right. And thanks for dinner."

"That's what big brothers are for." Jake had his hand on the doorknob when Matthew rushed to join him. "Well, Matt, I've given you something to think about. Anything else?"

Matthew pulled Jake down to whisper, "Why does my penis get hard and stick out sometimes?"

Of course, he should've explained it. He put his hand on Matthew's back and made eye contact. "That's called an erection. You might say that's nature's way of practicing, so you'll be able to, uh . . . have sex when it's time. You know, after you've grown up."

Matthew rolled his eyes. "Can I learn how to make it stop?"

Jake opened the front door and sighed. "Son, if you do, it's a skill that will serve you well the rest of your life."

REAGAN

CHAPTER TWENTY-NINE

Reagan's bedroom door squeaked open, and Matthew stuck his head in. "Mom, Charley's dad is here to pick me up."

She pulled herself up on her elbow. "Where's Lizzie?"

"Still asleep."

"Have a good time, buddy," she said, her voice so airless she wasn't sure it had carried all the way to her son. But apparently he'd heard her, because he ducked out of the room. She took a deep breath, wobbled as she stood, moved to the window that looked out on the street, and watched Matthew get into Mr. Walker's car. The streetlight shone on the crusty remnants of last week's snow. Reagan glanced at her phone. Eight o'clock. Charley's dad was always timely, but heavy, swirling clouds made it appear earlier and threatened nastier weather. She plopped back into bed and pulled the crumpled bedclothes up under her chin.

Reagan, you have to get up. It's eight o'clock. You'll never feel any better unless you get up and move. You need to get Lizzie up, dressed, and fed.

She didn't want to. She could hide from the voices when she slept.

It had been so easy to let Jake take over the "sex talk" with Matt. One of the best decisions she'd ever made, connecting with Big Brothers Big Sisters. People would be there to take over with the kids . . . if, for some reason, she wasn't around.

Sonny, Jordan, and Jake all cared about them. Sonny had a way with Lizzie that no one else, other than her father, had ever had. But could he really take care of her full-time? Matt adored Jake, but she really couldn't expect Jake to adopt Matthew. He only signed up for one afternoon a week for one year.

Jordan would take them . . . but she wouldn't move here— her business was in Atlanta—and she might place Lizzie in residential care. Reagan couldn't have them separated.

Mrs. Hamilton's voice broke through her resistance— *forgetting she had a daughter who loved her.* She forced herself upright and headed for the ornate box that held the letter from Scott. The proof that she had been loveable. She unfolded the letter, which had been folded and unfolded so many times it was tattered, and read the message Scott had asked Jordan to give her after his death.

Rea,

There is so much I want to say. First of all, I love you more than you can possibly know. Please don't remember me like I've been lately. Remember me throwing you over my shoulder to carry you into our new house, our starter home we're still in now. "Cake by the Ocean" is playing in my head as I write this. You want to know what floats through my mind when I'm all doped up? That's it. The good times.

Life goes so fast. Don't waste any part of yours. I want you to remember the good times we've had and have more, lots more.

I don't have a lot of regrets, but I do regret leaving you and the children. I hope our time together was as good for you as it was for me. I expect you to be sad for a while and grieve. That's okay, but only for a little while. I want you to move on. Never lose your joy of living. Find someone new who will love you and the children. I don't want you to be alone. Matthew and Lizzie need a father.

Don't forget, I'm watching over you for as long as you need me.

Love, S

He would be so disappointed in her. Scott was never a coward. He never went for the easy choices. He'd quit one job rather than lie to a customer as his boss had insisted he do. Reagan had been aghast. What would they do without his salary? But he had held firm to his principles and said it would be okay. And it *was* okay. He got another, better job working for a man who valued honesty. He would never have lied to the police, no matter what.

It took all the energy Reagan could muster to get up and put the letter back. With heavy arms and legs, she shuffled past Lizzie's room and peeked in. Still asleep. Good, she could go back to bed.

On her way back to her bedroom, Mrs. Hamilton's words

returned—*Vultures always hanging around . . . wouldn't leave her be.*

It had been a month since Angela withdrew from school, but her grandmother's voice, those words, still haunted her.

She went to the window again. Nothing unusual. Some folks were out early. A U-Haul was parked at the curb two doors down; the driver climbed the steps to the front porch. The sun shone from its usual early-morning angle. How could everything look so normal? Beyond comprehension.

JAKE

CHAPTER THIRTY

"Why don't you come with me, hon? Wouldn't it be great to get away for a few days, bask in the sun, take in a luau, play some golf?" Janet stood at the kitchen sink, preparing a roast for the oven. From behind, Jake slipped his arms around her waist and squeezed.

"Jake, you'll be busy with your meetings most of the time. You know how I hate being stuck alone while you work, plus the long flight. Besides, two of my patients are about to deliver."

He gave her an admiring gaze. The price he paid for marrying a woman of substance, a woman who knew her own mind, had her own career. How many wives of the guys he knew would turn down a trip to Hawaii?

"Well, it won't be the same without you there."

She patted his face. "You'll be busy, and I'm sure you won't have any trouble making a foursome for golf."

"Yeah, but it's not as much fun to watch those guys swing at a golf ball," he said, patting her on her backside.

"And I really don't like to leave Alex alone," she added,

slipping out of Jake's reach so she could slide the roast into the oven.

His stomach sank. *Of course. She's right. We don't dare leave Alex here unsupervised. If he were responsible—could be trusted—we'd have a number of options. Frances could come in, or he could spend a few days with a friend. But no, better not. Janet doesn't see that; she just wants to be available to Alex. Off-limits! The subject's off-limits.*

"Well, I think I'll bring my clubs up, clean them. Those guys are such show-offs with all their fancy equipment. I want to be ready for them."

Moments later, Jake returned to the kitchen. Janet was sitting at the table in front of the bay window with the paper and a cup of coffee—a pretty picture, framed by the frost around the window.

"Jan, have you seen my golf clubs?"

She looked puzzled. "They're in the basement, aren't they?"

"They're not down there."

Janet folded the paper and laid it aside. "They must be there. Where else would they be?" She headed for the basement.

"I don't think so, but you can look." The seed of a troubling thought sprouted in his mind.

The furnace rumbled loudly, laboring to keep the house warm on the cold February day. Jake moved from one light bulb to another, pulling every chain, illuminating the room with a yellowish glow. "They were here in the corner, next to this chest of drawers." He picked up a dirty T-shirt from the floor, looked at it suspiciously, then tossed it aside.

"Gosh, I didn't realize this basement was such a mess," Janet said, frowning. "I guess it's been a while since I've been down here." She climbed around boxes and old furniture, looking behind them for the clubs.

"It wasn't this big a mess." Jake rubbed the back of his neck as he scanned the room.

"I don't see them," she said.

"That's because they're not here."

Janet frowned. "Well, maybe Frances moved them for some reason."

"Why would Frances do that? She never even comes down here."

Janet shrugged. "Well, it was just a thought. I don't know, Jake. Do you think we could have been robbed?"

He quickly dismissed that possibility. "Have you noticed anything else missing?"

"Not really. But I haven't looked for anything, either."

"Janet, we have an alarm system. No one could have gotten in here without our knowing it unless he was let in."

She turned her palms up and shrugged. "Well, where are they then?"

"Where's Alex?"

"He's not here . . . and Alex doesn't play golf. He wouldn't have your clubs." Her tone was forbidding.

The muscle in his jaw twitched as he studied her.

How much are the fucking clubs worth to you, anyway? Remember the wall, the days of silence, the price for confronting her son the last time. You could just forget it. You can buy more clubs. He'll be out of the house in a couple of years.

Acid flooded his stomach. He just wasn't the kind of man who could let it go.

Dammit!

"He was the last one down here. He put away the Christmas things. Remember?" Jake had been suspicious then, when Alex so obligingly offered to take down the tree and decorations and pack them away. Not like Alex. Not at all. Jake said no more as he climbed the basement stairs.

While Janet was preoccupied with finishing dinner, Jake silently let himself into Alex's room and closed the door. He did not want Janet to hear him. She'd be livid. But he could not ignore the fact that a very expensive set of golf clubs was missing, and Alex was the logical person to have it. He didn't like himself much for doing it, invading someone's privacy. Sneaking around in his own house.

At first glance, no clubs. The room was a mess, but that was nothing new. Unsure what he expected to find, he carefully pulled out Alex's dresser drawers, one at a time, surprised by his own quickened pulse, and fished around stacks of clothes and other personal items. Just junk. Notes, loose change, unmatched socks, photographs. He peered into the closet, under the bed, into the bathroom. Nothing. Jake wanted to believe there was some other explanation, but deep down he knew Alex had taken those clubs—not the slightest doubt in his mind. He needed proof to confront him or the conflict with Janet would only get worse. There must be something there, some clue.

He scanned the room again, looking for possible hiding places. He picked up the bedspread and felt between the mattress and box springs, running his hand all the way around the bed. Nothing. Then he noticed a little pile of grit on the floor beneath the heat register. He stooped beside the bed, pulled his keys out of his pocket, and used one as a screwdriver to take out the screws. After pulling the cover from the wall, he carefully felt around in the crevice before he pulled out a bag of pills, different sizes and shapes, a bag of white powder, another of marijuana, and a receipt from a pawn shop in Kentucky for a set of PING golf clubs.

ALEX AND JAKE

CHAPTER THIRTY-ONE

Jake stood by the fireplace, his right arm resting on the mantel, his left hand tucked into his sweater pocket. The muscle in his jaw twitched. Alex immediately sensed danger.

"Hi, Jake. Hi, Mom." His mother sat opposite a crackling fire, casually sipping a martini. He walked over and gave her a rare peck on the cheek. "I'll be up in my room doing my homework." A lie, of course. He had no intention of doing homework, didn't even have books with him, but it was a good excuse to split.

"Alex, just a minute. Have you seen my golf clubs? Or do you have any idea where they could be?"

He froze, stunned. It was February. Why would Jake need his clubs? *Be cool, be cool!* He turned around to answer Jake.

"You gonna play golf? Now? It must be twenty degrees out there."

"I'm going to Hawaii next week—on business. How about it, Alex? Do you know where my clubs are?"

He knows, man, he knows! Focus. No proof. He couldn't have proof... could he?

No sign of anger. His mother seemed okay. Maybe Jake was just asking.

"Well, I think they're in the basement. That's where I last saw them." Solid eye contact, sincere smile.

"My clubs aren't in the basement. You're sure you have no idea where they are. Could you have loaned them to one of your friends? Could one of your friends have taken them with or without your knowledge?"

Alex furrowed his brow. "None of my friends would do that. They have their own clubs—if they want to play, anyway."

"Alex, did you take my clubs and sell them or—"

"Jake! Why the third degree? He said he doesn't know where your clubs are." Janet put her glass on the coffee table and glared at Jake, her chin raised slightly. "They must have been stolen. We'll call the police."

Alex smirked.

Jake pulled a yellow piece of paper from his sweater pocket and held it in front of him.

Alex's heartbeat skipped.

"How 'bout it, Alex? Do you recognize this?"

"Where'd you get that? Did you search my room? What gave you the fucking right to search my room?"

Janet looked from one to the other, grimacing. "What's the problem? Wh . . . what's that paper, Jake?"

Jake handed it to her. "It is a receipt from a pawn shop for a set of PING golf clubs. Four woods, one through nine irons, sand wedge, pitching wedge, putter. Sound familiar? It also has Alex's name, address, and signature."

Janet's jaw dropped. She turned to Alex, then back to Jake.

"Who gave you the right to search my room? Who are you, anyway, king? Who gives you the right?"

Janet gasped. "Alex, I don't understand this. What's going on? Why would you do something like this?"

Jake opened a drawer in the end table, carefully took out

Alex's bong and stash, and displayed them on the coffee table in front of Janet.

"Did you take my clubs just to piss me off, or did you want money for this crap?"

Trapped! Alex's vision narrowed to the plastic bag on the table. "Give 'em to me. Those are mine, man!"

Janet paled. "Alex, what's the meaning of this? What is that stuff?"

"Drugs, Janet!" Jake said. "Those are drugs: marijuana, cocaine, and—"

Alex snatched for the bag, but Jake grabbed his arm. Outmuscled. No way could he take Jake. Just too fucking strong. *Fuck* him!

"How long have you been using this stuff?"

Jake loosened his grip, and Alex pulled free.

"I'm out of here, man!" he screamed, spinning on his heels. Jake grabbed his arm again, but Alex shrugged it off. "Let me go! You got no right!" He kicked over the coffee table, grabbed a table lamp, and hurled it toward Jake. It crashed against the mantel behind him. The bulb shattered with a pop, showering the hearth with fragments of paper-thin glass. "You got no fucking right to search my room!"

Jake's face was crimson, Janet's white. They stared wide-eyed, mouths open.

"Who are you to tell me what to do? You're not my father. You're not my *fucking* father!"

Alex picked up a stack of books, the nearest thing handy, and threw them across the room, then a crystal vase, spilling water and yellow carnations. He punched the wall near the doorway, leaving a gaping hole. Then he fled.

Janet trembled, her face ashen. Jake moved toward her cautiously, unsure. Would she blame him for this? Possibly. He put his arms around her, pulled her head to his chest. She took a quick, gasping breath and relaxed beneath his arms. "Oh my god. I had no idea!"

"I've suspected it for a long time."

"What am I going to do?" Janet leaned against him. "It's mostly that Bryan's influence. What can I do?"

He folded her into his arms. She needed him. Hawaii could wait. "There are plenty of treatment programs. I'll check around. I don't have to go to Hawaii. I can stay here and help you with this."

She looked up into his eyes. "Thanks, but no. This is my problem anyway. I should be able to find someone who can help us. You go."

REAGAN

CHAPTER THIRTY-TWO

Reagan threw back the bedspread, then the blanket. She could not get comfortable. Angela came back to class and Reagan repeatedly hugged her, stroked her long, silky hair, and didn't want to let her go. She was bony, emaciated. Was she Angela— or Beverly? Reagan couldn't be sure. She sniffed behind her ear for lavender but smelled bacon. Scott cooked bacon for Sunday brunch. (No. It couldn't be that. It wasn't Sunday. She was sure of that much.) She followed the girl out of the building, but thick, menacing fog swirled around the school grounds and Reagan lost sight of her. A man popped out of a parked car. He had something on his arm. . . . What was it? *Don't go with him!* She tried to scream but the words caught in her throat.

She jerked upright but didn't want to wake up. She would rather sleep, even if she had nightmares. Several days in a row she had stepped out of her clothes and left them on the floor, making it difficult to walk without tripping. Her tangled hair hung across her face. She grabbed a half-full cup of coffee from her bedside table and took a gulp, hoping it would give her energy, but spewed it out. Disgusting! How long had she been asleep? The house was quiet. Thank god. She couldn't deal with the kids.

She knew it was Saturday. Other than that, she had lost all track of time. How long had it been since Beverly died, how many weeks? In Reagan's science lab, regardless of how much she tried to concentrate on teaching, Angela's vacant workstation haunted her, and she looked for the gunman everywhere. She would spot him sitting in a car, pointing a gun out the window at students walking away from school. Was she losing her mind? PTSD? She was barely functioning. The children's chatter pulled her out of her stupor, so she trudged to their bedrooms to investigate.

"There . . . that's nice." Matthew stood a few feet back and looked at Lizzie, like Da Vinci at *Mona Lisa*. Already wearing jeans and a red long-sleeved shirt, she seemed to think it perfectly normal for him to dress her.

Reagan stood quiet and motionless.

Lizzie sat on her bed and patiently allowed Matthew to brush her hair. With a tie stuck between his teeth, he pulled the hair back with both hands, then slipped the tie over it and said, "Voilà, a ponytail. Now then, don't you look pretty."

"Matt, what's going on here?"

The boy jumped. "It's okay, Mom." His eyes were larger than usual, his expression concerned. "I'll take care of her. You can rest. I'm just getting her dressed so I can get her breakfast." He rocked back and forth on his feet.

Reagan's chin quivered. Cracks began to form in the wall she had carefully constructed. My god! He's desperate to take care of me like Angela needed to take care of her mother.

So this is what it's come to. My nine-year-old son has to take care of his handicapped sister while his mother lolls in bed. Is this the way I help them through the grief of losing their father? By abandoning them? I have got to pull myself together.

She threw an arm over Matthew's shoulder. "Thanks,

buddy, but I can take care of Lizzie." She didn't realize she was crying until tears flooded Matthew's face . . . then Lizzie's. The more she tried to control herself, the louder the sobs. Matthew grabbed her around the waist and squeezed. Lizzie jumped up and joined them in a group hug. She didn't know how long they stayed like that, but it was a while.

"Boy, I needed that," Matthew said when he finally pulled away.

He needed that? Layer upon layer of emotion swirled inside her. Had she been sending Matt the wrong message? Did her being strong mean she hadn't given him permission to be himself? Come to think of it, the only time Matt seemed like a kid lately was when he was with Jake.

A box of Golden Grahams sat on the kitchen table next to an empty bowl and a bottle of milk. Matthew had already eaten. She glanced at her watch. Ten o'clock. No wonder. She grabbed a clean bowl from the cabinet, filled it with cereal and milk, and set it at Lizzie's place. As soon as her daughter sat down, Reagan raised the window. A draft of arctic air blew in, causing a rush of chills, but she didn't mind.

Bird stuck his head out the round door of the birdhouse and made eye contact with her.

"I've got to do something. I can't stand myself. I feel dead, but I can't be. I have children to take care of. They need me."

Bird moved to the windowsill, never losing eye contact with her.

Matthew sat down and pour himself more cereal. That didn't matter. He paid no attention to her when she talked to Bird.

"I don't know what to do. I keep thinking of the Serenity Prayer. Scott's gone; I can't change that. Lizzie needs more from a parent than other seven-year-olds; I can't change that. I am the only person who can identify a murderer; I can't change that. My student's mother became addicted to heroin and died of an overdose; I can't change that."

Bird looked frustrated, the way Lizzie did when she wanted to say something but couldn't express herself.

"I know what you're thinking: there *is* something I could change, but I don't have the guts." Reagan furrowed her brow, clenched her jaw, and gazed past Bird at nothing. "You don't understand. I'm not a brave person. I'm just an ordinary mother, teacher. Not extraordinary like Scott thought. I'm scared something awful will happen to one of the children . . . or to me. They need me."

On the other hand, they don't have me now. I'm useless. At least Jordan would take care of them, love them. What if something happened to one of them? No, that doesn't make sense. They can't identify the gunman, and he must know that if he hurt one of them, nothing would stop me from finding him.

Reagan scrutinized Bird, arched an eyebrow. "Are you just a bird? Was it some kind of weird coincidence that you showed up on the day of Scott's funeral? Or are you real, a messenger sent to remind me he's here, watching over us? Can you pull cosmic strings to keep us safe?"

One thing was perfectly clear: no matter what, she had to do something.

A L E X

CHAPTER THIRTY-THREE

Alex stood on the porch of a stately old house on a side street in Clifton, two blocks from University Hospital. The sign by the front door listed several names, mostly with *MSW* or *MD* after them. He walked inside, stomped crusty snow off his shoes, and wiggled his toes to warm them. The parlor had been converted to a pleasant waiting area lined with chairs. A large potted palm sat in the corner. Magazines covered the top of a coffee table. A pretty girl, not much older than him, sat behind a desk. She looked up and smiled as he approached.

"I'm here to see Dr. Blythestone. I have an appointment." He took off his coat and hung it on a rack. He was dressed in a crisp, clean shirt and jeans. Even had his hair cut for this occasion. The all-American kid. Anything to get his mother off his back. She had been different this time. Not as easy.

The receptionist picked up the phone to announce his arrival. Except for worn carpet, the place was pretty grand. Winding stairway in the foyer, high ceilings, lots of plants. The girl showed him into an office on the first floor.

Alex stifled a laugh when Dr. Blythestone stood to greet

him. He was old and thin, wearing a bow tie like somebody from one of those TV sitcoms filmed in the eighties.

"Good morning, Alex. So you're Janet's son. Good to meet you." He extended his hand.

Alex gave him a firm handshake. "Good morning. I appreciate you seeing me. Thank you, sir."

A sofa and chair were placed at right angles. Alex sat on the sofa, Dr. Blythestone in the chair. "So, tell me, Alex, why are you here?" His powder-blue eyes settled gently on Alex.

"My mom is making me come. My stepfather and her, mostly my stepfather, think I have a problem." A hairline crack snaked across the plaster wall behind the doctor.

"Do you?"

Alex squirmed and looked at the floor. "Uh, I don't think so. I shouldn't have gotten so upset, but my stepfather searched my room. I didn't think anybody had the right to search somebody's property without a search warrant. Don't you think people, even kids, should be allowed a little privacy?"

"What do you think?"

That technique was on TV a lot. Never give a direct answer. Answer a question with a question, that was how it worked. "Well, I know they pay the bills and stuff like that, but I don't think they should search my room."

Dr. Blythestone brought his elbows to his knees and steepled his fingers but remained silent.

"He found some weed and stuff. Now Mom wants me in counseling for a drug problem."

The doctor shook his head. "So, you think your using is not a problem?"

Alex snorted. "I don't have a *drug problem*. I mean, I can take it or leave it. Everybody uses once in a while. It's normal for a teenager."

"What drugs do you use?"

Alex shrugged. "Weed, mostly."

"When do you use?"

Simple question, nonjudging. "Just when I go out to party. On weekends. Not every weekend. Just once in a while when we go out. Everybody does it." He cocked his head. "What'd she tell you about me?"

"Not much. Just that you would be calling, mostly."

She hadn't told him about the golf clubs. That would've been harder to explain. Or had she? *Maybe I should mention it, blow him away with honesty.* He avoided the doctor's blue eyes and settled his gaze on the wall crack.

"Well, my stepfather hates me. He wants my mom all to himself. I can't do anything right. He criticizes everything I do. He's always hammering on my mom for not being strict enough." He took a deep breath, gritted his teeth until the muscle in his jaw quivered. "My mom and I got along fine until he came along."

"You really feel your stepfather hates you?"

"He does! I know he does. He was pretty old before he married my mom. Never had kids of his own. He doesn't like them."

"Hmmm." There was a long silence.

What the hell? "I took my stepfather's golf clubs and pawned them."

One of the doctor's bushy eyebrows jerked up. He studied Alex's face. "You must have been very angry with your stepfather to do such a thing."

Of course that was it. Angry. "You'd be angry too if someone was always trying to tell you what to do. Butting in between you and your mom. We had a great life until he showed up."

Tears. He willed them to come, reached deep inside himself. At first his eyes only watered, then he focused on how pissed he got about Jake finding his stash. He held the thought, the feeling of being trapped and desperate. Tears rolled over his lower lids and down his cheeks. "My stepfather—he's not my real father—my real father wouldn't treat me that way. He's got no right!" He got into it, worked up a really good scene with sobs and spit and snot.

"I see." Dr. Blythestone handed him a box of tissues, his pale eyes softening as he looked at Alex.

Alex suppressed a smile. He'd won.

REAGAN

CHAPTER THIRTY-FOUR

Reagan put her hand on her stomach to keep her insides from quivering. She hesitated to elevate her concern to family-meeting status because she didn't want to alarm Matthew, but she had to make an impression. Scott had started the tradition when they wanted to discuss something important. Family meetings were a big deal, scheduled a couple of days in advance, and nothing got in the way.

Sleet pelted the picture window. Matthew sat on the leather sofa, Scooter beside him.

"Buddy, I don't want to scare you, but I called this meeting to discuss something important."

Matthew drew his eyebrows together and rocked slightly against the sofa. "Okay."

She ran her tongue over dry lips. "Most people in and around Norwood are good people . . . like the Crammers. Right?"

He nodded.

"But you never know when you might run into someone

who's not. Remember when Lizzie was gone for a long time and we couldn't find her?"

He rolled his eyes. "Of course I do."

"Remember how upset Uncle Sonny was?"

He nodded, his eyes growing wider.

"Sonny thought someone lured her to get in a car and kept her awhile to scare me. We may never know if that's what happened, but even if it's not, it doesn't hurt to be careful."

Matthew's gaze drifted from Reagan to Scooter, and he ran his fingers through the dog's thick fur. "I don't get it. Why would somebody want to scare an adult?"

More than anything, she wanted to protect her children, let her son be an innocent kid rather than worry about her. It wasn't fair. He'd already watched his father get sick and die. But she had to enlist his help if she was going to do what she had in mind.

"A few months ago, I saw someone commit a crime, and I told the police. Your Uncle Sonny thought the criminal picked up Lizzie to let me know that if I identified him, he could hurt one of you. And he did . . . scare me. I was so worried about you and Lizzie that I told the police I couldn't remember what he looked like. But that was a lie."

Matthew snapped his eyes back onto her.

"Okay, I know that's not what I tell you to do—always tell the truth—but I was really scared when Lizzie went missing. I did the wrong thing for the right reason, to protect you and Lizzie. But it just made things worse. We live in a wonderful, safe community, and it's up to everyone to protect it, not let bad people get away with hurting others. You know that, right?"

He stopped rocking, leaned forward, and nodded.

"So if I go back and help them find this man, we both have to be smart. We can't let Lizzie out of our sight for even a second, unless she's with an aide. Also, I know you would never go off with a stranger, but sometimes bad people can be tricky. They might say, for instance, 'Your mom gave me a message for you.' That's not likely, but it could happen. We need to agree on a code word we would use in a case like that."

Matthew stood, jutted his chin up, puffed his chest out, and put his arm around her shoulder. "Mom, you don't need to be afraid. I'll take care of Lizzie."

Such a little man. "I know, son, but we need to have a plan if someone ever approached you like that. You would ask for the code word. If he or she didn't know it, you would not go with that person—you would run!" Scooter jumped off the sofa. "Can you think of a code word that neither of us would forget?"

Matthew seemed to give that some thought before a smirky smile spread slowly across his face. "I have a word." He leaned close to her ear and whispered.

"That's perfect, buddy. Our code word is *stupid*."

Reagan sat across from Detective Gabriel in his cramped office, her foot bouncing on the floor. She tried to calm herself. It had been five months since the shooting. Maybe the gunman had left Cincinnati. Maybe not. Whatever. Guilt was worse than fear.

"We've exhausted our resources and come up with nothing." Ron Gabriel's voice seemed weighted with worry. "There's been an increase in drug-related criminal activity in the area, more violence. I'm confident it's connected to that shooting in Pleasant Ridge. We just haven't put all the pieces together. I'm really happy you're here, Reagan."

He didn't look happy. His eyes were darkly circled, his jawline rigid, and his smile fleeting, not at all the easy grin he'd had before she withdrew her earlier statement.

"How're Angela and Mrs. Hamilton?"

He shook his head. "They're going through a lot."

"I wish I'd done more—sooner."

The lines in his face softened. "Well, you're here now and I'm grateful. I don't know if things would have been different for Beverly even if we had caught this guy. Unfortunately, these dealers multiply like roaches. When we take one off the streets, another one shows up to take advantage of these people—and addicts are resourceful when they need a fix."

Reagan appreciated his remark, but it didn't assuage her guilt.

"I've got a forensic artist waiting downstairs. Do you think after all this time you can describe the gunman?"

"Absolutely. That image is seared into my brain."

"Good. Just tell Joe everything you remember about the guy. No detail is insignificant. With your description, he'll be able to come up with a pretty good likeness."

She nodded. "I haven't mentioned this before, but there was something on the inside of his left arm just above the wrist—a burn scar maybe, or a birthmark. I only saw it for a moment, but I noticed it before I saw the gun. I meant to tell you about it earlier."

Detective Gabriel steepled his fingers. "So you think he was left-handed?"

"I don't know about that. He held the gun like on TV." She demonstrated the position by holding an imaginary gun with both hands straight out, pointed toward the door, her left arm slightly higher than the right, then slowly brought her arms around in front of her to point at the detective. "He shows up in my dreams, or I should say nightmares. His face isn't always clear, but I know it's him from the dread I feel when I see him, from the shudder that wakes me. Sometimes he has a gun, sometimes not. But even though I can't make it out, I always notice the mark. It's like my subconscious directs my attention to it."

The detective raised both eyebrows and nodded. "Maybe

so." He scribbled notes on a yellow legal pad. "Let's stop downstairs before we go any further and you can describe him to Joe." He led her down the concrete steps and past the lobby door.

Joe Lederman—sixtyish, with a receding hairline and a round belly—was waiting in an interview room. The artist reminded Reagan of Archie Bunker. He sat down at a metal desk behind a sketch pad and directed her to sit at a ninety-degree angle to the desk. A stack of large books was within his reach.

Joe leaned forward, elbows on the desk, hands folded. "Reagan, people are often nervous when we first meet. I know you want to help us catch this guy and you'll do your best. There are no wrong answers, and we're in no hurry. We'll keep at it until you believe we've come up with a reasonable likeness of him. I want you to relax as best you can."

She nodded.

"First, was he White, Black, Asian? What can you tell me about his race?"

Reagan looked off into the distance. "Caucasian. Tanned or olive skinned."

Joe pulled out one of the books. "Okay, the way this works, I have catalogs of different parts of the head and face. We'll take it one characteristic at a time." He opened the book to a page with sixteen impressions of different masculine face outlines without the facial features. "Look at the images and pick out the closest to the one you remember."

She ran her finger over the slick paper and studied the shapes: oval, round, square, diamond, heart, pear, and oblong. She came to one with a prominent jaw and square chin. She conjured up the figure she saw during the shooting . . . and pointed to a picture.

"Great, Reagan." Joe used a thick black pencil to quickly outline a square face. "Now let's look at the eyes."

She had no trouble with that. She had been transfixed by those eyes, and their unusual goldish-brown color.

Every time she pointed to a picture, Joe's pencil flew across the pad, adding that particular characteristic to the sketch. When he finished with the drawing, he tore the sheet off the tablet and held it up to her.

"What do you think?"

Reagan leaned back in her chair and gazed at the drawing, her head cocked, an eyebrow arched.

Joe asked, "On a scale of one to ten, how would you grade this resemblance to the gunman?"

"About a seven."

"Good. What would you change? How can we make it an eight or nine?"

"Hmm. I don't think his face was that square. It was longer, a little thinner."

He reworked the chin and brought the sides of the face in. "How's that?"

She squinted. "Better."

"What else?"

"The eyes. They were bigger and lighter, and the nose broader and flat, like a boxer who had taken too many punches."

Detective Gabriel, who was sitting in a corner of the room, behind Reagan, had been quiet until that moment. "You're doing great, Reagan. These details will be very helpful."

She turned to him. "I just wish I could remember more about the mark."

"I have an idea we can discuss when we're done here," the detective said.

After several more adjustments, the artist showed Reagan and Detective Gabriel the finished sketch. "Well, what do you guys think?"

Reagan nodded. "That's him."

JAKE

CHAPTER THIRTY-FIVE

Jake and Janet squared off in their kitchen. The dishwasher hummed in the background.

"Don't give me that bullshit! Is that what we're getting for three hundred bucks? A con job?"

"I'm just telling you what he said, Jake. Alex's behavior is not that unusual. It could be just a phase of rebellion, something he'll go through before becoming independent."

"Three wrecks within a year is not that unusual? Stealing my golf clubs and hocking them? Trashing the living room when he's confronted? Janet, have you forgotten how he was? What you saw with your own eyes? Alex's behavior is not normal. I'm worried about him."

"Well, he was provoked. I mean, you did search his room."

Jake threw up his hands and shook his head. "It's my fault? If I hadn't searched his room for my stolen golf clubs, and found his illegal stash, Alex wouldn't have punched a hole in the living room wall . . . and he wouldn't have a problem. Is that what you're saying?"

"Jake, I'm only telling you what Dr. Blythestone told me. He's the expert." She touched her fingertips to her forehead, a gesture indicating the beginning of one of her headaches, but he was unmoved.

"Well, I'll tell you what, Janet. You can do what you want about Alex. You can buy him another car when he wrecks this one, if he doesn't kill himself first. You can get him out of trouble with the police. You can make sure he gets everything he wants. But not me. I've had it! And he'd goddamn better stay away from my things!" Jake's face burned; blood surged through his veins.

Janet's eyes watered.

"I am sick of trying to parent him when he's not even civil to me. All I hear from him is 'You're not my father.' I can't compete with a fantasy. He's got this bond with a father he's never met, when I'm right here, doing my best to be his dad."

Janet stared at him as if trying to think of a response.

He didn't give her a chance. He grabbed his coat and stormed out of the house.

In his car, Jake doubled over with heartburn. "Jesus!" There was no use arguing with her about that boy. It was always like that and always gonna be. He groped through his glove compartment for Rolaids, snatched a couple from their wrapper, and popped them into his mouth. It took a moment before he could straighten up and take a deep breath.

He decided to clear his head by driving, pulled out onto Shawnee Run, and took a left. Sleet fell in the beam of his headlights and on his windshield. His wipers cleared it in rhythmic sweeps. The rush of adrenaline faded. The flow of blood through his temples slowed. He drove past the spot where Alex had hit the lamppost a few months ago. No commotion tonight; everything was quiet.

At a four-way stop, he idled until the car behind him

flashed its brights in Jake's rearview mirror. His face grew hot again when he glanced around. The only other car at the intersection was the one behind him. "Goddamn it, Jake, get a grip."

He accelerated with a jerk. Unconsciously, he moved through the dark night, going no place in particular, turning, braking, surging forward. Surprised to find himself on Kenilworth with no memory of a single turn he'd made to get there, he pulled to the curb across the street from the Ramsey house, turned off his headlights, and idled. Soft golden light glowed through the large picture window, enabling him to see clearly into the room.

Reagan and Matt—and Scooter, of course—sat in the living room across from the window, talking. It looked like a serious discussion. Matthew got up from the sofa, his chest stuck out like he'd just been named MVP, and gave his mother a half hug, arm around the shoulder—more like a friend than her nine-year-old son. She stood, squeezed him back, and brushed his hair from his eyes, a touch so personal and motherly it made Jake's eyes sting. Reagan was everything he missed about his mother. Warm and supportive. Involved. Mothers made all the difference. Some mothers.

Matthew disappeared from the frame, but Reagan sat back down on the sofa and drew her feet under her, a glass of wine within reach. She mouthed words to music he couldn't hear and swayed with the beat. He couldn't turn away, so he turned off the car and watched her for a while.

Christ, she's beautiful.

She looked at peace, almost happy. Good. She'd seemed in a dark place for a while, and Matthew was totally distracted. Maybe she had resolved whatever was bothering her. When she reached for the wine, her gorgeous hair, until then tucked behind her ear, tumbled to her chest, her breast . . . and now he was the one who was totally distracted.

Better move on before someone in the neighborhood becomes suspicious and has me arrested for stalking. Bet that cop would be all too happy to lock up my ass. I can always go to my office, where I can at least get some work done while I run away from home.

Jake's office was dark and cool, unfriendly at that time of night. He turned on the lights and checked the thermostat. His coat felt like lead. The act of walking took all his energy, but the thermostat read fifty-five degrees, so he left it on.

He sat at his desk. Thoughts came and went in no particular order. Jake and Janet on their honeymoon in Paris. God, he had been so proud to be with her. And the night they met, introduced over cocktails by Maude Taylor. He had never been so excited but yet so comfortable with a woman. From the first night, he knew he would pursue her to the end. It hadn't been that difficult. She liked him too. He couldn't believe it at first, then decided it was one of those matches made in heaven. It really did happen. And it was heaven, until his stepson made it clear he didn't want Jake in his life.

Scenes played tag through his mind—some good, some more like tonight's—until a siren wailed from the street outside his office. He got up and glanced out the window. Blue lights.

The police—that detective who had come to the house about a hit-and-run came to mind. Janet never considered the possibility that Alex had been involved, that he would lie. But of course he would. Jake was pretty sure Alex was involved, and he believed Trip's father thought so too, although that didn't stop him from pulling strings to make it go away. And it worked. They hadn't heard anything else from the police. At least not yet. Jake frowned. The privileged don't pay for what they do. There's always someone to bail them out.

He knew what it was like to do bad things and not be held

accountable. When he was a kid, people made excuses for him because of his mother. Vandalize, steal, smoke dope—he'd do anything to make himself feel better, get his father's attention. His behavior got worse in his teens, but his father always paid to get him out of trouble, which was easier than giving his son love and attention. Jake had no doubt he would have gotten into big trouble if Coach Majors hadn't intervened. But he did intervene, with a carrot and a stick. If Jake wanted to be on Coach's team, get his love and attention, he had to straighten up, stop using, improve his grades, and work hard. Coach wouldn't let anyone make excuses for Jake. It was hard, but he did it.

But parenting Alex like that was too hard. The price was always too high. Scene after scene played in Jake's mind, and he became resigned to the fact that his marriage wasn't working. Too many scenes like tonight. Too many walls between him and Janet.

Ice pelted his office window. This was no place to be at this hour. He sighed. Just last week the temperature was in the sixties—springtime. Now winter was back. If he was going home, he should go while the roads were still good. After all, why should he be here, rather than in his comfortable den watching the Lakers? He didn't have to care what happened to Alex. She'd made it clear. Alex wasn't his problem.

REAGAN

CHAPTER THIRTY-SIX

Reagan didn't totally believe in hypnosis, but then who was she to question it? After all, she believed in Bird. Detective Gabriel had set up the appointment. She didn't want to disappoint him, but she had no idea what was expected of her and worried that she wouldn't be able to deliver. The studio was in the therapist's home in Clifton—one of those big old houses with a large wraparound porch, ornate woodwork, and a dormer window on the second floor. Maybe at one time the grand old house had been subdivided into a duplex, since there were two front doors. But these days the second one provided a private entrance into the hypnotist's workspace. Janelle, the only name Reagan had been given, met her at the door.

"You must be Reagan. It's nice to meet you. Please, come in." Janelle's long dark hair fell in ringlets past her shoulders; the sides were pulled up and tied behind her head. Her wide smile and expressive eyes were welcoming. Her face looked freshly scrubbed, radiant with no makeup. She wore long, dangling earrings; an assortment of silver bangle bracelets; a long, straight dress; and flat shoes.

The room smelled faintly of cinnamon. Afternoon sunlight streamed through a picture window, bathing the surroundings in a soft golden glow.

"Honestly, do you believe this weather? Yesterday there was actually snow on the ground. Today couldn't be nicer. March in Cincinnati. Go figure."

Reagan had expected the therapist to be all business, like Detective Gabriel and Joe Lederman, but Janelle was warm and chatty. She pointed to a green leather recliner in the center of the room.

"Please, Reagan, have a seat. Ron told me why you're here. I think what you're doing is terrific."

Reagan eased herself into the cushiony chair and exhaled. She didn't feel terrific at all but silently added Janelle to the list of people she didn't want to disappoint.

"Tell me a little about yourself, Reagan. The only thing I know is you witnessed a crime and you're helping the police. I've worked with law enforcement myself for over ten years and love it. It makes me feel I'm doing something worthwhile."

Reagan found it easy to talk to Janelle about Scott, how much she missed him and how important the children's happiness was to her. They also chatted about Reagan's other passion, teaching—nurturing young people to be the best they could be. She explained how Lizzie's limitations made her better at it, more respectful of each student's individual needs. As they talked, her tension melted away like yesterday's snow.

"Reagan, if I had children—which unfortunately I don't—you are exactly the kind of teacher I would want for them." Janelle glanced at a small clock hanging among a group of drawings on the wall behind her desk. "How do you feel about being here today? Have you had an experience like this before?"

"No, and I'm a little nervous."

"Of course you are." Janelle's voice was mellow and confident. "That's normal, but most people say they enjoy it because it is very relaxing." Janelle adjusted the window blinds to divert the sunlight away from Reagan's eyes. "Essentially that's what hypnosis is, a deep state of relaxation. It allows you to access your subconscious, past all the obstacles your conscious mind puts in your way." She lowered her voice. "Trust me, you won't do or say anything you don't want to." She shook her head and pursed her lips. "Those stage hypnotists give hypnotherapy a bad name . . . but I digress. Everyone's different, but you may be able to let your guard down and remember things more clearly than when you are fully conscious. You want to go for it?"

Reagan nodded.

"Good. Can you tell me a time and a place where you felt safe and relaxed, a place where you could let your hair down? And if you were with someone, who were you with?"

Reagan leaned back in the chair. She hadn't thought about it like that, but it had been a long time since she had felt totally relaxed. After a while she said, "I was ten or eleven, in our playroom at home, a room furnished for kids: a large TV, big comfy chairs, thick carpet, and cushions on the floor. A bookcase crammed with books. Games and puzzles covered one whole wall opposite a big window that looked out onto the street. My happy place back then—mine and my sister's. It was our compensation for our parents spending so little time with us. One day a storm blew in while I was walking home from school. The dark clouds and intense lightning terrified me. The wind almost blew me over. My sister, Jordan, came looking for me, and we made it home right before a downpour that went on for hours. Or at least it seemed like that to me then. We stood at the window and watched the storm. I felt so safe and dry in that room with Jordan."

"Good. Now, I'd like you to get very comfortable. You can lean all the way back if you want. However you're most relaxed." Janelle waited for Reagan to adjust the chair to be fully reclined. "Good. Now look at that spot on the ceiling. I want you to focus on it until your eyes get heavy and close."

Soon Reagan's eyelids fluttered briefly and closed. Was she just pleasing Janelle or actually slipping into a trance? She wasn't sure.

"Reagan, I want you to listen to my voice and follow my instructions. Okay? Focus on your toes. How do they feel?" The therapist spoke with a slow, measured cadence. "Have they been crammed into tight shoes? Are they tired . . . cold . . . or warm? Squeeze them tight . . . tighter . . . as tight as you can." After several seconds, she said, "Okay, relax them. How do they feel now?" She hesitated before continuing. "Next, I want you to become aware of the balls of your feet. Do they ache from pounding the pavement? Are they cold . . . are they hot?" She waited a moment. "Now I want you to flex your feet so that the balls are flat against the chair. As hard as you can." After another moment she said, "Okay, relax them. How do they feel now?"

It was so easy to cling to Janelle's soothing voice and let it carry her away from the menacing thoughts that had been stampeding through her mind.

"You're doing great, Reagan."

She followed every new direction, focusing her attention like that up her body, eventually crumpling her scalp like an unwanted piece of paper before smoothing it with her mind. She had the sense of floating. The gentle hum from the furnace, voices from another room, traffic sounds all faded away.

"Good. Reagan, if you can, I want you to visualize the playroom of your childhood, your happy place, your safe place. Your sister, Jordan, is there with you." After a moment, Janelle said, "I'm surprised to see your forehead wrinkle, your face tighten. Is there a problem between you and your sister?"

Reagan responded with a weak, childlike voice. "Yes."

"Okay, would you like to share the problem with me? It's up to you."

Reagan hesitated a moment before responding. "She wants me to put my daughter in a home."

"I see. And you don't want to do that?"

"No . . . yes . . . I don't know."

"You are ambivalent about something important. Is there someone who can help you make this decision?"

Reagan's eyelids fluttered again before she answered. "Yes."

"Okay, Reagan, I want you to be in the most wonderful state of relaxation, so we should ask Jordan to wait for you outside the room. Can you do that?"

"Yes." A calming wave enveloped Reagan as she visualized Jordan leaving the room.

"Now, Reagan, I want you to go to the window and look out. There is a car parked on the street in front of your house. Do you see the car?"

"Yes."

"Can you describe that car?"

"It's big . . . black . . . a sedan."

"Reagan, you are safe, in your happy place, inside your home." Janelle's silky voice poured over her like syrup. "You feel relaxed as you watch the car. Can you tell me anything about the people in the car? You don't have to. It's up to you."

"The windows are tinted. I can't see inside, but they're not good people."

"I see. Can you guess what they're doing?" Janelle asked.

"Watching."

"Do you know who they're watching?"

"Just some people. Young people."

"Do you know them?"

"No."

Janelle was quiet for a moment. "What's happening now?"

"The passenger window is lowering."

240

"Good, Reagan. You're doing great. Can you see the passenger who lowered the window?"

"I can see his arms coming out the window."

"What can you tell me about his arms?"

"He's strong. They're muscular."

Janelle gave her a moment. "Anything else?"

"There's a dark spot . . . on the inside of his arm . . . close to his wrist."

"A dark spot? What does it look like? Can you tell me?"

She struggled to focus on the mark. She zeroed in on the wrist, but her attention immediately shifted to the hands . . . holding a gun. No. The wrist! She concentrated on the dark spot. *Important. It's important. What is it?* The gun was too big. Her mind wouldn't let her move past it. Her heartbeat quickened. Her jaw clenched. *They're gone.* The mark, the gun, the car all disappeared, and with them her sense of floating, of well-being.

"It's okay, Reagan," Janelle said, a tinge of disappointment in her voice. She pushed a lever on the recliner and brought Reagan's chair back to a sitting position. "It's not unusual for it to take more than one session to unlock a dark secret. We can try again, if you're willing."

Later at home, after the children were asleep, Reagan held her phone to her chest, thinking about what to say. She hesitated, practiced, shook her head, tried to calm her stomach, and finally punched in the number.

"Hey, you, I was hoping you'd call."

For only the second time in a long time, Reagan cried. "Hi, Jordi. I just called to say I love you."

"I love you too, Rea."

ALEX

CHAPTER THIRTY-SEVEN

Finally, Alex had wheels again. He'd gone to Dr. Blythestone, like they'd insisted he do after the golf club incident, and done what he could to get on their good side. It had taken a month to charm his mother into giving in again after she took his keys the second time. Jake hardly mattered. Alex hadn't mentioned Bryan to her, and for all she knew he only hung out with Trip. He was supposed to be in school, but tons of kids would be out today. Opening day for the Reds.

Shit, I'm at eighty again. He wasn't going much faster than the rest of traffic on I-71 South, but he could *not* get a ticket. No use giving them any more ammunition. But even a ticket wouldn't quell his excitement today. He was finally free of his walking cast, and he *loved* his car.

He'd stop in the 'wood and get some weed from Bryan, and they'd both go downtown.

He was only twelve his first opening day. He'd been practicing an ollie for at least two hours—crouching on his new skateboard, picking up speed on the downslope—but his balance was off. Popping harder didn't help. A cool breeze blew through his hair. At least he was out of the *boring* house. All Mona did was watch TV and talk on her phone. His mom called Mona the housekeeper, but he knew the truth. She was there to babysit him during spring break.

Twelve is too old for a babysitter.

He heard the racket before he saw the boys. Three of them, older than him: one he'd seen before, Sebastian something; another with rust-colored hair; and a Black kid. They were laughing too loud, being obnoxious, shouting at drivers on Smith Road, messing with each other.

He felt like something was crawling around in his stomach.

"Hey, skater, cool board," Rusty screamed. "I want a board like that. Don't you, Sebastian?"

All three boys rushed Alex. Sebastian hollered, "Let's skate!" They surrounded Alex, forcing him to stop and pick up his board.

Sebastian jerked the skateboard out of his hand, hopped on, pushed off, performed the perfect ollie, and rolled out of Alex's reach. The other boys whooped with laughter.

Alex's knees turned to rubber. "Give it back," he yelled as he ran after his board. Tears sprang to his eyes. He *could not* let those assholes see him cry.

"Boo-hoo! He's gonna blubber like some little girl," Rusty yelled, dancing around Alex.

Out of nowhere, another boy flew into Sebastian, like some avenging ninja, and grabbed him around the waist, knocking him off the board.

"What the fuck?" Sebastian shrieked. They rolled on the pavement, pummeling each other with quick, sharp jabs.

Rusty grabbed the board. The Black guy dove between Sebastian and the ninja, fists flying.

Now Rusty had his board. Alex latched onto Rusty's arm and pulled. Rusty turned around and punched Alex under his left eye. The blow stung but didn't slow Alex. His breath came in short, hard gasps.

"Cops!" Sebastian yelled.

The boys froze and looked toward Williams Avenue. A squad car slowed. Blue lights flashed on as it turned onto Smith Road. The assailants abandoned the skateboard and took off running, cut through a Shell station, and split up, leaving Alex and the boy who came to his rescue.

The police car pulled to the curb.

Shit! We're in trouble.

Guys in his class talked about being hauled in to the police station. But never him!

The cop got out of the car. "What's going on here?" He looked the boys up and down. "Oh, it's you, Bryan."

"I was just tryin' to help this kid. They ganged up on 'em."

The cop shook his head.

"It's true," Alex said. "They stole my skateboard."

The officer took a close look at Alex. "You're going to have a pretty nasty shiner there. You okay?"

Alex touched his tender cheek, raised his chin, and nodded.

"Well, lucky for you boys, it's opening day, and I don't have time to run you all in. No more fighting. You got that?"

Alex diverted his gaze to the ground and nodded.

"And Bryan, see if you can stay out of trouble."

They watched the officer get into the squad car and pull away. "Thanks," Alex said to his rescuer.

"No problem," Bryan said. "I seen them take your board. They're assholes. This ain't my first run-in with them." He flipped his dark hair out of his eyes. "You live around here?"

"Yeah," Alex answered. "On Evergreen . . . 8533."

"Oh yeah? I live on Evergreen too. The next block down. I was gonna find a place to watch the parade. Maybe try to sneak into the ballpark later. You wanna come?"

Alex hesitated. He had promised his mother that he would

stay close to home, and that if he went out, he would let Mona know where he was. His mother would be mad—real mad—if he didn't. He straightened to his full height of five feet. "Hell yeah! That'd be great."

"My bike's around the corner," Bryan said.

The boys stopped by Alex's house, quietly left his skateboard on the porch so they wouldn't alert Mona, and got his bike. He had never done anything so . . . exciting.

They pedaled through Over-The-Rhine, a neighborhood just north of downtown. Bryan seemed to know how to get around, so Alex followed him. Most of the main streets had been closed to traffic. They walked their bikes when they reached Music Hall, where bleachers had been set up for temporary seating. Up and down Race Street, people sat on the curbs and crowded the sidewalks, waiting on the parade, creating an ocean of red: sweatshirts, hats, sweaters, all with the team's logo. A woman walked by with a poodle on a leash, its fur dyed red. Drums and horns sounded in the distance.

The weather was great. Sixties and sunny. The atmosphere was festive, thrilling. They crossed the street to Washington Park, where Bryan led him to a food truck set up on the lawn. Alex stuffed his hands in his pockets and frowned.

"I didn't bring any money."

"No problem. I got some." Bryan bought them each a hot dog and a Coke. They found an empty picnic bench near the dog park and ate while they watched kids playing in the gazebo. A car horn blared to announce the parade was underway. The boys hopped onto the table and looked over the heads of others. A convertible carrying Davey Concepción, 2014 grand marshal, glided by.

"It's really crowded today," Bryan said out of the corner of his mouth. "It'll be worse on the Banks. Good chance we can get into the game." He raised both eyebrows and gave Alex a devilish grin.

Alex pressed his lips together and slowly nodded. "Sure. Let's do it."

They rode their bikes along the parade route to Fountain Square, where local television stations had media people commenting on the day's events. One of the high school bands played "The Stars and Stripes Forever." Alex had never really paid attention to band music before, but he liked that song a lot.

People packed the sidewalks leading down to the area known as "the Banks," with bars, restaurants, apartments, boat access to the Ohio River, and Great American Ball Park.

Alex had a white-knuckled grip on his handlebars and a pit in his stomach as he biked down the steep hill, trying to keep up with Bryan without wiping out or running into a pedestrian. No way would he ask his new friend to slow down. They finally parked their bikes at Second Street and walked. At the stadium's entrance they stopped at a life-size bronze statue of Joe Morgan and scrutinized the nearest ticket taker.

"Let's hang around here for a while. Wait for the right time," Bryan whispered.

"What are you waiting for?"

"I ain't sure, but I'll know it when I see it."

The breeze off the river was cool and refreshing. Puffy white clouds drifted by, leaving plenty of blue sky and warm sunshine. Horns honked; a small Cessna pulling a Reds banner droned overhead; boisterous fans yelled at each other as they crowded around the entrance. The whole scene was noisy and exciting, not quiet like at home, where it was just Mona or some dumb soap on TV.

After several minutes, Bryan said, "There!" He pointed to a woman leading several boys about their age. "We'll pretend we're with them. Keep your head down. There's cameras everywhere."

Bryan turned up the collar of his jacket and fell in behind the group. As he followed, Alex held his breath, his insides quivering. The woman handed the attendant a fistful of tickets. He scanned them one at a time and counted the kids.

"Let's go!" Without looking back, Bryan took off running past the other boys. Alex hesitated for a couple of seconds before adrenaline kicked in. He ran too.

"Wait!" the ticket taker hollered.

The boys sped through the gate past folks milling around the stadium and didn't stop until they reached a crowd waiting in line at a beer vendor. Alex doubled over to catch his breath, his heart beating wildly.

Bryan glanced all around. "Ain't nobody chasing us now. Too busy. Watch out for guys with yella shirts talkin' into radios."

When Alex could breathe, he turned up his jacket collar, modeling his newfound friend. They roamed around the ring of the stadium, trying to avoid obvious cameras. Bryan bought them nachos to share. Every once in a while, they stopped to look at the field for a few minutes. But the game never seemed to be the point.

It was the most fun Alex had ever had. Bryan was the coolest guy ever.

"What happened to you?" Janet moved to within two feet of Alex's face; her eyebrows knitted together. "Have you been fighting?"

Alex looked round the room, at the floor, anywhere but at her. "I, uh . . . I—"

"I told you if you went out to let Mona know where you were at all times, but when I called, she said she had no idea. She had looked but couldn't find you."

"Mom, I'm twelve years old. I don't *need* a *babysitter.*"

"Apparently you do! Look at yourself. Where were you?"

"All I did was watch the parade!"

Her eyes flashed open like a camera lens. "You did what? Where?"

"Over by Music Hall."

"How did you get there?"

"I rode my bike."

Her jaw dropped. "You're telling me that while I was at the hospital, you rode your bike all the way to Music Hall?"

He nodded. "It's not that far."

"How did you know how to get there? And that doesn't explain the black eye!"

"You're always at the hospital. You don't care that it's spring break, and I'm supposed to hang around here and listen to Mona blab on the phone to her friends. I want to be with my friends!"

"What friends?"

"I have friends. Bryan is my friend."

"Is he the one who gave you a black eye?"

"No. You don't understand. Just leave me alone!" He stormed to his room and slammed the door.

Alex's door crept open, and the aroma of fresh popcorn drifted in. He rolled over and pulled the sheet over his head. Janet sat down on his bed, put the bowl of popcorn near his face, and pulled back the cover. "Can we talk?"

He wanted to stay mad, stand his ground, but he felt bad about yelling at his mother. And the popcorn smelled really good. "Okay."

"I know I'm gone an awful lot, but we discussed this. It won't last much longer. As soon as I'm done with residency, I won't be working as much."

"But I'm twelve. I don't need a babysitter."

"Mona's not a babysitter, because you're not a baby. But

when I have to work twelve-hour days while I'm in my residency, I do need someone I can depend on to take care of you like I would if I was home. It's just for a few more weeks. Then I'll be done and take my boards. I'll have mostly regular hours. We can do things together." She put her arms around him. "I'm sorry I haven't had much time for you, with medical school and all, but that's almost over. We'll have more time *and money*. We'll take a vacation, just the two of us. And next year, you won't need to risk your life biking to Over-The-Rhine. We'll watch the parade together."

Alex shoved a handful of the warm popcorn into his mouth.

Janet gave him a peck on the cheek. "I'm doing this for you, you know. I want so much for you. A good school, a good life. I don't want you to have to struggle like I have."

Alex nestled up against her and smiled.

"It's always been just you and me, hasn't it?" his mother said.

He nodded.

She embraced him and whispered in his ear, "You'll always be my main man. Always."

REAGAN

CHAPTER THIRTY-EIGHT

Wind howling, whistling, a loud slam against the outside of the house. Reagan forced her heavy eyelids open, but the room was pitch-black. She rose up on one elbow and tried to orient herself. *What time is it?* Instinctively she patted the bedside table, searching for her phone until she felt its familiar smooth surface. She pushed the home button. Dammit! Just a thin, red battery outline. Dead. No problem—it was Friday night, or Saturday morning. No need for an alarm. Matt was sleeping over at Charley's, and Lizzie slept late on weekends.

Good. She didn't want to wake up yet. If she rolled over in a hurry, she might be able to catch up with that dream. Within seconds she was dozing, not fully awake or sound asleep, pleasantly drifting from one image to another. Hilton Head . . . seagulls standing on one leg . . . warm sand underfoot . . . the surf pulling away from the shore.

A flash of lightning illuminated the room for a brief moment, followed by a roar of thunder. Reagan burrowed into her bedclothes, glad to be safe and dry, with that same floaty sense of well-being she'd had in Janelle's office. She was there, could smell a hint of cinnamon, could feel the sunshine coming through the windows, warming her face and shoulders. The car was there too, like before, on the street outside . . . the car window came down—that new song, "Thunder," was playing on the radio—the arm came out . . . but she didn't want to turn away like before. She snuggled against her pillow, and it was okay to look. The arm . . . the gun . . . the mark.

She moved closer, peeked around the gun to the arm: no birthmark, no burn, no scar. A tattoo. She jolted up. Of course it was a tattoo. Why didn't she realize that before? An odd place for a tattoo, the inside of the arm, but it was clearly a small, dark tattoo of a wolf's head with a skull in its mouth.

Creak.

What was that? Footsteps on the other side of her bedroom door. Apparently Scooter heard it too, because he was going nuts in his crate in Matt's room. Her heartbeat quickened. The light switch was all the way across the room, by the door. Why was it so dark? Another bolt of lightning illuminated her closed bedroom door.

That would explain the unusual darkness—no ambient light from Lizzie's room—but why was Reagan's door closed? She always left it open so she could hear the kids. She stood, groping for her clothes. No use. Wearing only a T-shirt and underwear, she left the warm bed and felt her way across the room, her thoughts rampaging. She touched the doorknob first and flipped the switch. The light flashed on, then off again.

"Dammit!" *This old house. The circuit always trips when you need light the most.*

She grabbed the useless lamp to use as a weapon, just in case; held it above her head; and slowly pulled on the antiquated door, which screeched open. She kept her left hand on the knob in case she needed to slam it shut again and peeked into the hallway. Light spilled from Lizzie's room, creating just enough brightness to keep Reagan from tripping over Georgie, the large stuffed bear that was lying in the middle of the hall floor. Nothing out of the ordinary.

She looked both ways, still holding the lamp, and crossed the hall into Matthew's room. Scooter stood up in his crate, barking.

"You're okay, boy. Calm down." Reagan squatted down and petted him until his barks trailed off to a whimper. Then she rose up, stepped into the hall, and looked through the glass door into Lizzie's room. Her daughter lay tangled with her colorful bedspread—lots of hearts and flowers—her dark hair splayed across her face. Reagan unlatched the door and went in. Her baby slept, softly snoring. Reagan's own breathing slowed and synced with Lizzie's—in and out. Her thoughts jumbled. She loved this child, and like most mothers would, she wanted to protect her. But there were times—those she didn't want to admit even to herself—when she wondered if being Lizzie's caretaker was going to be her life.

Scott had been adamant: Lizzie would always live with them. It hadn't been that difficult then, when he had taken on more than half the load. Anaya made it even easier. Lizzie essentially had three parents, at least one of whom was always around to take care of her. Reagan's parents—never supportive, even when she and Jordan were children—had distanced themselves from both daughters after Lizzie's birth. They seemed embarrassed by their granddaughter. Now Scott and Anaya were gone. She was alone. Jordan had forced her to confront a monumental dilemma. She suspected that was the reason she had been so upset with her sister, her dearest friend.

Wind shrieked outside, rattling the windows. Of course, the storm had been the source of the noise earlier. The old house creaked and moaned with the slightest provocation. She should be used to it by now. The knotted muscles in her neck and shoulders relaxed, and suddenly she was cold. She looked at her watch. One o'clock. She quietly closed Lizzie's door, unconsciously latched it behind herself, and went back to her room. There, by the light from the hallway, she plugged in her phone and went back to bed.

Reagan's dreams turned gloomy—menacing—and after a time she awoke again. Something wasn't right. The dim light from the hallway cast the bedroom objects into shadows. At the end of her bed a dark figure stood, holding something she couldn't make out. She screamed and bolted upright, her heart pole-vaulting into her throat.

After her initial moment of panic, she said, "What are you doing in here?"

Lizzie, clutching Georgie under her arm, crawled into bed with her mother.

Reagan took a deep breath and tried to calm herself as she pulled Lizzie close, snuggling against her back, her chin touching the top of her daughter's head, her arm over her chest. The child's hair was damp, her skin smooth and warm to the touch, her breath sour. Lizzie placed her small hand in her mother's and fell back asleep.

Reagan searched her memory. She had latched Lizzie's door; she was sure of it.

A heavy blow to Reagan's chest knocked the wind out of her. Her eyes popped open. Lizzie straddled her, the child's grinning face so close that Reagan couldn't focus. Her small hands held Reagan's face, one on each side, as she jabbered something undecipherable.

"And good morning to you too."

Lizzie giggled and bounced, causing Reagan's eyes to bulge. "*Oomph!* That hurts."

She gave Lizzie a gentle shove, sat up, and took a good look around. Sunlight streamed through the window, giving the old bedroom furniture a new, polished glow. Nothing scary there. Reagan got up, opened the window, and breathed in the fresh evergreen scent. The sky looked clear and clean, as if last night's storm had washed away all haze and pollution. She felt foolish for letting a storm frighten her in her safe, dry home. Debris from nearby trees cluttered her front yard.

"Okay, kid, let's go downstairs, let Scooter out, check on Bird, and have breakfast."

Scooter scampered out as soon as Reagan opened the back door. She put the coffee on, poured milk into a sippy cup for Lizzie, and went to the kitchen window. Broken twigs clustered under Bird's tree, but his house hung straight and stable, in its usual place. Bird hopped from limb to limb, appearing to survey the area himself for any damage.

Reagan enjoyed the aroma of freshly brewed coffee and lingered over her second cup while Lizzie ate pancakes. Then, her empty plate pushed aside, she made notes about what to say to Ron Gabriel about the tattoo. It was possible she'd been dreaming, but she didn't think so. She was pretty sure she had seen that tattoo on the gunman's arm.

The sequence of events last night had been scary, but she'd seen nothing scary this morning, and she chided herself for panicking the night before. She wasn't a wuss. She had never been afraid to be alone.

"Ipa," Lizzie said to her mother, her eyes gleaming, a maple syrup drip on her chin.

"No iPad until after you get dressed." Reagan refilled her coffee, helped Lizzie wipe her face and hands, and followed her upstairs, supporting Lizzie with one hand and clutching her coffee with the other. At the threshold of Lizzie's room, Reagan stopped abruptly and screamed. The cup slipped from her hand, spilling coffee on the carpet.

"What the hell!"

Her arms and legs turned rubbery. There on Lizzie's bed, propped against her pillow, was her rag doll, Annie.

ALEX

CHAPTER THIRTY-NINE

Avoiding the heavy pedestrian traffic, Alex carefully maneuvered his Mustang down Clifton's main drag, past sleek little foreign cars parked alongside jalopies. A bald man wearing grungy clothes approached the driver's window to ask for a handout. Alex swerved and raised his window, barely missing a parked Volkswagen on his right.

"Weirdo. You should've taken him out," Bryan grumbled. A group of demonstrators stood on the sidewalk in front of a family-planning clinic—chanting, waving signs, and offering brochures to pedestrians, most of whom ignored them and hurried on. A dark-skinned woman wearing a red-and-gold sari crossed in front of them. On a bicycle, a young man with powerful quadriceps glided along the sidewalk, steering with one hand, a backpack slung casually over his shoulder. The street was alive with people.

"You never know what you're gonna see down here, it's so close to UC," Bryan said. "There's a cool head shop two blocks down that way."

Alex sighed. "We're never going to find a place to park."

"There's a Kroger a block over. We can park in the lot and walk."

"That's a long way back to the car." Alex surveyed the scene.

"Bruh, nobody's gonna fuck with us. You're paranoid."

"Maybe, but we're coming out with a lotta dope."

"We'll put it in my backpack. Regular college kids. Nobody'll know," Bryan said.

Alex made a left turn, then pulled his car into the crowded lot and parked between an SUV and a van. A dark sedan with tinted windows pulled into the lot behind them. Bryan glanced at it briefly before turning away.

"The shop's over this way." Bryan pointed as they got out of the car and locked the doors.

Inside, the old building had scuffed wood floors and dingy walls. An acrid smell hung in the air. The boys casually browsed through the jumbled merchandise: rock posters, incense burners, T-shirts, fake books and pop cans for hiding a stash, an assortment of bongs. A silent storekeeper watched them suspiciously from behind a paperback. They killed half an hour paging through *High Times* and admiring ingenious little pipes disguised as fountain pens and compacts that easily tucked into a pocket.

"What time are we supposed to be there?" Alex whispered.

"Three thirty."

"It's three thirty now."

"Okay, I'm ready. Cool shop though, ain't it?" Bryan replaced a magazine, and the boys left under the watchful eye of the clerk. After a short walk they stood at the front door, waiting.

Alex unconsciously picked at flaking paint and peeled off a long strip as the door opened a crack.

One hostile eye glared out. "Whatcha doing?" Mose growled.

"Shit!" Alex dropped the paint strip and wiped his hands

on his jeans. "It was coming off. I just helped it a little. Uh, probably needs to be stripped."

Mose opened the door wider and grunted recognition when he looked past Alex to Bryan. "I got your stuff."

"All of it, I hope," Bryan said.

He nodded. "You're taking a lot. You bein' careful?"

"Of course. Always."

"What about him?" He nodded toward Alex.

Alex swallowed hard.

"I told you, he's cool. We go way back, man."

Mose leaned into Bryan's face, then Alex's. "Just so you know, I don't do time. Ain't gonna go good for nobody tries to take me down if they go down. Got it?"

The hairs on Alex's neck stood on end, but Bryan seemed undisturbed.

"Dude. Take you down? Ain't nobody gonna take you down." Bryan shook his head. "We got a good thing going here. We're careful. Besides, who'd have the balls to take you down? You're getting paranoid, you know that?" he said as he entered the house. "You really oughta lay off the coke."

Alex hesitated. Bryan sure had nerve.

Mose showed the boys to the kitchen, then disappeared into a back room. When he returned, he was carrying an empty Nestlé candy case the grocery store had discarded. He unpacked several plastic bags, some filled with weed and others with white powder. Bryan opened a bag with the powder, dipped his finger in, and rubbed it on his gums. He fluttered his eyebrows and grinned.

Mose transferred the bags into Bryan's backpack as the boys watched. "You want any Big H?"

Bryan shook his head. "No, man." He slapped a stack of bills onto the table and zipped up his backpack. "See ya."

"Yeah," Mose grunted as he counted the money.

Bryan, who had not had a book in his bag the whole school

year, hoisted the backpack over his shoulder, flipped his hair out of his eyes, and walked out of the house and down the street toward the car, quickly blending into a background of rushing students.

Alex hurried alongside him. "Why does he hate me?"

"He don't like rich kids, I guess. Mostly he's just paranoid."

After leaving Clifton, Alex drove to BW3 and parked next to Bryan's Pontiac, which they'd left there before going to Mose's. The two boys sat in Alex's Mustang for a few minutes, sharing a joint, talking.

"I'll unload a lot of this before Randy's party Saturday night," Bryan said. His eyes darted to the rearview mirror each time a car drove in.

"You waiting for somebody?"

"I thought maybe Stephanie might show up. I told her I'd be here."

"You getting anywhere with her?"

Bryan shrugged. "Her ol' man's a real dick. Don't let her out much. We've gotten high after school a few times, but that's about it. She bought some weed from me. Shit, I tried to give it to her, but she insisted on paying for it, like she don't want to be in debt to me." He smiled. "I like that in a woman."

"Yeah. She's different."

"How much you want of this?" Bryan asked.

"Three bags."

Bryan opened his backpack but looked distracted by something in the rearview mirror. He moved closer to the mirror before eagerly lowering the passenger-side window. Stephanie pulled her car in alongside Alex's Mustang.

"Hey," Bryan yelled.

She lowered her window. "Hi. What's happenin'?"

"Not much. Come on over." Bryan passed the backpack to Alex, got out of the car, and opened Stephanie's door. She casually swung her legs out of the car, looked up, and smiled coyly. She wore a long-sleeved sweater and a short skirt that exposed smooth, tanned legs, a strawberry tattoo on her ankle, and a silver ankle bracelet.

"Okay. For a while," she said.

Bryan got into the back of the Mustang, offering Stephanie the front passenger seat. Her long black hair fell loosely around her face. Bryan passed her the joint.

She rolled her eyes and waved the joint away. "Can't today. My dad might be able to tell."

Alex handed the backpack to Bryan.

"What're you guys up to?" Stephanie asked.

"Oh, just making a little transaction," Bryan boasted, hanging over the front seat, grinning.

"Hmm. Looks like a big transaction to me."

"I've got anything you want," he said as he handed three bags to Alex.

"How about coke?" she asked.

"All you want."

"Wow. How do you get all that stuff?" She eyed the contents of the backpack.

Bryan cocked his head. "I have important connections. If you want something I don't have, I can get it." He flipped his hair out of his eyes. "How 'bout we go out Saturday night? We could go out to eat and then to Randy's party."

"Bryan, I told you, you would never pass my dad's inspection."

"What about Alex? He's a rich preppy kid. Would your ol' man let you go out with Alex? He could pick you up and meet me someplace."

Stephanie laughed. "I don't know. Why don't I just meet you guys at the party?"

Bryan looked dejected. "I guess."

"I'll tell you one thing," she said. "I'm out of there as soon as I turn eighteen. No more letting my dad run my life."

"Yeah. Me too."

"Me three," Alex joined in.

"Problem is, I don't know what I'll do to make money yet. I put a job application in at Walgreens, but they only pay minimum wage. I've got a little money saved, but not much. It's really stressing me out. I'll be eighteen in three months, and I can't wait to get out on my own."

"No problem," Bryan told her.

"What do you mean?" She cocked her head and gave him a crooked smile.

"I got lots of money. I could help you out. We're friends, ain't we?"

She shook her head. "No, Bryan. You know I don't want to be indebted to anybody. I want to earn my own way. Maybe the way you do. You could introduce me to the guy you work for. I could supply the kids from my old neighborhood, just until I make enough to move out on my own—like three months. Don't worry. I wouldn't cut into your business."

Bryan shook his head. "No. Mose is a bad dude. I wouldn't want you to get mixed up with him."

She laughed again. "Mose. That's a funny name."

"For a fucking funny character. Big dude in Clifton. But he's strange. Real paranoid." Bryan gave her a long, appraising look and grinned. "Besides, he might decide to keep you."

Stephanie shrugged. "Well, I guess I have some time to figure out what I'm going to do. I have to get out of there, but right now I have to get back. I'll probably see you guys at Randy's. I'll have my coke money with me then, okay?"

Both boys watched her get out of the car, their eyes lingering on the hem of her skirt.

Saturday night, several high school kids stood around the

firepit in Randy's small backyard. The fire was great because the night had turned cold when the sun went down.

"Alex, have a drink." Randy handed him a beer. "How you doing?"

"No complaints." Heavy metal blared through unseen speakers. Alex took a gulp of the beer and scanned the crowded yard. "Where's Bryan?"

Randy chuckled. "Bryan's been busy dealing since he got here. Must be making a fortune."

Alex shrugged. That was Bryan. Obsessed with making money.

"I suppose you heard the latest," Randy said.

Alex shook his head. "What's that?"

"That hot new girl, Stephanie—you know who I mean? She's a senior at Norwood."

Randy had his full attention. "Yeah?"

"She's not in school anymore. Word's going around that she's a narc."

"A narc?" Alex's stomach bottomed out. "Are you sure?"

"That's what I heard. Nobody's real sure, but the rumor's going round."

"Shit! I better tell Bryan."

"Why? Did he sell to her?"

Alex pushed his way through the crowd of kids and found Bryan in the middle of a group, laughing with the others. Alex jerked him out of the ring and dragged him to a corner of the yard. Trip followed.

"What the fuck?" Bryan shouted to be heard over the music.

"You're in trouble, man. Big trouble!"

"What's the fucking *problem*?"

The music stopped abruptly. Several people close by turned and stared at Bryan.

Alex moved closer to Trip and Bryan and whispered, "I just heard Stephanie's a narc."

The music blared again. Bryan's face turned red and he screamed, "Bullshit! Steph's no narc!"

He turned to walk away, but Alex grabbed him by the elbow and steered him toward the front yard, where it was quieter, darker. "How can you be so sure she's not?"

"What makes you so fucking sure she is?"

"There's something different about her, man. For one thing, she wouldn't let you come to her house." Alex scrutinized Bryan. Maybe that wasn't a valid point. Even he no longer let Bryan come to his house.

"That's 'cause her ol' man's a dickhead, just like my ol' man, and yours." Bryan's voice softened, like doubt was settling in.

"Did you sell to her?" Trip asked.

Bryan nodded.

"That's another thing, Bryan. You told me yourself she wouldn't let you give it to her. How many girls you know wouldn't take drugs for free?"

Bryan ran his fingers through his hair. "I need to think. Let's get the fuck outa here." They walked in silence to Trip's Nissan. When they opened the car door, the dome light illuminated Bryan's ashen face, his glassy eyes. He looked sick. "I should have known. I should have fuckin' known she didn't really like me. Just a fuckin' bust!"

"Maybe not," Trip said. "This could be just gossip. You know how guys love to start rumors. If her cover's blown, why hasn't she already busted you if she's really a narc?"

"Maybe she planned to do it tonight, at the party. She knew I was gonna be here with lots of dope."

Alex stared at Bryan. "Or maybe she wasn't as interested in busting you as someone else. She seemed awful curious about who supplies you."

Bryan punched the back of the driver's seat. "Fuck! Let's go to Clifton. Fuck, fuck, fuck."

"No, Bryan, you gotta stay away," Alex said. "If Stephanie really is a narc, the cops may be watching you."

"I can't. I gotta warn him. He'll kill me if he's busted."

Trip said, "We'll be in my car. They won't connect it to Bryan."

I shouldn't go anywhere near there. That dude hates me. The nagging thought tormented Alex all the way to Clifton, but he couldn't turn back now.

Trip wound through the narrow streets, stopping for pedestrian traffic, still heavy at this hour. Students mostly, hitting the bars on Jefferson.

"What are you gonna tell him?" Alex asked.

"Fuck if I know, but we gotta warn him."

Trip turned onto Mose's street and stopped abruptly. Up ahead, blue lights flashed in the darkness.

"Fuck!" Bryan shrieked.

"Maybe it isn't for him," Alex said. "Get closer. Just drive by the house."

"Hell no, man! Get the fuck outa here!"

Trip pounded the steering wheel. "I can't turn around now, and I can't just sit here. Be cool. We have to drive by." Trip slowed to a crawl.

Bryan dove for the floorboard. "I don't want nobody seein' me."

Trip negotiated past the first of two squad cars idling in the street. It was a tight squeeze. As they pulled even with the second, two officers escorted Mose out the front door of his house, his arms cuffed behind him. Trip stopped the car to let them pass. Just as the police stuffed Mose's massive body into the second squad car, he looked up, into Trip's car, and pierced Alex with a glare full of rage.

REAGAN

CHAPTER FORTY

Reagan tried to convince herself she had overreacted. Spring storms were often violent, loud enough to wake her from a sound sleep. That alone could be disorienting. She should be grateful the dreadful winter was finally coming to an end.

A gentle cross breeze drifted through the house, bringing with it the pleasant fragrance of early spring flowers. Sunlight streamed through the living room windows. Nothing at all scary.

But the doll—she couldn't stop obsessing about that doll. Maybe there was an explanation for how Annie had reappeared after she and Matt had both searched for her for days, but she couldn't think of one. And Lizzie's door . . . she always latched that door, a safety thing, the only way they had been able to keep Lizzie from wandering around at night, getting into trouble. The only way the rest of the family had been able to get a good night's sleep for years.

She dreaded calling Sonny. She loved him, but there were times he steamrolled over her. Scott never tried to control her, but somehow Sonny thought the promises he had made to

Scott gave him license to tell her what to do and how to do it. It was nice, of course, to have someone she could depend on. A confirmed bachelor with no kids, he loved Matthew and Lizzie as if they were his own.

"Hi, Sonny, are you busy?"

"I'm at work. What's up?"

"Do you remember Lizzie's doll, Annie? The rag doll with the red hair and blue dress?"

"You mean the one she carried under her arm everywhere she went for months. Of course I do. Come to think of it, I haven't seen it lately. Why? If she's having a meltdown 'cause she can't find her doll, tell her I'll take her shopping and buy her another one. Like she doesn't have a room full as it is."

Reagan could sense Sonny's eye roll from across town. "The day she disappeared, did she have it with her at McDonald's?" she asked.

"No. She didn't have anything."

"Are you sure? Maybe the officer with her saw it and stuck it in her bag for safekeeping . . . or maybe Lizzie dropped it in one of the squad cars?"

"She didn't have the doll. What's this about, Rea?"

"Something strange happened last night. I heard creaking—"

"No kidding. Creaking in that old house. What a shock."

"Will you listen a minute?"

"Sorry. Go ahead."

"I thought someone was outside my bedroom door last night. I heard creaking, like footsteps, and Lizzie got out of her room this morning . . . and Annie was in her bed." Her voice climbed a couple of octaves. She hated that.

"So, what are you thinking?"

"I think whoever took Lizzie returned her doll last night."

Sonny hesitated. "I'll be there in a few minutes."

Simultaneous relief and dread flooded through her. Was

that even possible? Half an hour later, a car pulled into her driveway. Reagan met Sonny on the porch. Scooter burst through the screen door, pranced around him, yapped, jumped on his leg. Sonny crouched down and ruffled the dog's fur.

"Some guard dog you are. Where were you last night?" Sonny looked up at Reagan. "Do you really think a stranger could have broken into the house without him raising hell?"

"He was asleep in Matt's room in his crate. He raised hell alright, but he always does during a storm." Sonny stood up, erect in his police blues, hands on his hips. "Are you sure it's the same doll?"

She shoved it into his hand. "It's the same doll. Trust me."

He scrutinized Annie. "Maybe you just thought she had it with her that day."

"She had the doll with her on the porch swing the day she disappeared. I'm positive. I was on the phone, but I watched her through the window. She was swinging with Annie."

"Could she have dropped it somewhere around here before she walked away?"

"Maybe, but how would it have gotten into the house? Onto her bed?"

"Where's Matt?"

"He spent the night with Charley. They're going to the zoo today."

"He probably came across the doll and gave it back to Lizzie without telling you."

"No. I called him already. He said he hadn't seen it either. Sonny, it might have been the storm that woke me up last night, but the creaking in the hallway sounded like someone walking by my bedroom, so I got up to check on Lizzie. She was sound asleep. I chalked the noise up to the storm."

Reagan crossed her arms and regarded Sonny. "When I left Lizzie's room, I'm *sure* I latched the door, but after a while she got in the bed with me. This morning the doll was in her bed."

"Before I left the station, I talked to Michelle, the officer you met at McDonald's. She reminded me that Lizzie was never in her car. Someone at McDonald's phoned after Lizzie walked in unaccompanied. Michelle didn't see a doll 'cause Lizzie didn't have a doll. The only Norwood police car that child was in that night was mine, and there was no doll in my car. Were your doors locked?"

She had known he would ask that. "Yes, of course. I locked them both before I went to bed, and they were still locked from the inside when we got up this morning."

Lizzie came out onto the porch grinning and held her arms up for Sonny.

"Not now, Lizzie Lu, Uncle Sonny is working." He lifted his gaze to Reagan. "I'll take a look around outside. If there was a prowler, the storm probably washed away any sign, but I'll check it out. You try to figure out if anything is missing. Oh, I also asked Jerry to have a talk with Bryan Butler. Ask what he was doing last night."

Reagan took Lizzie inside. After a few minutes, she went to the front door to investigate a loud slam outside. Sonny had leaned a ladder against the house. In the living room, Lizzie turned on her iPad to "Wild World" loud enough to be heard next door.

Reagan poured herself a cup of coffee and sat down at the table. Bryan Butler. As a seventh grader he had been a sad kid. She had taken him under her wing, staying after school when she could, tutoring him. She had reached out to his parents twice, but they didn't want to meet with her—unusual for the parents of her students.

After an hour or so, Sonny walked down the inside stairs, his expression grim. "Yep, I think someone got in by climbing onto the porch roof and jimmying open Matt's window."

Reagan's jaw dropped. Chill bumps raced down her arms.

"The ground's soft, and he left clear footprints. Some kind of athletic shoes."

"Oh my god! Someone really did break in!"

"Looks that way. The storm washed away most of the evidence, but the porch roof shielded the flower bed from the heaviest rain. I'm going to cast a print, see if we can figure out which brand. It's possible we could match it if we catch the guy. It has to be the perp who took Lizzie, trying again to scare you. Since nothing's missing, I can't see any other motive." Sonny shook his head. "He's got some balls, climbing up the front of your house when you're at home." He drilled her with his eyes. "It's a damn good thing Matt wasn't there last night."

Her face flushed. Someone had actually broken into her house. It was not her imagination. She swallowed hard. "Sonny, those doors were locked, I'm sure of it. And nothing was taken . . . a doll was left."

"I told you not to get involved in this shit, Rea. Someone broke into your home when you guys were sleeping. What if your son had been in his bed when this . . . I don't know who . . . climbed in that window? It's all related to that shooting, I know it is. I told you not—"

She heard her father's voice and she was ten again, trying to think of ways to escape.

"I know you, Rea. You just can't believe there are bad people out there. People who would harm you or your kids. But I'm here to tell you there are. I don't want Matt walking to school alone. If he can't ride with you and Lizzie, I'll take him myself."

His words hammered into her brain, making her head pound.

"Another thing: Jerry called. They couldn't find Butler, but they're looking for him. I know he's mixed up in this somehow, so I asked Jerry to bring him in when they find him. I'll stay here tonight, crash on the sofa—"

"No, you won't!"

"It's no problem. I promised Scott I'd take care of you—"

"I don't want—"

"Maybe next time you'll listen to me, Rea."

"You aren't listening to me! This is my home. You will not crash on my sofa. Lizzie and Matt are children. I am not."

Sonny took a step back and raised his hands. "Hey, you called *me*, remember?"

"I know I called you, to ask a question—not have you chastise me for being a responsible citizen."

He shrugged. "I don't know what you want from me then."

The expression he gave her, that damned look of superiority with his nose in the air and his eyebrow arched, sent her over the edge. "I'll tell you what I want. Just do your *fucking job!*"

Bird stared at her with his *I can't believe you said that* expression, then stared back at the joint she'd just rolled. Not even noon. Was she going to light it? Was it being a responsible adult to smoke illegal weed? It's not like she actually bought it from some connected gangster—it was a friend she'd known for years. More like sharing.

Matt and the boys planned to spend the day at the zoo. He wouldn't know. Bird wouldn't tell; he never said anything. She was on her own.

ALEX

CHAPTER FORTY-ONE

"Aren't you going to answer your phone?" Frances asked, after jerking a headphone away from Alex's ear. "It's been ringing nonstop!"

Alex looked at her through a red-eyed haze, nodded, and listened as she mumbled her way out of his room: "Have to stop what I'm doing when I'm tired and trying to get through cleaning. Always got those things stuck on his ears."

He rolled across his bed, grabbed the phone from the floor. "Yeah?"

"Hey, man, whatcha doing?" Bryan whispered into the phone. He sounded funny, nervous.

"Just hanging. Where've you been?"

"Around. I'm sorta trying to avoid Mose? You know what I mean. How 'bout meeting me and Trip at BW3 later?"

Alex glanced at his phone and struggled to bring the time into focus. Four thirty. "Sure. When?"

"Tonight."

"All right. When tonight?"

"After dark. About eight."

"Okay. Mom and Jake are going to a hospital fundraiser. They'll be out late." He started to hang up, but Bryan stopped him.

"Don't mention where you're going, man. Who you're gonna be with."

Alex snorted. "Bryan, I never mention I'm gonna be with you."

The phone went dead. Bryan was gone. Strange of him to say that.

I'm being paranoid.

Alex started to get up, wobbled slightly, decided to wait for a while. He clamped his headphones back onto his ears and turned up the volume.

Megadeth pulsed from Alex's stereo as he drove down Madison Road to BW3. He was getting annoyed with a dark SUV dogging him. Seemed like it had been following him for a while. He stared into the rearview mirror but saw only headlights. Fear seized him, then absurdity.

I'm really paranoid.

Just to make sure, he made a quick right at the next street, keeping one eye on the mirror. The SUV turned right. Queasiness gripped him. The area was darker and more deserted than Madison Road, mostly warehouses that were closed that time of night. Confused about where he was, he took a left, trying to get back to Madison. When the SUV didn't turn, he breathed a sigh of relief.

At the next stop sign, the SUV showed up again. Just a coincidence, he told himself, until it pulled within a foot of his rear bumper. Intimidating. Probably some bullies from Northside trying to pick a fight.

They don't like kids from Indian Hill.

He sped up, the SUV sped up; he slowed, the SUV slowed.
Fuck!

He stared in his mirror, trying to make out the occupants.
No use. Just outlines behind glare. Two of them. He accelerated again, but the SUV matched his speed, staying right on
his bumper. He moved to the right lane. The car ducked into
the right lane behind him.

Fucking assholes!

He shot them the bird in the rearview mirror.

The SUV flashed its brights, blinding Alex as it zoomed
past his Mustang and swerved diagonally in front of his left
bumper and stopped, blocking a getaway. Too late, he saw
Mose in the passenger seat. Alex locked his car door. His irri-
tation streaked into terror.

Mose got out of the SUV swinging a baseball bat, and with
one powerful swoop shattered Alex's door window into a million pieces. Glass flew all over him, pricking his skin, settling
in his hair, sticking to his clothes. Stunned, he couldn't think.
He stared dumbly at Mose's forearm as it reached into the window and unlocked the door.

"You goin' for a ride, fuckface." Mose grabbed Alex by the
shoulder and pulled him from the car.

This can't be happening.

Mose was bigger than Jake, a Hulk Hogan replica; he would
make three of Alex. Totally powerless, Alex was petrified by
fear.

Mose shoved him into the back seat and the SUV shot forward, speeding like a bullet onto Madison. The blond girl was
driving and didn't look at him. Mose sat sideways, his back to
the door, so that he could see Alex as well as the cars behind
them and the road ahead.

"I told you, be careful. Now look what you done. You set
me up!"

Alex tried to answer, to say he didn't do it, but his throat tightened.

"Pull in there," Mose told the blond. "Where that big yella sign is."

They pulled through an open gate into a lot inside a tall chain-link fence. Their headlights shone on a weathered wooden building that looked like a warehouse with a large garage door in front. Mose got out and pulled a cord hanging by the door. The door creaked open. The blond drove the SUV inside, concealing them from passersby, from anyone who would help Alex if he called out.

His thoughts raced. He had no idea where they were. Mose was going to kill him, and nobody would know where to find his body. *Shit!*

He thrashed his arms wildly as Mose dragged him out of the car. Mose brought his powerful fist up into Alex's solar plexus, thrusting him several inches off the floor. Pain—heavy, suffocating—racked his lungs. His eyes watered. Choking, coughing, Alex gasped for air, but his lungs wouldn't fill. Another gasp, a tiny breath, then another vehement blow. He grabbed his chest and doubled over, gagging, certain he would suffocate.

"You wanna impress girls, huh? You wanna show 'em what a big shot you is! Well, let 'em see your pretty face after this!" A mighty hooking blow under the chin sent Alex reeling, slamming him against the SUV.

His mouth filled with warm, coppery-tasting blood. A blow from the other fist caught the left side of his face. The drab surroundings exploded into a kaleidoscope of color. He went down, hearing Mose's garbled ranting, but he couldn't understand him. Blunt, heavy boots kicked him in the chest, the legs, the arms. The pain and Mose all faded into blackness.

• • •

Acceleration, slowing, zipping from one lane to another, roused him. Rough, dirty carpet chafed his face. His head pounded, every muscle in his body hurt. His chest burned when he inhaled. He couldn't breathe through his nose, and broken teeth and swelling crowded his mouth. Blood gurgled in his throat as he gasped for air.

Bits and pieces of conversation floated into his consciousness, then receded, like ocean surf on a moonless night. The blackness came again, washed over him. Later shrill, nervous chatter of two people made it past the buzzing in his ears.

"What'll we do with him?" It was Bryan's voice, sounding far away. "What if he dies?"

"Hell, what do you think we should do?" Trip asked.

"There's the river. We could dump him there."

"You've lost it, man. You know that?" Trip's voice sounded incredulous. "I can't believe you let this happen. We have to call the police."

"Oh yeah? Well, what's your fucking father gonna say this time? Think Daddy's money will buy us out of this one?"

"We can say Alex called us."

"Sure. Cops will believe Mose stood idly by while Alex gave us directions *in his condition* to private property we had no fucking business being in or even knowing about. Private property that'll lead 'em back to Mose. He's already pissed about us showing up. If you hadn't been with me, he'd for sure have killed Alex and me both."

Again the voices faded, and Alex slipped into blackness.

Bryan! The thought awakened him. Bryan must have set him up. It had to be. He tried to move, but the pain was unbearable. He moaned.

"What was that?"

Trip's voice made it past the buzzing in his ears. The movement slowed.

"He's waking up." Trip leaned over the front seat and touched Alex's arm. "Say something, man."

Alex could only groan.

"Bryan, we've got to take him to the emergency room. He needs help! This is your fault anyway. You're the one who got mixed up with a narc."

"Fuck. Mose hates Alex. He wouldn't have believed it wasn't him who got 'em fingered. Even if he knew it was me, he would've got him too."

"If you don't take him to the hospital, I'll call the police myself."

Bright light flooded the back seat of Bryan's Pontiac; it warmed his face, his eyelids. The car slowed. He struggled to open his swollen eyes. Glare from the bright University Hospital sign shot daggers to the back of his skull. He squeezed them closed again.

"Shit! There's a squad car at the entrance," Bryan shrieked and accelerated.

"You've got to stop. He needs help."

Disconnected from the body on the floorboard, Alex watched himself in his own nightmare, wondering how it would end. Blood trickled from his nose before his thoughts faded.

Someone tugged at his arms, trying to lift him off the floorboard.

"You gotta help, man. Come on!" Trip sounded breathless.

Alex wrenched his eyes open to slits and tried to focus.

"Alex, get up. I can't lift you by myself." Trip pushed his back as he rolled Alex up from the floorboard and sat him upright, his legs splayed out the door. White-hot pain almost took him back to darkness. He moaned.

"We got to hurry!" Bryan said. "His ol' lady will call the

cops for sure if she sees my car in the drive. I'll drive around the block once, then pick you up. That should do it."

"All right," Trip gritted his teeth. "Alex, can you stand up?"

Alex moaned.

"Come on, man. Let's try." Trip inched him through the car door and placed his feet on the driveway. "Okay, let's stand." He threw one of Alex's arms over his shoulder and helped him teeter upward.

Waves of nausea from the pain gripped him. He motioned for Trip to stop, doubled over, retched from the pit of his stomach, puking bile and blood into some marigolds planted by the driveway. Through watery, swollen eyes, Alex saw the front of his house and wavered, his knees weak. He straightened again, leaned heavily on Trip, and shuffled to the front porch. Trip carefully leaned him against the doorbell, then vanished.

"What?" Jake responded to the irritating nudging. "What is it?"

"It's the phone," Janet answered in the raspy, feeble voice of half sleep. "For you."

"Why would it be for me?" he snapped. "It's always for you in the middle of the night."

Jake sat up on the side of the bed, shook his head, tuned in to the unrelenting, grating noise from downstairs. "It's not the phone, Jan, it's the doorbell." He looked at the clock. "It's three thirty in the morning. Who the hell—"

Janet shot up. "I'll go." She grabbed her robe and tied it tightly around her waist.

"I'll go too." Adrenaline shocked him awake.

Jake led the way downstairs. He looked out the window and saw no one, heard nothing but the eerie, incessant call of the doorbell. Cautiously, with Janet looking over his shoulder, Jake opened the door and barely caught the sixteen-year-old who fell into his arms.

Janet's scream pierced the quiet of Shawnee Run.

JAKE

CHAPTER FORTY-TWO

The ambulance sped down the interstate—siren screaming, lights flashing. Jake was right on its tail. It was early morning, before dawn, and the trauma center at University Hospital was a chaotic scene, uniforms going in and out from every direction: fire department EMTs, police officers, doctors, nurses. Alex's ambulance pulled in behind another already in the bay. Medical personnel who were lined up to receive the injured looked stunned when they recognized Janet, her ashen face, her rigid expression. The staff repeatedly checked on her, offering their support.

Jake put his arm around her shoulder, and she leaned against him. After a while, a police officer approached them. "Dr. Petersen and—"

"Yes. This is my husband, Jake Dekker."

"I'm Officer Burke with the Cincinnati Police Department. I'm sorry you're going through this, but I need to ask you some questions. We can't get much out of your son. He tried to speak, mumbled a few unintelligible syllables, but nothing we could use. We've located his car, abandoned on a side street near Madison, the window busted out. That was no accident."

Janet blanched.

"Do either of you have any idea who would do this?"

"No. No idea," Janet said, her voice strained, hollow.

"He's in no condition to talk now, but we'll be back. We'll find whoever did this."

Jake nodded and tightened his arm around his wife.

Dr. William Witherspoon walked out from behind double doors. His stiff demeanor softened when he approached them. He put his hand on Janet's back. "He's got some serious cuts and bruises, and I'm concerned about internal injuries. I don't know the full extent of those yet. We're getting X-rays now, including a CT scan. Sit tight. We'll know more after we get the results."

"Thank you, Bill."

"You look beat, Janet. Need something for stress?"

"No, but thank you."

After a while, Dr. Witherspoon returned. He sat down beside Janet and took her hand. "When Alex was in X-ray, he stopped breathing and we had to resuscitate him."

Janet whimpered.

The doctor gave her a sympathetic smile. "We got him back, but we're sending him to ICU after we finish the tests and get him cleaned up and made comfortable. We're having a helluva time getting all the glass off him. It's in his hair and on his clothes. There are even splinters in his socks. He's in a great deal of pain, too."

"Thank you."

"You should go home and get some rest. We'll call you the moment anything changes, I promise. He's stable right now, and the team's busy with him, so there's nothing you can do."

Janet shook her head. "I couldn't. Really."

Dr. Witherspoon nodded. "The waiting room outside ICU

is reasonably comfortable. You can hang out there if you like. Janet, we'll take good care of him. Don't worry."

Jake and Janet talked very little on the way upstairs to ICU. The resentments of the last year festered—the unvoiced accusations, bricks in the wall between them.

It was quieter on the fifth floor, and the doc was right. It was okay.

Jake asked her, "You want coffee?"

When she said no, they settled down and waited, each lost in thought. An elevator pinged in the hall. A staffer wheeled an elderly patient on a gurney past the waiting room. Jake's mother had been only forty when she was wheeled out of surgery the last time, but she looked old and pale like that patient. Thirty-two years ago now. Her gurney had rattled, while this one glided down the hallway without a whisper. Her hospital had smelled sour; this one smelled fresh and clean. This was different—Jake was no longer an eleven-year-old, dependent on the dying person on the gurney—but the feelings were the same. Fear, powerlessness, and the notion that he didn't matter.

Late the next day, Dr. Blythestone walked into the ICU waiting room. "Well, how's he doing?" the psychologist asked.

"How's he doing?" Jake's sarcastic voice pierced the quiet of the waiting room. Other visitors sat up, wide-eyed, anxiously looking from Jake to the doctor. "Didn't you say his behavior was just an adolescent thing? Well, your so-called professional nonadvice just about got him killed!"

Dr. Blythestone took a step back and frowned.

"Jake, please!" Janet grabbed Jake's arm. "This isn't his fault."

"We sent him to you because my wife trusted you to do your job."

"I know, and I'm sorry. Let's go into the consultation room and talk."

Dr. Blythestone led them into a small room off the waiting room. Once there, he spoke to Jake. "There's good reason people shouldn't treat family and friends. That should also go for family members of friends. I made some assumptions because Alex was Janet's son, and I shouldn't have. People are complicated. My primary judgment was that Alex was jealous of you. After all, he'd had his mother all to himself until you came along. But I misjudged him.

"I just read Alex's chart. The results of the blood work are in. He tested positive for an assortment of street drugs, including marijuana and cocaine. He needs more help than I can give him. He's too good a con. That's what he was doing with me—conning me. I see that now."

Janet dabbed at tears with the back of her hand. Dr. Blythestone's pale-blue eyes rested on her face for a moment. "Janet, no woman wants to hear that her child is an addict, but there's good treatment available. He's not a bad kid, really, but he's on a path to self-destruction. There's a program I've visited, been very impressed by, actually. Please check it out. It would be better to send him straight from the hospital when he's able to be discharged. Here's the number."

Tears streamed down Janet's face. Jake reached for the card Dr. Blythestone held.

Dr. Witherspoon came in later and confirmed that Alex had a litany of drugs in his system, but he also stressed that Alex's pain needed to be managed. They would worry about the addiction later.

ICU allowed two people at a time to visit briefly every four hours, but Jake stayed in the waiting room because Janet wanted to go in alone. That was fine with him. Alex was seldom conscious anyway, and even if he were, he wouldn't want to see Jake.

He wanted to get out of the hospital, get some exercise, go

back to work. Sitting in the waiting room all day was agony, but Janet needed support.

As if she could hear his thoughts, she looked at him. "You should go to work. There's really nothing you can do . . . but thank you for being here."

Thank you for being here? The way she said it struck him as odd, like she would thank a minister for stopping in, not her husband, her boy's stepfather. Where else would he be?

"Are you sure you don't need for me to stay?"

Janet appeared relieved. "No. You should go to work."

"Code blue, ICU" blared over the intercom. People in white stampeded into the ICU and chatter in the waiting room stopped. All eyes fixated on the door into the unit.

Jake sat back down next to Janet and took her hand.

Twenty minutes later—it seemed like hours—a doctor he hadn't met before came through the double doors. Jake's heart pounded hard enough to break a rib. The others in the waiting room watched as the doctor walked over to Jake and Janet and pulled up a chair.

"I'm Dr. Clawson. We had to resuscitate Alex again, but he's young and fit and we got him back pretty quickly. He's got a strong heartbeat now. We're good." She smiled at Janet. "Don't worry, we'll take good care of him."

Janet slumped against Jake. He exhaled. He'd been holding his breath since the doctor walked out. He pulled out his phone.

"Dave, I won't be coming in. I don't know how long it's going to be. Take care of things."

JAKE

CHAPTER FORTY-THREE

Three days later, Dr. Clawson sauntered out of the ICU, the most spring to her step since they'd been there. "Your young man seems to have turned a corner." She grinned. "I think we're on the road to recovery. Are you ready to go in?"

For the first time in days, Janet smiled like she meant it. She followed the doctor through the double doors into the ICU. Jake took a deep breath, rolled his head from side to side. The muscles in his upper back relaxed. Sounds of the hospital— the rumble of food carts, foot traffic in the hallway, muffled conversations—made their way back into his consciousness.

Janet seemed two inches taller when she came out of the ICU, and her face several shades lighter. "He actually complained about the food. Can you believe it?" She almost giggled as she looked at her watch. "It's only ten, Jake. You should go to work."

Jake suppressed a grin. "Are you sure you'll be okay?"

"Absolutely."

Jake got home around seven o'clock to a dark house and was

glad to be alone. They'd given Frances time off since "the event." He flicked on lights as he walked into the cold kitchen, checked the thermostat, turned up the heat, and opened the refrigerator. He pulled out a cold Heineken, opened it, and gulped.

It had felt good to be at work today and now good to be home, in no rush to get back to the hospital. He noticed a covered dish on the shelf under the ice maker and pulled it out. Roast beef, potatoes, and gravy. God bless Frances!

He slipped the meal into the microwave and set it for two minutes. Within seconds the kitchen smelled like Sunday dinner. He retrieved it from the microwave, uncovered the dish, then stuck his nose two inches from the roast and took a whiff. "Ahhh."

It was then he noticed the note sealed in a yellow envelope, Janet's stationery, sitting on its side, wedged between the salt and pepper mills on the kitchen island. The envelope read *Jake* in Janet's handwriting.

He didn't need to open it. He was pretty sure what it would say. Other than growing the business, finally making his father proud, all he had ever wanted was a happy family, children—especially a son—but maybe that wasn't in the cards for him. He got a fork and a knife out of the silverware drawer, sat on a stool at the island with his dinner, and opened the envelope with the knife.

Jake,

I don't know how to explain this, so I won't try. Alex and I will not be coming back to Indian Hill when he's discharged. I have leased a furnished apartment near the hospital. We'll go there. Maybe by the

time we see each other, I will better be able to express my thoughts, but right now I'm at a loss. I just know this is best. Please don't come to the hospital.
  Sorry,
  Janet

She didn't know how to explain herself. Huh. Neither did he. He read the note again, folded it, put it back in the envelope, and set it aside. With gusto, he dove into his dinner, enjoying every morsel. For months this had been his worst fear, but now . . .

The tension in his neck and back, the tension he'd grown accustomed to, the tension that caused his whole body to ache, slowly disappeared like the potatoes and roast beef.

JAKE

CHAPTER FORTY-FOUR

Matthew bounced on one foot, then the other, as Jake pulled items out of the duffel bag he had propped up on the Ramseys' kitchen table. He had picked Matthew up from school as he did every Thursday. Rather than go to one of their favorite parks, they planned to surprise Reagan and Lizzie with a special meal that Matthew, with Jake's help, would cook. Reagan had a meeting after school and would be late.

"First off, sport, we get in the mood." Jake pulled out a small CD player, and soon Pavarotti's beautiful tenor voice filled the room with "Santa Lucia."

"My mother, she was Italian." Jake threw up his hands, mocking her gestures and the way she talked. "Fast food. Terrible! Food is to be savored." He kissed his fingertips. "People should eat together . . . talk . . . listen to good music. For me, first I cook, then everything else." He gazed at Matthew, expecting him to turn up his nose at the music, and was pleasantly surprised when he didn't. His big green eyes were fixed on Jake.

Scooter pranced into the kitchen, jumped up with his

front paws on Matthew's legs, and howled. Matthew giggled. "He's trying to sing with the record."

"He thinks he's getting spaghetti," Jake said as he pulled out a Kroger bag stuffed with onions, garlic, a chunk of parmesan, ground beef, and pasta. Then he held up a package of bacon. He looked at Matthew. "Everything's better with bacon, don't you think?"

"That's what my dad used to say. He loved bacon."

"Your dad was a wise man."

Jake loved his Thursdays with Matthew, the way the kid beamed with excitement when he showed up, the way he leaned in to hear every word Jake said, the way he bounced on his feet as he listened. Jake had been a lonely kid and had never connected with his father. Maybe that was why he had no clue how to relate to Alex. It was easier with Matthew. Matthew was always glad to see him.

Last week he'd told Jake he wanted to cook dinner for his mom, the way Anaya use to, because she'd been really busy and stressed out. They'd planned the menu over several phone calls, and Jake was as eager as Matthew for the big surprise. It occurred to him that he may have gone a little overboard, especially with the bottle of Brunello he'd retrieved from his wine cellar. But, what the hell—you couldn't have Bolognese without a good red.

Next came a garlic press, a food chopper, and two aprons: one kid's size and brand new, which Jake slipped over Matthew's head and tied in the back; the other, for himself, well-worn and frayed, with writing across the chest.

"Did your dad like to cook?"

"He liked to grill. And on Sundays he'd fix pancakes or bacon and eggs and biscuits . . . before he got sick." Matthew glanced down at his hands.

"Did you help him?"

"Nah. I was just a kid then."

"Ah. My mom would pull a chair up to the kitchen counter for me to stand on and I would peel and chop vegetables. We'd sing along with the music and talk about everything. Those were my favorite memories. I was just a kid—your age. She called me her sous chef." Jake stopped unloading and looked at Matthew. "Right after my mom died, I couldn't stop thinking about her being sick—all caved in and stuff—but now what I remember most are the good times. Like when we cooked."

Their eyes met. Matthew's expression said it all. *Yes, I'm ready for the good memories.*

The next item in the bag was a book, *The Usborne First Cookbook*, which had simple recipes and large, colorful illustrations on every page.

"We have to have a cookbook with instructions."

Jake turned to the spaghetti page. A tiny man with a tall, poufy chef's hat twirled pasta around a fork as big as he was, while another cook spooned tomato sauce into a skillet. "You know, Matt, you can learn almost everything you need to know from books. I have about a million of them."

Matthew nodded. "We go online to learn new stuff."

Jake rolled his eyes. "Of course you do. But it's really nice to hold a book."

They spent the next hour preparing dinner with the cookbook propped open and a garbage pail next to the sink, washing up as they went. The music flowed from one Italian song to another. Jake delighted in the way Matthew leaned against him as they both stood at the counter, the boy on a step stool. He showed Matthew how to peel onions, use a garlic press, and grate cheese, and all the while they talked about their deceased parents, Sunday brunches, football games, picnics at Coney Island, and movie nights in the living room with popcorn and Milk Duds.

At Jake's direction, Matthew drizzled olive oil into a cast-iron skillet. As soon as it was hot, he threw in the onions and garlic. An explosion of incredible fragrances filled the room. Scooter jumped up on Matthew and almost knocked him off the stool.

Jake took a deep breath and kissed his fingers again before breaking into a wide grin. "Ah . . . *bello*."

He cut the bacon into bite-size pieces and when the onions were soft, added the meat, breaking up the ground beef with a wooden spoon. "O Sole Mio" competed with the clanging of skillets and pots.

Jake leaned closer to the window. "Matt, there's an odd-looking bird on the windowsill watching us."

"Oh, that's just Bird."

Odd the way it watched them with those big eyes. "It looks too small to be an owl, and that dark streak . . . What kind of bird is it?"

Matthew reared back and folded his arms across his chest. "It's a mystical bird."

Jake jerked his head back. "Oh . . . really?"

"Yeah. That's what my mom says, but I have to be honest with you, I don't tell my friends that. They'd just laugh at me. But my mom doesn't care if they laugh at her."

"We'd all be better off if we didn't care if people laughed at us," Jake said.

He dipped a spoon into the Bolognese sauce and tasted it. "Hmm. I think it needs something more. Get a spoon and have a taste."

Matthew moved his stool to the stove, stepped up, and submerged his spoon into the bubbling sauce. "Maybe salt?"

"Yes, that's what I was thinking. Salt . . . and something else." Jake walked to the duffel bag and fished around the bottom. "I must have left my spices, but I'm sure your mom won't mind if we borrow hers." He pointed to Reagan's spice rack. "I think we need a pinch of basil and a good amount of oregano."

REAGAN

CHAPTER FORTY-FIVE

An incredible bouquet of garlic and onions welcomed Reagan at the front door. A white tablecloth covered the dining room table, and a vase in the middle held a bunch of yellow daffodils she recognized from their front flower bed. Andrea Bocelli's amazing tenor carried "Con Te Partirò" throughout the house. The sights, the sounds, the smells overwhelmed her senses and made her eyes sting. What a marvelous surprise. She arched an eyebrow as she looked around, expecting Jordan to pop out of the kitchen to surprise her.

Instead Matthew appeared, wearing an apron and a wide grin. "Mom, I cooked dinner for you and Lizzie," he said, bouncing from foot to foot. "Don't worry. Jake helped. We have baloney sauce and spaghetti, garlic bread and salad and wine." Scooter pranced into the living room beside him, the fur around his mouth tinged with something red. "Jake taught me how to test the pasta—to see if it's all dented." He kissed his fingers like Jake had. "And we always listen to Italian music when we cook."

Reagan laughed as she helped Lizzie out of her backpack

and laid it on a cabinet by the front door. "Honey, Matt has made dinner for us, and you love spaghetti, don't you? But we have to wait until it's ready." She tossed her purse on the cabinet, next to the backpack.

"We're almost done. I need to set the table. Jake is opening the wine." Matthew jerked his eyebrows up. "It's an Italian red. It has to breathe." He abruptly stopped bouncing and looked at his mother. "I have no idea what that means."

Reagan followed Matthew to the kitchen, but he stopped her at the door. "No admission. Just men in here."

The air was warm, moist, and fragrant. Jake's back was to her as he counted out silverware. He wore snug jeans, a deep-blue shirt with his sleeves rolled up to his elbows, and a long apron tied in the back. He turned and gave her one of those charming, dimpled grins. "Always Kiss the Chef" was written across the front of the apron.

Wow! The first time a man had been in her kitchen in over a year. She felt an unexpected surge of excitement.

"Mom, can Jake have dinner with us?" Matthew held a stack of plates, his mother's favorites: blue and white with windmills.

Jake blushed and responded quickly, "Matt, this is supposed to be a family dinner. Your mother's been working all day, and she probably wants to eat and relax. Remember, this is her special evening."

Matthew ignored Jake. "Mom, please let's ask Jake to have dinner with us."

She didn't know what to say. Matthew was so excited; she didn't want to disappoint him. And, actually, she would love to have Jake stay—get to know him better, more as a friend than just Matthew's "big brother." But she didn't want to put him on the spot.

"Matt, of course, I'd be happy for Jake to have dinner with

us, but he's been with you all afternoon. He probably just wants to go home."

"Mom, please."

She smiled at Jake—a little too broadly, she feared. "Please, join us. We'd love to have you share this dented spaghetti and baloney sauce that you spent all afternoon helping Matt make for me and Lizzie. If Frances wouldn't mind, that is." She glanced at Lizzie, whose expression was inscrutable.

"Actually, I gave Frances the night off, and I don't have any place I have to be. I was planning on going home to a plate of delicious cheese and crackers, but I could be persuaded to forgo that appetizing dish and join you guys. If you insist."

"Well then, I insist."

"Oh boy," said Matthew. "I'll get another plate."

Lizzie signed, "Eat, eat."

"Baby, it's almost ready. Doesn't it smell wonderful?" Reagan held Lizzie's hand, trying to keep her out of the way as the guys finished up.

Lizzie looked skeptical but calm.

The master chefs scurried back and forth between the kitchen and dining room. Jake placed a large soup tureen of spaghetti and Bolognese sauce in the center of the table. Matthew set four places and brought out garlic bread and a large bowl of salad.

"I hope you like the sauce," Jake said as he poured wine into Reagan's long-stem glass. "I have a heavy hand when it comes to the spices." He flashed a mischievous grin that reminded her of one of her teenage students.

"I'm sure I will. I love Bolognese."

Jake raised his eyebrows. "I forgot mine, but I borrowed yours. You had plenty of really good oregano."

"Okay."

Jake's sheepish grin confused her. So, he used her oregano. What's the big—

Oh, the oregano.

Her eyes popped wider. She tried to squash the giggle she felt coming from her ribcage. "I can't wait to try it. I bet you make one mean Bolognese."

"Well, I think you'll be happy with it," Jake answered. "Okay, let's eat."

Lizzie was the first to take her usual seat, then Reagan and Matthew. Jake stood by the soup tureen, dishing out a healthy serving of spaghetti to each plate.

"Jake," Reagan mouthed, "the oregano?"

His deep-dimpled grin gave him away despite his obvious effort to keep a straight face. Before he ducked back into the kitchen for the shredded parmesan, and tea for the children, he gave her a quick shake of his head. "I used the Kroger brand oregano. You have two."

Lizzie watched Jake, her eyes narrowed, as he returned to the dining room. He set the cheese and drinks on the table, pulled out the chair her father always used, and sat in his place.

"Noooo!" Lizzie screamed as she swiped her plate of spaghetti off the table with such force that it crashed against the wall, breaking the plate into three pieces.

Reagan jumped up, knocking her chair to the floor with a loud slam.

Fury radiated from Lizzie's eyes. Her lips were curled, her fists drawn into her sides.

Matthew shot up, wild-eyed. Little gasping sounds came from his throat before he screamed at Lizzie, "How could you do that?" Uncontrolled tears flooded his cheeks. "You always ruin everything!" He stormed out of the dining room, stomped up the stairs, and slammed his bedroom door.

Angry red splatters embroidered the off-white wall, the oily meat sauce trickling to the floor. Scooter lapped up spaghetti off the hardwood. A blue windmill from a piece of broken china poked out of the chunky red mess.

Suddenly Jake was standing in front of her, his large hands on her shoulders. "Reagan, it's okay. I understand. Don't worry. I'll go talk to Matt. He'll be fine." He glanced around the room, toward the dining room table with the uneaten dinner, the wall weeping spaghetti sauce, then down at Scooter nonchalantly cleaning up the floor. He shook his head. "I'll help you with this after I talk to Matt."

Reagan righted her chair and flopped down, dropped her elbows onto the table, and rested her head in her palms. Lizzie moved to Matthew's place and popped his garlic bread into her mouth. The house was quiet except for "O Sole Mio" drifting from the kitchen. Reagan took a sip of the wine, then a gulp. Despite everything, all she could think about was Jake—the warmth of his touch, the smell of his aftershave, the vibration of every nerve ending in her body. Feelings she hadn't had in over a year.

REAGAN

CHAPTER FORTY-SIX

Four days after the spaghetti incident, a large blue-and-white X of tape stating POLICE LINE—DO NOT CROSS barricaded Matthew's bedroom door. Reagan arched an eyebrow and maneuvered herself over and under the tape without pulling it down. Matthew sat on his unmade bed, playing with Stretch Armstrong action figures, and ignored her. Clothes were strewn haphazardly about.

"The tape's a little overkill, don't you think?"

Matthew shook his head without looking up.

"I don't have to ask where you got it, do I?"

"Uncle Sonny."

"I figured. How long are you going to punish her? You know she probably doesn't understand."

Matthew shrugged.

Reagan took a deep breath. She had put off this conversation for months. She had not wanted to put something so monumental on Matthew's nine-year-old shoulders, but one way or the other, the issue affected him. He should have a voice. Not the final say . . . but a voice. Maybe it was time.

"Matt, I've been meaning to discuss something with you."

Matthew put Stretch Armstrong aside and looked at his mother.

"How would you feel if Lizzie didn't live with us?"

He sat straight up, his mouth open and his eyebrows bunched together. "What?"

"There are homes for children like Lizzie, where people would always be there to take care of her. She would still go to school, and we could pick her up on the weekends—"

"Mom, just because she did a bad thing doesn't mean she's a bad person!"

Reagan's words came back to her. How many times had she told Matthew that very thing?

"Buddy, I love you and Lizzie more than anything. You know that, right?"

Matthew nodded.

"This has nothing to do with Lizzie's behavior the night Jake was here. I've been meaning to talk to you about this since Christmas. Your Aunt Jordan and Cheryl—you remember, Lizzie's social worker—they both think Lizzie would do well in a group home. For one thing, she would be safer away from, you know, the bad man we talked about when we set up the code word. And she would get the help she needs from people trained to take care of children with special needs. You and I wouldn't need to watch her all the time and—"

She was talking way too fast, her speech out of control. She took a deep breath and tried to slow down. "There would be people there twenty-four seven to take care of her."

Matthew shook his head.

"Aunt Jordan thinks you would be better off."

He leaned back and stared at his mother, looking incredulous. "Why?"

"Buddy, Lizzie is always going to need someone with her. She's not going to become independent or be able to take care of herself. She has no regard for her own safety, so someone has to look after her, always. You're getting older, and you'll want to go places and do things like other kids. Things other than caring for your little sister."

Matthew considered that for several minutes, gazing past his mother at the blank wall behind her, until finally answering. "Nope, Lizzie belongs to us. She needs to live here, with people who love her. We'll just have to find someone else until Anaya comes back."

He made it sound so simple—just like his father, so sure of himself. No dilemma, no stress. They'd work it out. Maybe it *was* that simple. Lizzie would live with them because they belonged together. They were family, and they loved each other. Nobody would scare them apart, not even a man with a gun. Reagan wasn't sure which had caused the most stress: the dilemma she'd been wrestling with since December or the thought of discussing it with Matthew. Either way, the anxiety faded away like yesterday's news.

She hugged Matthew. "Okay, buddy, you're right."

She tousled his hair and stepped back through the tape. At least for now it was settled, or maybe it was just easier to decide not to decide. It would come up again, she was sure of it. Maybe many times as Lizzie developed. But for now it had been decided.

Before she went downstairs, she peeked into Lizzie's room. Her daughter sat on her bed, undressing Annie. On Reagan's way down, she heard the tape being ripped from Matthew's door.

The next afternoon as she packed up to leave school, her phone rang. The screen read Unknown. She started to reject the call, but something stopped her. "Hello."

"Hi, Reagan. Ron Gabriel. Would it be okay for me to stop

by your place this afternoon? I have something I'd like to talk to you about in person. New developments."

That was odd. He had never come to her house before. They'd always met at the station.

"Sure. I'm at school now, but I'll be home in about half an hour." Butterflies fluttered around in her stomach. He hadn't said what the developments were. That made her anxious.

By the time she got home, her anxiety had changed to excitement. Bright sunshine shone on a brilliant-green lawn, and her flower beds were bursting with yellow daffodils and red tulips. The boys next door played basketball on the driveway, in short-sleeved shirts. Sure signs of spring. Reagan hurried around the living room, picking up toys, shoes, and socks, even a coffee cup and an empty cereal bowl. She opened the kitchen window and turned on the TV in the living room for Lizzie, with the volume on low.

Lizzie was stretched out on the floor watching the movie *Home* for the hundredth time when the detective knocked. Reagan's heart pounded louder than the basketball hitting the concrete next door.

As always, Ron Gabriel was nicely dressed in a sports jacket over a collared shirt and dark slacks. Unmarked car. Nothing to identify him as a Cincinnati police detective. Reagan had brewed coffee. The aroma filled the room by the time she invited him in.

"Ron, it's nice to see you. Your call surprised me."

"Hey, Reagan." He looked relaxed and younger than the last time they were together, the deep lines in his forehead less noticeable, his smile more genuine. "We've had some developments I wanted you to hear from me first."

For some reason Reagan couldn't explain, her stomach fluttered. "Really? Why don't you come into the kitchen, away from the TV, and I'll get coffee?"

The detective followed her into the kitchen and took a seat at the table. "First, I want to thank you. Your help made all the difference."

"Oh?"

"Absolutely. Pieces started clicking into place almost as soon as you came back on board. Actually, it all started before then, back in October, when you notified Norwood Police you had information that Bryan Butler was dealing drugs to middle school kids."

"Really?"

"Oh yeah. They borrowed one of our undercover officers, Brandy Arnold, to plant in the school."

The day seemed so normal, so innocent—not the kind of day she should be talking about drug dealers and undercover cops. A soft breeze blew in through the window; sunlight brightened the room. Reagan wrapped her hands around her coffee cup and enjoyed the warmth, the steam reaching her face.

"Brandy," he laughed. "I swear that's her real name. Since you teach in the middle school, you may not have seen her, but you'd remember her if you had. She's brunette, very attractive, looks young, and can easily fit in with high school kids. She used the name Stephanie Benedict. That's her perverse sense of humor.

"She recognized right away that Bryan was associated with people who were connected, but it took her a while to get him to talk about his supplier, Moses Haydon, known as Mose on the street. After watching Haydon awhile, we realized he was a major player bringing in a shitpot full of drugs, so we contacted the DEA and they brought him in." Ron blew on his coffee, then took a sip.

"None of us had any idea that Butler or Mose was connected to my homicide until you came back in. The drawing you and Joe put together helped, but it was the tattoo that broke things open. Once I put that out, I got calls from just about everyone who came into contact with him during that initial arrest. You notice something like that when you slap bracelets on a person . . . or take them off. I was fielding phone calls for days. Anyway, we apprehended Haydon and went looking for Butler but couldn't find him. Turned out the Norwood Police had picked him up for something else."

The boys' loud voices from outside and the ball pounding the driveway interfered with their conversation, so Reagan got up and closed the window.

"We went to Norwood and interviewed Butler. The kid was scared to death. Not of the police, but of Haydon. He said he'd been hiding ever since Haydon got out on bond after that first arrest. Of course, anyone who watches TV knows to ask for a lawyer, and Butler did. When we called his parents, they said they wanted nothing to do with him and hung up on us." Ron shook his head.

Her experiences with Bryan's parents came to mind.

"Anyway, we brought in a public defender, and on the advice of his attorney, Bryan agreed to turn state's evidence if we charged him as a juvenile. He won't be eighteen until next month. He'll get off pretty easy. He may do some time in a juvenile facility, but he could get probation. For sure he'll be free of everything when he turns twenty-one.

"When that was settled, he rolled over on Haydon, testifying that he shot and killed Andrew Jenkins, the young man in Pleasant Ridge. When he did it, Butler was driving the car. He swore he had no idea that Haydon was going to do it, or that he even had a gun. He also gave him up for almost killing a kid from Indian Hill."

She was taken aback. Jake had told her about his stepson. Was that him? It seemed like too much of a coincidence, but it fit.

Ron continued. "I know the DA. No way he would have

gone along with such a sweetheart deal for that budding sociopath, except for one thing: Butler said that he was shocked when he recognized you at the scene, and that Haydon got a good look at you too. He convinced the prosecutor that ever since the shooting, he'd been protecting you and had gone to great lengths—in his own idiotic way—to keep Haydon from knowing who you were. He told Haydon he would find out, just to keep him from looking for you himself, and then lied to him repeatedly about your identity and whereabouts.

"He even told the prosecutor he'd made friends with your daughter and would have turned himself in but had to return something to her first. Right after he did that, he was picked up by the Norwood police."

The doll—the threat. Reagan shook her head. "I know what he was talking about. But why was he protecting me?"

"The reason he gave was that you were the best teacher he ever had. Besides his grandmother, you were the only person who ever really cared about him, even if it was your job. And you respected him. That's why. He couldn't let you or your children get hurt."

Tears welled in her eyes.

"Because of you, Andrew's killer will be brought to justice. His family will at least have that. The DEA is on the trail of several members of a drug cartel that has flooded our city with cocaine, fentanyl, heroin, and anything else some poor addict could crave. I'm not naive enough to think this arrest will single-handedly take care of Cincinnati's drug problem, but you have made a difference. You care about kids and people. You wouldn't turn a blind eye. Your kindness to that kid in seventh grade created a tsunami of ripple effects."

Tears trickled down Reagan's cheeks. It would take a while for this to sink in, for sure. At least she wouldn't have to worry about the gunman anymore. That was huge. But it was all so sad, really: the young man who had died, and his family who were still grieving; the seventh grader who believed no one cared about him but his teacher; the fact that people made bad choices that ruined their lives.

Ron got up to leave, and Reagan walked him to the door. Matthew had joined the other kids to shoot hoops.

When Ron reached the steps, he swiveled back to her and smiled. "You know, Reagan, I'm reminded of a saying we have in the district: Be nice to everybody. You never know who might turn up on a jury."

REAGAN AND JAKE

CHAPTER FORTY-SEVEN

Reagan threw open the kitchen window and breathed in the earthy smell of spring. Grass, still damp from early-morning dew, glistened in the bright sun. A soft breeze ushered in a sense of new beginnings. The first birdsong last spring had held no thrill at all. No sense of anticipation. She had pushed her feelings down so deep, she had sleepwalked through the spring and summer. Maybe it was true: it takes about a year. Time did make a difference.

She'd read and reread the email from Anaya and felt a little guilty about being so overjoyed. Her sister died. But now Anaya was coming back and Reagan couldn't wait. She'd told the children and now she wanted to tell Bird.

Soon his house would be partially obscured by the oak's thick foliage, but this morning the blue-and-yellow structure stood straight and still, attention grabbing. She leaned closer. Where was Bird? She glanced from the top of the tree to the lower branches without seeing her odd little friend, but she didn't have time to worry about it. This was the last day of school. She still had to take a shower and get Lizzie ready. Bird was somewhere in that tree. He was always there.

Noise from Reagan's happy seventh graders ebbed and flowed as they busied themselves in groups of two or three. The ear-splitting bell had already rung. Kids in the hallway shouted to one another, slammed metal lockers, and ran through the building like stampeding horses, but none of her students seemed in a hurry to leave.

Reagan wandered through the room, handing out T-shirts to kids who quickly pulled them on over their other clothes. She talked to each student, laughed about their hair, asked about their summer plans, and encouraged them to read over the break. Most of them wouldn't.

Max, one of the seventh graders, pulled up iTunes on his laptop and played "Celebration." Reagan directed Charmayne and Greta as they packed up posters, displays, and other science accoutrements to be stored away for reuse next fall. They moved to the rhythm of the music.

As she had done ever since Anaya left for India, Jean Smith, Lizzie's teacher, escorted her to the science lab after school because her class got out half an hour earlier than the middle school. They hadn't been able to find another aide to take care of Lizzie during the afternoons.

Reagan opened the door. "Welcome to the last day of school," she said to the newbie, who was fresh out of college and enthusiastic about working with children with special needs. "Jean, you've been wonderful to do this every day, and thanks for everything else you've done to help us. I really appreciate it." Reagan handed her an envelope containing a thank-you note and generous gift card.

As if on cue, Lizzie turned and gave her teacher a hug and

patted her on the back. When she spotted Reagan's students, she rushed to join them.

Jean laughed. "Well, I guess you don't need me anymore."

"I guess not. Enjoy your summer."

Over the months Lizzie had been coming to her class-room, Reagan's students had adopted her. They treated her like a younger sibling—watching over her, making sure she didn't get into any of their stuff, also making sure she didn't leave the room if Reagan's back was turned. Lizzie loved their attention.

Jake had never been inside Norwood Middle School, with its high ceilings, plastered walls, and sturdy classroom doors. He guessed it had been built sometime around 1910, and it was *old*. The vinyl tile floors in the hallway looked passable, but attempts to repair cracks in the plastered walls had been botched, and the patches were covered with paint that didn't exactly match. Doors to some of the lockers were missing, and one hung askew, straining against its hinge.

He wondered what it would cost to have one of his crews come in and renovate. Ideas flickered through his mind as Matthew led him up the wide staircase to Reagan's classroom. They'd need scaffolding in the cavernous hallways and stair-wells, but that'd be no problem if the school was empty.

Dave could probably get volunteers to do the painting after the walls were prepped. He lived in Norwood. He knew people there. They could knock it out before the kids came back from summer break.

As Jake had done every Thursday for months, he'd picked up Matthew from Sharpsburg Elementary, a few blocks from Reagan's home, for their regular "mentoring"—the highlight of Jake's week, especially since he and Janet separated. Matthew wanted to do something special as it was the end of the school year, and they'd decided to ask Reagan if she and Lizzie wanted to go with them.

They walked up the stairs against a strong current of schoolkids rushing down. Music and laughter filled the stairwell, and it grew louder the closer they got to Reagan's classroom. Jake smiled when he looked through the window.

"Matt, you didn't tell me your mom's class was having a party."

Matthew shrugged. "I didn't know."

"Did you know about the hair?" A wide strip in the front of Reagan's hair was . . . green.

Matthew peeked into the room. "Oh, I knew about that. Mom had hers dyed yesterday at a salon."

When one of the students opened the door to leave, music blared into the hallway. Jake rapped on the glass.

Reagan stopped in her tracks and looked at them over a box of books she was carrying. She smiled—a genuine smile that said she was glad to see them, maybe even excited, a smile that excited him back.

"Matthew, Jake, I'm surprised to see you here."

A large, half-eaten sheet cake and an almost-empty gallon of green punch had been positioned on one of the workstations. All the students wore blue T-shirts with "I'm a WINNER" written across the front in large white letters and, on the back, the Samsung logo and "Solve for Tomorrow." They were paired up, spray-painting each other's hair.

He loved Reagan's spunk. No matter what life threw at her, she maintained her sense of humor. Janet would never have dyed a streak in the front of her hair like that, no matter what the cause. Everything had to be perfect.

"Mom, do you want to go with us?"

Jake grabbed the gritty box from Reagan. "Let me take that. Where do you want it?"

"Thanks, it is heavy." She pointed to one of her students. "Jamal, please show him where these go . . . and Matt, how about feeding the fish? The food's by the aquarium."

Boxes were stacked waist-high in the small closet, which smelled of old wood and dust. When he returned, Jake tilted his chin slightly to the left, raised his brows, and said to Reagan, "That's an interesting hairstyle. What do you call it?"

Reagan laughed. "Green. I call it 'winner green.' I challenged the kids to enter a contest and we struck a bargain. If they won, I would dye my hair. I really didn't think they would win, but they did." She pointed behind her with a nod. "Now they all want green hair too." She shook her head and threw up her palms. "Go figure."

He laughed with her. She *was* fun.

"I furnished the spray dye, and they furnished permission slips signed by their parents. I have to be honest with you, a couple of signatures were *a little iffy*." Reagan cocked her head and lifted the corner of her mouth. "But when I called the parents, they gave their okay." Reagan ran a hand through her green streak. "At least I had the good sense not to commit to how long I would wear it. You know, *it's not easy being green.* I've already made an appointment to have it colored over. School's out. Who will know?"

"I like it, Mom," Matthew objected as he wandered back from feeding the fish.

Reagan gave an exaggerated shrug. "Well, Saint Patrick's Day is only ten months away."

Jamal carried more boxes to the closet and came out holding something behind his back. Reagan didn't seem to notice.

"Where are you guys going?" Reagan asked Jake.

"We thought we'd go to Sawyer Point and walk across the Purple People Bridge to Newport. Or . . . play on the giant piano in Smale Park and eat at Moerlein's . . . or do something else downtown."

Reagan's eyes widened. "Guys, that sounds wonderful, but I don't have a sitter."

Suddenly the music blared and a burst of laughter sounded behind them. The students stood in a circle, clapping in time with the song. Jake moved closer to see why they were laughing. Lizzie, a look of total delight on her face, stood in the middle of the group, singing, her ponytail bobbing with the rhythm. Jamal, the kid Jake noticed a moment earlier, handed her a cordless microphone and she held it like a pop star without missing a beat. She clearly had the right melody. The lyrics were unrecognizable, but the kids knew them and sang with her, calling out her name, egging her on. The louder they got, the more she bounced, until she was jumping up and down, clearing the floor.

Jake grinned and looked at Reagan. "You don't need a sitter. We'll take her with us."

Reagan looked at him through hooded eyes. "Jake, are you sure? You found out the hard way, she can be a handful."

He threw up his arms and said, "We have six hands between us."

Reagan arched an eyebrow. "Sometimes that's not enough."

Jake laughed. "We'll be fine."

After everything had been put away and all the students were gone, Jake and the kids waited for Reagan by the door. She took a long look around the room and tried to figure out what she was feeling. She had become a teacher because she was convinced of the job's importance—the molding of young minds, helping kids get excited about learning and become responsible members of a community. She'd wanted to make a difference.

That was her identity: teacher, wife, and mother. Scott's death had thrown her off balance. For a time, she didn't know how to be herself. How to trust herself. Now she was at a crossroads that was both scary and exciting.

"Okay, guys, we're out of here," Reagan said as she closed and locked the door.

"Yeah, let's do this!" Jake responded.

As Reagan watched the three of them, Lizzie slipped her hand into Jake's. Suddenly it became clear: For months she had pushed down her feelings, like turning down the volume on a radio. But when she did that, she also couldn't hear the music—and she wanted to hear it all.

ACKNOWLEDGMENTS

While people come and go from critique groups depending on their work in progress or their interest in writing, there are regulars to the Cincinnati Writer's Project, who, like me, have been participating for years, even decades, and without whom this book would have been unreadable. Kandy Witte, Mary Ann Back, the late Barbara Kuroff, and I took great pleasure in solving the world's problems as we drove together to the weekly meetings held in whatever bar would offer us free space. For years that was Molly Malone's in Pleasant Ridge and is currently, as of this writing, St. Bernard Pub. Thanks to the owners and staff of these venues and the regular members of the group, each of whom diligently read every word of the manuscript, chapter by chapter, and offered their unique perspective on how it could be improved. Besides Kandy, Mary Ann, and Barb, those members are Mark Bois, Sarah Eckstein, Sally Christopher, Joe Terbeck, Karen Andrew, Lauren DiMenna, Marcia Eckstein, Mary Fitzpatrick, Dana Kisor, Tom Groh, the late Joe D'Amato, Jim Fiorelli, and Shannon Hall.

Reading the finished book with an eye on flow, pacing, and overall narration requires a considerable commitment of time and energy. Many thanks to my beta readers extraordinaire: Peter White, Paige Jarrell, Tracy High, Mary Ann Back, Betsy Smith, Elizabeth Walker, Tracey Stinson, Feriel Feldman, Camille Prado, Pat Ludovici, and the unnamed readers from Spun Yarn.

Thank you to the wonderfully professional team at Girl Friday Productions, who filled in the gaps in my "know-how" and saved me from spending another ten years working on this novel.

I very much appreciate Chief William Kramer of the Norwood Police Department, who made time to meet with me one morning when the officer I had scheduled for an interview became unavailable at the last minute. His generosity demonstrates the small-town culture of Norwood that I find so appealing. I repeatedly found it when talking with past and current residents of the city and teachers at Norwood Middle School.

And, of course, I garnered bits of information I needed from friends and neighbors, such as Cami Geraci and Thom Brannock. Thanks to them for helping me add authenticity to my scenes involving their respective organizations.

Hats off to all the volunteers who make Women's Fiction Writers Association one of the most valuable resources a writer can have. Like writing and publishing a novel, it takes a village working behind the scenes to make that organization the gem that it is.

Lastly, and most important, thanks to my daughters Paige Gipson Jarrell, who repeatedly illustrates to me and 750 Facebook friends how to show love and humor while living with a severely disabled child; Tracy Gipson High, whose enthusiastic encouragement enabled me to push past the impostor syndrome and publish this book; and my husband, Jan-Willem, whose support for this project means the world to me. Love you guys more than you know.

READER'S GUIDE
DISCUSSION
QUESTIONS

1. What do you think of Reagan's teaching style? Would you like to have her teach your child or grandchild? Why or why not?
2. Jake apparently loved Janet and wanted their marriage to work. Were you surprised by the note from Janet?
3. How does Reagan respond to embarrassing situations (outside Kroger, for example, or on the flight to Atlanta)? Does her response style work for her?
4. What do you think of Bird? Is he really mystical . . . or just a bird? Does Reagan actually see expressions on his face?
5. Reagan feels comforted by her belief that Bird watches over her family. How is that different from or the same as the comfort others receive from prayer?
6. How do you feel about Reagan smoking weed? She is a staunch supporter of law enforcement and adamantly believes she should help the police find the killer even if it puts her in danger. So how

does she reconcile that belief with smoking illegal weed?

7. Discuss the impact of good parenting—or the lack of good parenting. Who in the novel would you say practices good parenting, and who doesn't? How does that impact their kids? What in Jake's background causes him to feel so strongly about holding Alex accountable for his actions?

8. Jake is Matthew's "big brother." What kind of mentor is he? Who benefits the most from their relationship, Matthew or Jake? Why?

9. Janet refuses to hold Alex accountable for his behavior. Why is it so hard for Janet to accept that Alex's behavior is troublesome?

10. Mrs. Hamilton, Angela's grandmother, is grief-stricken when she tells Reagan about her daughter's death. What does she mean by "Nobody brought us casseroles?"

11. Jordan suggests that Lizzie be placed in a residential facility. Why would she do that? Why does Reagan get so upset with her? Would it have been a good choice for the family?

12. Several characters in the novel address the issue of powerlessness. Who becomes powerful? When and how?

13. Guilt is a theme throughout the novel. Other than Reagan, which characters are impacted by guilt and why?

AUTHOR'S NOTE

I've always been interested in people—what makes them alike, what makes them different . . . what makes them tick. So I studied psychology. I could have taken any one of a number of career paths after finishing my master's, and it just so happened a nonprofit treatment program for chemically dependent adolescents in my area was looking for someone and I was looking for a job. The course was set. I learned a great deal from those kids and their families and loved it most of the twenty-something years I spent there.

During those years, my younger daughter finished high school and college, got married, and started her family. Her second child, a daughter, was born with Down syndrome. I'll call her Lizzie. We had not expected that and grieved a little, but we soon changed our expectations and moved on. We noticed kids with DS working at Kroger, eating out with their families, and enjoying themselves other places in the community. One evening a bunch of young adults with DS from a group home nearby showed up at a neighborhood concert and danced together like they were on *Dancing with the Stars*.

I loved watching them obviously having so much fun. They seemed happy and functional.

As Lizzie developed, I noticed behaviors that I would *not* associate with Down syndrome. She was super sensitive to certain sounds. If I turned on one specific water faucet, she would put her hands over her ears and scream. She became mesmerized by ordinary visual stimuli such as water pouring or the garage door opening and closing. She also did not develop speech.

When she was four and my daughter had another child, Lizzie became aggressive with the baby and other younger, smaller children—pulling hair, scratching, pinching, and similar antisocial behavior. We could not leave the baby unguarded, and we could no longer take Lizzie anyplace where other children played. No parks. No parents' nights out.

As is common in people with Down syndrome, my granddaughter had hypotonia, meaning her muscle tone was weak and her joints loose. The loose joints meant she could fold her body up like a contortionist. She had a tendency to bolt away from whomever she was with. Restraining her was made difficult by her loose shoulder joints and unusual strength. If we grabbed her around the chest to safely lift her, she could easily slip out of our grasp. We called it "disappearing armpits." When she started school, she could also slip out of her restraints on the school bus, which meant an aide had to ride with her.

Her pediatrician repeatedly told us she felt there was something different about Lizzie, something more than Down syndrome, but she didn't know what. We sought help from a behavioral therapist and, in desperation, made an appointment with a psychiatrist at the Thomas Center for Down Syndrome Services at Cincinnati Children's Hospital. Lizzie was immediately dually diagnosed with Down syndrome and autism spectrum disorder (DS-ASD).

I had no idea that a child could have both Down syndrome and autism. It seemed too much of a coincidence. Despite studying psychology for six years, I had never heard of it. Apparently, Lizzie's pediatrician hadn't either. But I've since discovered it is not a coincidence and not that unusual. Research indicates that 16 to 18 percent of children with Down syndrome also are autistic. Some experts estimate that the percentage is much higher.

The Centers for Disease Control and Prevention (CDC) states this: "Although the cause of ASD is known in some people and not known in others, genetics, biology, and environment are all important factors. Having older parents, a difficult birth, or infections during pregnancy are all examples. Beyond these factors, certain people are at higher risk than others. . . . People with certain genetic disorders, such as fragile X syndrome, tuberous sclerosis, and Down syndrome, are more likely to have ASD."

A plethora of information about DS-ASD can now be found online at DS-ASD-Connection.org, and a search on YouTube will pull up several different videos on the subject. The Down Syndrome Connection of the Bay Area presented an especially informative webinar by Noemi Spinazzi, MD, FAAP, medical director of the Down Syndrome Clinic at UCSF Benioff Children's Hospital, and Teresa Unnerstall, DS-ASD consultant and the author of *A New Course: A Mother's Journey Navigating Down Syndrome and Autism.*

One thing is clear: research is ongoing, and the information is relatively new. In the 1990s it was believed children with Down syndrome could not develop autism. That explains why Lizzie's pediatrician did not recognize it.

During Lizzie's school years, my daughter was a professional who needed to leave for work at about six in the morning and sometimes didn't get home until after six in the evening. Lizzie's father was deployed a year at a time. Lizzie needed help getting ready for school before her bus picked her up and supervision in the afternoon before her mom got home. A Medicaid waiver provided the funding for an aide, but finding dependable people to provide care was hard. My part-time job required traveling, so I wasn't always there. After my daughter tried three different agencies, I quit my job and became Lizzie's care provider. And I decided to write this book somewhere along the way.

I wanted to give readers a glimpse of life with a severely disabled child. It has its challenges for sure, and they impact the whole family, but it also has its rewards. Lizzie's brother and sister are two of the most compassionate teenagers I've ever known. Her brother is studying to be a special ed teacher, and they both have volunteered at Stepping Stones, a camp for children with disabilities. It's hot and hard work, but they love it. Lizzie doesn't necessarily enjoy the same things other kids enjoy because she is her own person. Just as the experiences with Lizzie portrayed in this book are unique to her, my thoughts in this note are my own.

ABOUT THE AUTHOR

 Penny Walker Veraar is retired from decades of work in the nonprofit addiction treatment field. She now spends time as a caregiver for her granddaughter, who has special needs. In addition to writing a story people will enjoy reading, her goal for *Owl in the Oak Tree* is to increase awareness by providing a glimpse into the life of a family who shares her experience. She lives in the Cincinnati area with her husband.

Lightning Source UK Ltd.
Milton Keynes UK
UKHW042203150223
417096UK00010B/162